The Weight of Echoes

Erin Giannini

Praise for Erin Giannini:

"Quite enjoyable."
-Coco's Reading

"Fantastic book."
-Aprimavista

"A great addition to any collection."
-Valerie Estelle Frankel, author

For Keith Huff, playwright, friend, and the best mentor anyone could ask for.

CHAPTER ONE

All I did was shake a hand. People do it all the time, and the worst that happens to them was a clammy palm or a few germs.

I should have known better. I did know better, but sometimes, the pressure was too much and coming from too many places all at once. *Behave, Veronica.* And sometimes, it drew more attention to me if I refused, and that was the last thing anyone wanted.

Maybe there were other reasons—fate or curiosity—that I didn't want to admit, even to myself.

Whatever the reason, there I was in the aisle of Faith Fellowship Church, all-over relief that another Sunday service was over and done. I could go home and change out of my stupid navy blue dress with its itchy lace collar choking me that Dad insisted I wear, pretend this stupid place didn't exist until next Sunday.

Dad had his right hand in an iron grip on my shoulder, like I might cut and run—if only—and steered me down the aisle like a prized cow, giving a nod or a brief hello to whatever other Faith Fellows did so first.

"Matthew Simon! Just the man I wanted to see."

In front of us stood Mrs. Phelps, whose first name I'd never remembered. Since we'd moved to Dalesville five years ago so Dad could join up with his beloved Faith Fellowship Church, I'd been treated to more than one lecture on the disrespect of using an adult's first name. The first time, I'd snarked back, asking him at what age it would be appropriate. He'd sent me to bed without supper. Mom wouldn't have let him do that, but she wasn't here, barred from contact by Dad's Faith Fellowship lawyers.

Dad gave her a small smile and nod. "How are you, Retha? How's Frank?"

Her answering smile was big and bright and toothy. "Really good, thank you for asking." She turned her klieg-light smile on me, stuck out her hand. "And how are *you*, Veronica? My, you've grown." She said that like she hadn't seen me in years instead of days.

I stared at her outstretched palm like I was trying to read it, buying time to either figure out how to gracefully refuse, or dig my gloves out of my coat pocket before I took it.

My pause left her hand hanging in the air for a fraction too long for Dad, and the full weight of his stare hit me like an iceberg.

Caught, I took her hand, managed a "Fine, thank you," and a brief, shining moment of feeling nothing but the scrape of callouses against my palm and a surge of relief I'd finally gotten myself until control when it hit me.

The pictures in my head, the ones I tried—and mostly succeeded—in blocking out in the past five years, were back, as clear as if I was watching them on TV. Except these were all the same. A woman lying on a bed, viewed from a distance. Her eyes were blank and her mouth slack with only slight variations: her chest rising and falling, her head turned toward the wall. The smell of industrial cleaner assaulted my nostrils. I knew this unknown person, but whether that feeling came from me or Mrs. Phelps wasn't clear. I staggered where I stood, yanking my hand from hers as I made a blind grab for something to steady me.

I shut my eyes, the images still there, and took a deep breath. The world around me righted itself again, and I opened my eyes to Mrs. Phelps's concerned frown and Dad's angrier one.

"I'm so sorry. The light hit my eyes." I gestured up at the triangular window above the door, where the late morning sun was streaming in.

Phelps's smile seemed relieved. A glance at Dad also showed a slight modification of his scowl.

"Maybe I'll go sit down while you talk?"

Dad gave me a curt nod, and I hurried over to the doors, sank bonelessly into the chair where the greeters sat before the service.

Crying seemed like a viable option, but that was the last thing I'd want to do in this place. What I really wanted to do was swear, to make all those grown-ups in their golf shirts and print dresses turn and gape at me like caught fish on a boat deck. All that time keeping my distance, wearing gloves if needed—even in summer, even at school—hoping if I ignored it, it'd go away like an imaginary friend no longer needed, was for nothing.

I didn't cry. I didn't swear. I rubbed my temples, tried to ease the band of pain behind my eyes. Watched Dad chat with Mrs. Phelps, her smile still as broad as the shoulder pads on her dress. The ability—the curse—hadn't just gone away. It had gotten stronger, building up behind the mental wall I'd erected to keep it in.

I stared at Dad, giving Mrs. Phelps the smile he never had for me.

Bless me, Father, for I have sinned. It has been five years since my last confession. I see things when I touch someone.

No, that wasn't the whole truth. Not anymore. Feel. Smell. The scent of orange cleaner and hopelessness lingered in my nose, in the back of my throat.

And I would never confess that to my father. He thought he was one of God's chosen. It was hard to trust someone with no doubt.

I leaned my head against the wall, closed my eyes, let my thoughts linger over what I'd seen. What Mrs. Phelps had seen, I amended. How this little freak of my brain worked I was never one hundred percent sure, but it was always from their perspective: a face contorted, a road stretching ahead through bug-splattered glass. This one was odd: a figure seen at a distance through a small space.

I briefly considered walking back and asking her. And how would that go, exactly? *Hey, Mrs. Phelps, looked through any tiny windows lately? Why do I ask? No reason.* But one glance at the two of them, still deep in conversation, put a damper on that idea. Dad was death on kids—I was his height, and almost eighteen, but whatever—interrupting adults, and the best I could expect was a scowl and no answers simply for violating one of his prohibitions.

And he had so many prohibitions.

Finally, he shook her hand and headed my way, the weak sunlight catching his lapel pin—two hands clutching a cross that all the Faith Fellowship bigwigs wore—as he marched forward. I sat up straight as he came closer, hating myself for doing it.

Without a glance at me, he went to the door, opened it. "Come along, Veronica."

I stood and followed him out, seething. *Come, Veronica. Sit. Stay. Good girl.* I dug my sunglasses out of my purse, even though the sun was peek-a-boo-ing behind the thick gray clouds above. All the better to hide. Dad didn't require me to smile except in front of people like Mrs. Phelps or Reverend Ash or the guys that came over for his Tuesday prayer group. My eyes, though, they always gave me away.

We drove home in our usual silence, past the fast food joints and strip malls on Sunset, dominated by McClellan's Sporting Goods's college campus-sized store, the other big deal in town besides Faith Fellowship. As we crested the hill where City of Light Acres brooded over Dalesville, I stared at the entrance sign with its name in huge, weathered letters, complete with a carved likeness of its head honcho, Robert James Jr., staring at me with dead oak eyes. I turned to the side window instead, the toast and coffee I'd scarfed before church reduced to bile in my throat. The endless rows of tan houses with green doors blurred as we sped past.

Dad finally spoke as we pulled into the garage, and he tapped the remote to close the door behind us. "I trust you're feeling better."

It took me a good thirty seconds to remember I was supposed to be recovering from my faintness at church. *You're slipping, Veronica.* "Yes, better. Thank you."

A curt nod. "I'll be working in my office for most of the afternoon. Please strip the beds and wash the linens before you make supper."

"Yes, Dad."

I followed him into the house, his back ramrod straight as he marched up the two stairs and through the door, down the hall to his office.

As I changed into jeans and a t-shirt and hung up my church dress, my only thought was, at least he said "please" this time.

It was the little things.

I left my bedroom door ajar, the sound of the washer soothing as I sprawled across my bare bed and stared at the metallic star Mom had given me a decade ago, bought after a day of boring errands when she'd caught me staring at it in the window of a paper shop. It caught the sun and winked light on the wall and into my eyes.

Dad told me she'd walked out on us. He'd wanted to move us here after he got a job offer from a place and man he admired. Mom had refused. At first, quietly, and then with more heat, finally kicking him out of our little house in Denver after some of his Faith Fellowship guys had shown up and tried to convert me. Two weeks later, she surprised me with a trip to Camp Serenity, a sleep-away camp up in the mountains I'd begged to go to ever since I saw their commercial on local TV.

It didn't occur to me at the time why she'd finally given in. As I watched the star spin as the heat kicked on and blew hot air from the vent, I knew now she'd wanted me away from a father who was becoming hard to recognize. Or predict.

The washer stopped. I bounded off my bed and stomped down to the laundry room, yanking out the sheets with more force than necessary. Hadn't worked, had it? I was stuck here with him, and she was gone. I'd tried to talk to Dad about it as he'd slammed around the house taking down pictures and stacking boxes by the door, but all he would say was, "She abandoned us."

I stuffed the sheets in the dryer, slammed the door shut, and pushed Start. Sighed.

I didn't buy it then. I still don't. I scowled at his office door. It was a battle, and he'd won.

Back in my room, I went to my closet, rolled up on the balls of my feet to retrieve the keepsake box I'd hidden behind a troop formation of stuffed animals. Dad may have purged anything that reminded him of Mom, but I'd managed to rescue a few bits and pieces. I pushed aside old Field Day ribbons and dried rose petals and pulled out the picture I kept there. Mom, caught in the act of pruning a rosebush, grinning, with a smear of dirt across her forehead. Younger than I remembered her, but still exactly the same.

I touched her photoed cheek. "Soon, Mom."

I stared at it long enough to burn her image into my retinas, to see her when I put it back in the box and closed my eyes. In my head, she moved, bent to snip one of the just-opened buds, and handed it to me. Laughed. I drifted closer to her, closer to sleep, but as I reached out, she changed, her face drawn, her eyes a chilling blank as she dropped the shears. Her knees buckled, and she fell as I ran forward, trying to catch her before she hit the ground.

Instead, I was yanked backwards, Mom receding farther way until she was a forlorn figure viewed through a small window.

The dryer stopped, its bored beep waking me up. I stared at the star turning over my bed, my heart gonging in my ears like I'd sprinted the length of the house. I knew. That sense of familiarity was doubled. Maybe I didn't quite understand how this talent of mine worked, but I could make a few guesses. That image leapt to Mrs. Phelps's mind when I'd shaken her hand because I reminded her of someone else in that fleeting, *deja vu* way.

The same feeling I got when I looked in a mirror.

The woman in the bed was Mom.

Four Months Later

I sat at my desk, reading the school paper. Mom had found the desk abandoned on a street corner on our way to the grocery store. We'd chivvied it into the back of Grandpa's old truck that stood wheezing and idling as we grunted and sweated, finally getting it in. She'd spent the summer between my fourth and fifth grade year sanding and staining it between planning her lessons for the fall and a brief week of all three of us heading to the coolness of the mountains to escape the July heat.

And she was here in Dalesville. Seen by a member of Faith Fellowship, no less. When? Where? Why? I had to know what happened, why she'd be here, and what I could do without revealing to anyone exactly *how* I came by this information. Not that they'd believe me, anyway.

I filled up my calculus notebook with more ideas than equations, made more than a few lame attempts to get info out of Dad. No dice. Possibly because I had a hard time even looking at him lately, although I was sure he assumed I'd finally learned my place.

I stared down at my hands, splayed across the newspaper, half covering the scowling face of Dalesville High's recently fired geometry teacher, Richard Peterson, caught playing favorites with grades and exposed by *Dalesville High Journal*'s star reporter, Chris Mulligan.

Well, I thought he was a star. And I never liked how Mr. Peterson said "Veronica Simon" during class, with a little extra creep sauce in his tone. Chris's investigative skills were one idea that might be possible, if I could figure out how to ask him. We shared no classes, but I'd had a few ideas where to look outside of school, and had been on my best behavior for months in the hope Dad might loosen the chain.

The door opened behind me. I spun in my chair to face my father, who'd perfected the art of looming and scowling half a decade ago.

He spied the school newspaper on my desk and his perma-frown went all Grand Canyon. "I take it your homework is finished."

I stood, tried to strip any sarcastic inflection from my voice, if not from my head. "Yes, sir."

His expression eased a fraction. "I'll be back Sunday. I'm trusting you to behave while I'm gone."

"Yes, Dad." In my head, I was doing backflips, so I didn't trust myself to say more than that, but he seemed satisfied.

He turned to leave. "Remember, God is watching," was the only good-bye he bothered to give me before shutting the door.

In five years, this was only the second time he'd left town without roping a Faith Fellowship biddie into staying the night. If he thought I didn't know the first time was a test or that he'd have neighbors like Mrs. Sneed keeping an eye out for any infractions, he clearly thought less of my brain than he used to.

I sank back into my chair, listened for the sound of the garage door opening and closing before I allowed myself a relieved laugh, and got up to go to my closet for a change of clothes.

Half an hour later, having watched Mrs. Pimms heft herself out of her chair and turn off her TV—I could spy, too—I turned off my bedroom light, turned on the desk lamp, and slid out my window.

After I pulled it shut and twitched the curtain closed, I made my way down the alley that ran the length of our subdivision toward Sunset, the road that ran east-west through this crappy town. Toward downtown, where all the freaks hung out, hoping this was the time I'd run into Chris. I thought he might be able to help me keep my promise to myself to find out what happened to Mom. Whatever other motivations I had I did my best to deny as I walked down the hill leading to Sunset.

"I'm trusting you," Dad had said.

More's the fool him. Trust was for suckers.

I moved, they moved, we moved together. The bounce and sway of the mosh pit, the black-clad mass pressed against my body, the music pressed against my eardrums, colored lights pressed and flashed against my eyes. We were one. I flailed and fell, drowning. I leapt up and slammed against another. So much noise, I couldn't hear my own thoughts...or anybody else's. I was no longer Veronica Simon, alien and alienated. I was no longer alone. Just because I had a plan didn't mean I couldn't have a little fun, right?

The song ended, segued into a slow jam suitable only for the love sway, couples hugging one another with no visible rhythm.

Of course, my mocking was only the slim coating over a bitter pill. Seventeen-years-old, and the only commandment I'd managed to break, goddamn it, was not taking the Lord's name in vain. I still honored my mother, but Dad cared more about his stupid Faith Fellowship Community than me, so he didn't deserve it.

And maybe I'd done a bit of coveting of a certain sharp-faced, black-haired boy reporter with a quirky little smile. The thought of him made me smile as I plowed through the crowd, trying not to touch anyone. I wouldn't mind breaking a few more commandments with him. Much as Dad and his cohorts tried to convince us otherwise, "Thou shalt not engage in sex before marriage" hadn't actually made it onto Moses's big stone tablet.

I almost wished it had, for the fun of breaking it.

Then again, I thought, as I got closer to the bar, who knew what would happen with that much closeness? I shuddered. Keep my distance. Tamp it down. Caution: use only as directed. And if a few things still slipped through the cracks, all the more reason to keep to myself. Best to concentrate on this opportunity.

I rapped my knuckles on the bar to get Mike the bartender's attention, and gave him what I hoped was a winsome smile. I hadn't had a lot of practice with talking to people since we'd moved to Dalesville, but the few times I'd made it to *The* Club, talking to Mike had been easy. Someday, I might even be able to talk to someone else.

He grinned when he saw me, his natural expression. He had a kind of teddy bear face and physique that was made for tapping kegs and giving the highest of fives. "What can I get you, Veronica Simon?"

"Vodka tonic, if you'd be so kind, Michael Higgens." I matched his tone.

He crossed his arms, tried unsuccessfully to settle his round face in hard lines. "ID?"

"Mike. Do me a solid. Jesus'll love you for it, you know."

The grin reappeared before he could stop himself. "You could go to hell for saying shit like that."

I felt my good humor crack a bit. It was a reminder of things I wanted the drink to forget. My smile and banter felt rubbery and fake, but I pushed on regardless. "My bad. I thought this *was* hell."

He coughed and laughed simultaneously. "Fine. Three bucks."

I put four on the bar. "Price-gouging bastard. Thanks, Mike. May God bless you."

He laughed all the way down the bar.

I swiveled in my chair, sipped my drink, and watched the dancers. An involuntary sigh escaped me, and I took a large gulp of my drink. Pathetic. I lit a cigarette from the pack I'd bought at the beaten-up little store around the block and commenced watching again, but the dizzy dance-induced endorphin rush was long gone, replaced by the slow-simmer anger I'd carried for the past four months.

What did I expect, coming to this place? I didn't know anybody. Five years of home, school, church, or church-related activities had rusted any social skills that didn't involve quoting the Bible or praising Jesus. Even with Nancy, my best friend until Jeremy Barnes asked her out and proceeded to monopolize her, every word had to be monitored and measured, so I wouldn't offend her. She'd never be caught dead in a place like this.

And Mr. Mulligan, sadly, was nowhere to be seen.

I crushed out the cigarette, half-smoked, polished off the last of the vodka, adjusted my gloves, and slid off the stool. I snaked again through the dancers to the exit and out into the cold night air to be actually alone.

I wasn't alone.

On the outer rim of the streetlamp outside the parking lot of *The* Club was a guy, leaning against a station wagon festooned with an array of discordant bumper stickers from an NRA "from my cold dead hand" to an Earth Day decal. He held a cigarette between long pale fingers, nails painted black to match both his hair and ensemble.

My laugh was both unstoppable and loud.

He looked up and saw me, then shoved himself off the car and ambled in my direction. Despite the vampire drag and the dark parking lot, I wasn't remotely scared. I knew who he was, the reason I'd started haunting *The* Club in the first place, hoping it might be one of the places he'd hang out.

Finally, risk met reward.

I leaned against the wall of the club, bass thrumming through the plywood, a soothing counterpoint to the fluttery sensation in my stomach as he came closer. I told myself it was the nervousness of asking for a favor from a stranger.

He reached into the pocket of his coat and produced a pack of cheap cigarettes, offering me one. I took it and the offered lighter. It was only then he spoke.

"Were you laughing at me?" No accusation in that deep, soft tone, only curiosity.

I darted a glance at him, smiled. "Yes."

He returned it. "Just checking."

I took a drag of my cigarette, exhaled the smoke toward my boots. "Are you offended?"

"Terribly." His somber voice was immediately undercut with a laugh.

I chanced looking up again, and let my smile widen. "Then please accept my deepest apologies..."

"Chris Mulligan."

"Veronica Simon."

He squinted at me as if the fluorescents above the door hurt his eyes. "You look familiar."

"I think we go to the same school, although your distinctive style should've made you more...distinctive," I finished lamely.

I was lying. I'd been noticing him for a long time, a math class here, an English class there, sneaking glances at his profile over my copy of *Huck Finn*, reading his stories in the *Dalesville High Journal* with a little more interest than a profile of Coach Blake necessitated. I didn't want to open with that, though. I thought I might come off as a stalker, especially since I'd never actually worked up the courage to talk to him until now.

I watched him as he took a drag on his cigarette, the sharp plane of his cheek sucked in slightly. It should've made him look gaunt, but his face was softened by long lashes and lips whose curves always seemed to quirk on the edge of a smile.

Not that I'd ever visualized kissing those lips or anything, or thought about running my hands through that shiny black hair. Nope, not me. I wasn't remotely disconcerted by his proximity and was in no way having any problem paying attention to what he was saying. Absolutely not. This was purely professional.

"...anyway, there's a day-Chris and a night-Chris. Mostly 'cause day-Chris has enough to do getting up and getting dressed without killing someone to manage more than jeans and a shirt. Then again, my dad hates it when I dress like this."

"That's enough of a reason to do it, yeah?" My voice didn't shake at all. Go me.

"Pretty much." He finished his smoke and ground it out under his boot. "My friends are going to think I died. I should get back in. I'll look for you."

"Do that."

He smiled and was gone again into the bowels of *The* Club, so named because it was the only one in town.

I hefted myself upright from the wall, turned and stared at the door that shut behind him. In the minute after he left, I knew I could pull open the door and follow him inside. Hell, maybe I could ask him to do the sway. Instead, I crushed the smoke, turned again, and made my way through the parking lot and out into the streets of downtown Dalesville.

The night was sullen with silence as I walked past alleys lively with trash and their furry inhabitants, boarded or soaped windows of stores and restaurants, victims of the now decades-old mall where the shinier kids took their economic and social business. As I meandered past the shuttered Blue Moon Café toward the square, I wasn't sure why I hadn't gone back inside, found him, and asked him to do the clutch and sway on the dance floor. I'd been waiting for this opportunity.

Keep your distance. Find out what happened.

All my planning and thinking hadn't given me any idea on how to achieve both. Focus on the latter, I lectured myself as I continued my walk, the square coming into view. That was the important thing, wasn't it? Not the way his smile quirked on and off, like a shorted-out lamp, or his gangly walk, or the shock of black hair he kept pushing back from his forehead. I wanted *him* intrigued, not me.

You could just ask him.

My foot stumbled over a rock on the sidewalk. I kicked it hard into the street.

When had asking nicely ever gotten me anything?

The nip of night air felt nice on my skin, and I let my sudden bad mood trail away. I dug another cigarette out of my bag and lit it, focused on the fact I'd kept my head around him, and known to quit while I was ahead.

The light from a trashcan fire in the alley next to the St. James Hotel—formerly the "jewel of downtown Dalesville" and now home to anyone who could pay the ten dollar a night charge—illuminated the stark dark branches of the catalpa in the center of the square. I ambled over there, took a seat on the warped wooden bench under the tree, and leaned back, sending smoke up toward the icepick stars above.

Alone was better. Dad would be home on Sunday, in time to drag me to church, where I had the joy of being surrounded by people whose only connection was how much they hated everything not like them. I wasn't like them, and the effort to hide that was exhausting. Worse, the collective crazy of Dad's church of freaks had a way of sneaking through the chinks in my mental armor even without touching them.

I hugged my arms more tightly around myself. Alone was definitely better.

The square was deserted, and the silence loud. My ears strained to pick up a sound, any sound. Relief came in the form of an idling car nearby. A door slammed, and I stood, turned away from the street. It was time to move on, sneak back into the house.

"Hey. I thought it was you."

I spun around again, on my guard, and was facing Chris, giving me that same flickering smile.

He stepped back, the smile gone. "Unless you didn't want to be bothered."

I let my face relax. "No, it's fine. I wasn't doing anything important."

It quirked on again. "Cool. We're," he gestured toward the station wagon, where two shadows lurked in the depths of the car, "going to Sam's for some coffee and grease. Wanna come with?"

"Well…" I thought about the walk and the pleasure of solitude, that smile and the sharp teeth of the wind. Thought about sitting next to Dad and being harangued for my sinful nature in this our sinful world, anger like incense lingering in the air. Smiled, because it worked. "Why not?"

We walked together toward the car. Chris opened the passenger door for me. Up close, I noticed two boys in the backseat sporting a motley collection of piercing, tats, and other blasphemous attire, and scrambled right in and slammed the door behind me.

Chapter Two

The smell of incense was worked into the wooden pew. In front of him was the doleful face of the suffering Christ. He saw no judgment there, no expression carved into the face that said, "Chris, you have sinned. You are cast from my kingdom."

There was enough of that in the pinched faces of the communicants' heel-toe-ing it up the aisle. He stared instead at the lip of the pew where he was kneeling, trying not to slump and lay his head there. The wages of sin were falling asleep in church and waking up to see the red creep up his father's neck, and the disappointment in his mom's eyes. His father—his Dad's friends called him Big Pat, and so did Chris in his head—was always angry about something lately, and thus easy to dismiss. Mom's disappointment was rarer and harder to take.

Be a good boy.

When he was little, he'd wanted that life. A modern-day Saint Francis, working with the sick and poor. A life of service to the greater good. Christ's representative on earth.

That was all gone. He wasn't sure exactly where it had gone. Maybe it was as simple as getting old enough to be horrified at the idea of never getting laid. Maybe it was Catholic grade school and the bitter nuns and pietistic priests and the hypocritical good boys and girls they praised, who were no better than anybody else. If it hadn't been hard for him to figure out they were full of shit, shouldn't people who'd devoted themselves to God be able to see through all that crap, too?

There was one thing left that could still give him an echo of that old magic. The darkened church, priest in the nave with a large candle, and then the parishioners lighting their candles, each to each, until the church was full of hundreds of flickering flames. Easter vigil: the return of Alleluia, the return of the Lord from the hell of death.

Eventually, the candles were snuffed, and he'd start counting the hours until the vigil was done.

"The mass is over. Go in peace to love and serve the Lord."

The organist crashed into the recessional like he was playing Notre Dame rather than a mid-sized Midwestern Catholic church. Chris wasn't the only one who jumped. He suspected Big Pat actually had dozed off, given the wide-eyed bleary gaze he returned to the priest. Still, he managed to get himself together to lead the procession out of the pew as soon as Fr. Nickols and the altar boys had swept past. Chris outdistanced his family almost immediately, pulling on his jacket as he walked down the aisle and out the doors into the sharply cool sunlit Sunday morning.

He lit a cigarette the minute his feet hit the mended asphalt of the parking lot, picked out their rust-bitten station wagon among the shiny sedans and SUVs of the other parishioners, and strode in that direction. Their newer truck was in the shop, and money was tight while Big Pat was on disability. From that vantage point, he could watch his parents nod and smile at Fr. Nickols, watch his sister Meg squirm with irritation at being forced to stand still after an hour of sitting in church.

He took a drag of his cigarette and followed the lazy drift of his thoughts to Friday night and the girl who got into the car. They'd driven over to Sam's, the mangy twenty-four-hour diner on Sunset amid with strip malls and dollar theaters and fast food joints like neon pimples on the green backside of the hills surrounding the town. The fries were undercooked, the pie was rubbery, the coffee could either strip paint or be thin enough to read through, and the air was thick with cheap cigarette smoke, old grease, and beer sweat from the good ole boys who'd stumble in when The Rambler across the street closed, but it was theirs. The girls with shiny hair, the guys with visible biceps? They never set foot in Sam's. It was the boys clad in black, pale from choice or from spending hours in their parents' basement reading *Lord of the Rings* or playing Dungeons and Dragons, the girls who pierced their noses or dyed and spiked their hair in electric blue or Kelly green or cherry red. Even more subtle outcasts—the girl who'd rather read English lit or was too fascinated by string theory, the boy who liked to draw, or even the ultimate crime in a mid-sized Midwestern town in the mid-nineties, the boy who like other boys—flocked to Sam's.

Sam's, *The* Club, the Blue Moon coffee shop, Lou's Used Records—those belonged to all of the above. To hell with the rest of the town. Chris was counting the days, and his savings, until he could leave for good.

They'd stood in the doorway, and he could recognize almost everyone under twenty. Mark, who could quote verbatim from *The Hitchhiker's Guide to the Galaxy* and laughed at any mention of the number forty-two, or Cecilia and Tim, with heads both shaved on one side so when they sat together, it looked like one head of dyed black hair. They were the town's answer to Kim Gordon and Thurston Moore, and played their brand of odd, intellectual rock every other Saturday at the Blue Moon.

Veronica? He couldn't remember her at any of those places, only coming out of the ground fog at *The* Club, laughing at him, or sprawled on a bench under the worn catalpa in the square, staring up at the sky. That was weird. She was memorable. Tall, with dark brown hair in a careless ponytail, and a glance so sharp, it could cut glass.

The four of them had wended their way through the crowd, pouncing on a table under the incongruous white pergola in the center of the restaurant mere seconds after the two old dudes with trucker hats stood, adjusted their droopy jeans, and with deep scowls as they eyed the four of them up and down, walked pigeon-toed to the door. They paired off—his best friends Laine and Julian, Chris and Veronica—across the table from each other. Chris noticed Laine's grin and knew he'd planned it. The easier to talk without awkwardly craning one's neck.

Before any of them could say a word, Shirley appeared, exhaling annoyance along with a faint tinge of Juicy Fruit. She knew well enough they stayed too long and ordered too little. It vanished, in the smoothing of her wrinkled nose and a smile lurking behind her eyes, when she saw Veronica. "Hey, sweetie. What are you doin' here this late, and with these losers?"

Veronica grinned. "Making new friends."

She laid a bony talon on Veronica's shoulder, green sparking behind the brown of her eyes. "You could do better."

Laine's expression matched both of theirs. "How come she's 'sweetie' and we're 'losers'?"

Shirley filled up their cups and started to walk away, then turned back, still smiling. "She tips well."

Laine snorted as he stirred sugar into his coffee. "There, see, you're ruining it for the rest of us."

Veronica winked at him. "That was the plan."

A car on Sunset backfired, jolting Chris back to the reality that he'd been half asleep leaning against the car with a lit cigarette. Stupid. He dropped the butt, yawned, and glanced over at the church. His parents were finally making a move away from Fr. Nickols, Megan danced with impatience against Mom, who still had a grip on her hand.

He stood up straight, watched as the last cars eased out of the church parking lot. Both of them volunteered at Our Lady of Peace—Mom as Eucharistic minister, Big Pat disclaiming the Word in his booming voice for the first or second reading. They were probably discussing schedules or something boring like that. He was glad he was too far away to overhear.

He'd watched Veronica talk to Laine, who looked smaller than usual next to her. She was tall, with angular long arms and hands that seemed built for grand gestures, discussing bands they liked (none of whom would have set foot in Dalesville), while the smoke from her cigarette curlicued upward. When she wasn't smiling, her face looked cold. He glanced toward the church and saw her resemblance to the stone-carved virgin above its doors. Still, it was interesting—and a little disturbing—how well she fit in with the three of them, a piece he hadn't realized was missing.

He'd been so intent on his examination of her that he didn't at first realize she was staring at him. When their eyes met, he'd had the disconcerting sensation of being looked through, felt an odd shudder deep in his gut like some ancient machinery coughed to life.

"X-ray vision," he'd said before he realized he'd said anything. She jumped a little, red tinging her face and making it less stone, more human.

She fumbled another cigarette out of the pack, eyes down, before looking up at him again. The unnerving gaze was gone. "Sorry. I do that sometimes. I'm not great at people."

He returned her smile with one of his own, shrugged. "Forget it. It's all good."

"Yes." What that was an answer to, he wasn't sure. Leaning against the car, watching his family come toward him, he still wasn't sure. He turned the moment over in his head, trying again to figure it out. Something else. He glanced toward the church again, Fr. Nickols' vestments blew out behind him like a cape, and he wondered when Nickols knew he'd wanted to be a priest. Nickols was always banging on about vocations, that sense of being called, and that Chris never felt it was another reason he'd dropped that particular life plan. His cold hands balled into fists in his pockets as he realized what it was: he felt chosen. But for what?

"Who wants to go out for breakfast?" Mom asked as the three of them came to a stop at the car.

Megan hopped up and down, braids bouncing. "I do, I do!"

Mom cocked an eyebrow at him. "Chris?"

He shrugged, his mind still on the night before. "Sure. Why not?"

His parents shared a wry look, but it was Mom who spoke. "Your enthusiasm's overwhelming."

"I'm dancing on the inside."

She swatted him on the arm. "In the car, reprobate. You'll eat with the family and like it."

"Torture." He dismissed all thoughts of Veronica and vocations, winked at his mother, and dutifully got into the car.

Chapter Three

On those plush chairs, hard words flung at us like kids spitting cherry pits, Dad sat as he always did—on the dining room chairs at dinner, on the easy chair in the living room—as if a broomstick stiffened his spine, and slumping would snap it in two. Or maybe he was like a tree, feet planted in black polished shoes the shiny roots of a banyan tree, like the ones we'd seen in Hawaii—the last vacation before everything went to hell—grey cotton twill pants as a trunk, and the white shirt the spreading leaves that threw me in shadow. His branches twined so tight around me I could hardly see daylight, wooden bars that both held me in and kept me out.

Dalesville called itself "City of Light", but shadows obsessed me. They crept around the edges of the congregants at Faith Fellowship every Sunday. If I concentrated, I could see their colors, tinged red for rage, the sick seafoam of jealousy, and the indigo of defeat. I tried not to concentrate too much anymore. All of them tasted rotten, like the limning of vomit in my throat and nostrils after a bad migraine. I did what I did any time I was around these people, bricked myself off and imagined myself away, a little tip from Mom.

"I know what it's like, sweetheart, to feel too much." A game of Red Rover had sent me home from school. Frankie Pyle, twice the size of the rest of us and four times as mean, had crashed into me, his hand grabbed mine as we both fell, but the real blow had been the sight of his dad, belt in hand as Frankie (me) cowered by the front door. I hadn't been able to stop shaking, even as the playground monitor took me to the nurse's office. They finally gave in and called Mom. On the car ride home, Mom's touch was gentle as she took my scraped hand, eyes still on the road. "It's better than feeling nothing at all, but if it gets to be too much, imagine a wall, and you safe behind it." I started wearing gloves whenever I could, but if my teachers noticed, they usually told me to take them off, thinking I'd forgotten after recess. Keeping my distance from other people got me branded as a snob, a more painful protection than gloves or mental walls.

"And on that day, the tree will provide no shelter, the rock will not protect you." Dragged from my memory of Mom, I looked up at Reverend Ash as he intoned those words, his face bloodless and cold. He wasn't telling me anything I didn't already know. "The sinner will cry out—the secularists, the sodomites—but too late. It is justice for those who pervert Jesus' way."

I glared at Ash, as if he'd notice. Thought about Chris' friend Laine, a grin as he tried to draw me into the conversation the night before, or quiet Julian and the way he listened then managed to express in a few words something relevant or insightful. Nothing evil or dark about either of them. Ash was full of shit. Well, that wasn't news.

"Before we depart from one another this week," he said with all the fervor of an airline pilot droning about safety procedures, "Our illustrious shepherd and founder, Mr. Robert James, would like to address you."

I shifted in my seat next to Dad, who for once didn't notice since he was staring at Mr. James with the same mind-blown look of a newborn. I looked around, barely bothering to be slick about it, at the assembled Faith Fellows whose looks matched my dad's. Only then did I let my gaze rest on this object of worship. He was as he always was, a small man, lithe despite the apple he carried in front, his broad face a little flushed. There were a thousand twins of his in every state—well-fed, round-eyed—nothing in his appearance spoke of anything extraordinary. Until he started to talk.

"Destiny." He grinned like a man facing a porterhouse and a martini. "Now, you might ask yourselves, well, why is old Bob throwin' around big words like that? Why, that sounds darn near prideful, and as you well know," a wink to all and sundry, "that's the same sin that got the Morningstar thrown in the pit."

His pudgy hands gripped the podium and his head bowed ever so slightly, so that the light reflected off the smooth plane of his forehead like a halo. "I hope I don't suffer from the sin of pride when I say that word, though, when I tell you we are a people of destiny."

"Amen!" rose up from everyone—except me.

"Amen is right!" Mr. James looked up then, gifted us all with his smile. "When my grandfather said to those Godless Easterners, 'Enough!' he had only his faith to guide him here and the faith of those wise enough to follow and they suffered." The corners of his mouth turned down, eyes shimmering with a grief about as real as spray cheese. "Oh, they suffered like we can't even think of, coming to a strange land, with none of those comforts we have now. The way to the Promised Land is always hard, and what did they find when they arrived?"

I could feel the tension in the congregation, like children at story hour, spellbound by what's next. Behind my wall, I was untouched by any of it.

"Nothing!" His voice echoed through the church. A murmur broke through the congregation, like a soft wave kissing the shore. "No Golden Arches! No mall to buy shoes and new shirts! No McClellan's to buy fishing poles and buckshot! So, what did those poor souls do? They built it—they built the Promised Land with the labor of their hands and the sweat of their brows. They shivered, they coughed—husbands lost wives, mothers lost children—and still they pressed on! Alleluia!"

Everyone stood together. I was pressed up against my will, pulled by my father and the woman sobbing next to me. I kept my eyes on Robert James and felt nothing but cold, as if I was one of those settlers, stupidly shivering in a tent because I followed a madman.

His voice dropped then, like a hand over the clapper of a bell. All his tricks, loud and soft, simple words for simple people, flattery, I could see through them all. Under the cover of my hair and behind the shelter of my mental wall, I glanced at Dad again, who was as transported as the rest, and felt as far from him as if he'd left me back in Colorado. How could he fall for this?

"Now, my good people, our destiny turns again. We stand on the threshold, as my grandfather and his followers did." His voice was conversational, like he was sitting at everyone's kitchen table, eating fresh baked muffins, and complimenting the coffee. "We will spread our good news far and wide. We will turn the world—yup, I said world!—from error. Will you stand with me?"

As one, they shouted, "Yes!"

He nodded, jowls bobbling in that aw-shucks way he had. "Well, I knew you would. The sinful world we live in stops at the doors of

Faith Fellowship. Already our good news is reaching far and wide and you can help us with that, can't you?"

I stared down at my feet and grinned. All that song and dance for money. I heard the tearing of checks all around me, the furtive scramble to find a few coins among the less blessed, dredged from linty pockets, from the cracked leather of ancient purses. Only when all the baskets were lined up at the altar did Robert James address us again. I watched his own hastily concealed grin at the fullness of all of them. "You don't know what you have done."

My breath caught in my throat at those words, the first thing he'd said that touched me. I stared at him like I'd never seen him before, like he hadn't been the looming presence of my life for the past five years. In that moment, it was me and Robert James, and the cold crawly feeling in my scalp that told me I'd heard him speak the truth for the first time. He stared back at me with a soft smile. "No one will stand in our way."

"God bless you all." With that, he bowed the Reverend Ash, and snapped his fingers at his number two, Paul Barnes. Paul and the men with him gathered up the baskets and followed Robert James into the chapel.

I slumped where I stood, dizzy with relief.

We walked out after, Dad shook hands with Reverend Ash, my friend Nancy gave me a quick wave and the "call me" fingers as she got into her parents' sedan. I scowled as I stared at the ground. Sure, she had time for me, as long as her boyfriend Jeremy was busy. As I passed under the shadow of the giant cross that threw the entrance into gloom, my shiver had nothing to do with the cold bite of February air after the close warmth of the church. Like the lurid red-paint bleeding Christ above the altar, his peach-colored face a tortured rictus of pain, it scared me. I couldn't ever say that, because I was afraid of what

Dad would think that meant about me, that I feared God because of the devil inside me. Jesus didn't scare me, but his followers at Faith Fellowship did. Because I had my own cloaked places, a damning strangeness in a place without unity, only a safe, Novocain sameness.

In the after-church crowd, I could feel all those ugly emotions trying to chip away at my wall, and I held my breath, held myself, trying not to touch anyone. I kept my head down through the crowd, Dad already at the door, my gloved hands fisted at my side. Wasn't making that mistake again.

Dad caught my eye, made an impatient come-on gesture. I nodded and followed. As we drove through downtown, past the Old Saint James, around the square where Chris picked me up on Friday, and up toward Sunset to the way home, I couldn't get my mind off that speech. My stomach squirmed as it always did when I thought about Robert James. He was, on the surface, not that different from all the other men that showed up Tuesday nights to our house—for fellowship, as they called it—as they thumbed through their well-worn Bibles and furrowed their brows while bitching about liberal humanism, feminazis, "the gays," the brilliance of Limbaugh and the evil of the Clintons, flop sweat and resentment oozing from their pores. Like the houses in City of Light Acres, with their identical dark green doors, tan siding and green shingles, it was hard to tell one from another, with their constant been-done-wrong songs, wife left me, affirmative action keeps me down, immigrants taking my jobs, kids have no respect. I would drift in with a tray of food and they'd fill their plates without meeting my eyes. I didn't bother to look at them either, or even learn their names. I rechristened them as "Stumpy," "Baldy," "The Asshole," and "Never-Gotten-Laid-Guy." But him—Mr. Robert James ("Bob to my friends," but I never heard anyone call him anything but Mr. James)—he stayed in my head, even though he only came to our house once, said little, and left quickly.

I came into the living room with a tray of deviled eggs, in the high-collared navy blue dress Dad had picked out for me to wear. Dad gestured for me to serve Mr. James first and so I obediently and unobtrusively positioned the tray in his eye line and myself out of it. He took an egg with pudgy fingers and looked up at me. His eyes were round and blue, protruding from a soft, multiple-chinned face. I knew that face. He looked me up and down, but there was nothing covetous in it. His face morphed into a smile belied by an emotion I couldn't read. My hands went cold, nerveless, and I almost dropped the tray. "Thank you, Veronica." His voice was soft, a little high and it wormed itself into my head, like I was being hypnotized.

He finally looked away, folded the egg into his mouth in one bite, and I could move again. As soon as each had been served, I ran back into the kitchen, setting the tray onto the counter with a loud clatter that went unheard over the volume of one guy's diatribe about teaching evolution in schools and I leaned against the counter and shook so hard I thought I'd break into pieces.

When I'd finally gotten myself under control, I steeled my spine and reemerged with the sandwich tray. The relief at seeing Mr. James gone nearly made me drop the tray again. Yet, that night I felt boiled alive by nightmares in which Mr. James ordered Shorty and Stumpy and Never-Been-Laid to enact biblical justice on me. "Why?" I managed to ask before I woke up with my fist in my mouth to keep from screaming. His voice was a bell ringing across a wasteland. "For your presumption."

The nightmares gradually diminished over the week that followed, and the dream of routine reasserted itself. I slept-walked through my days. Up at six, shower and dress, Dad's alarm at precisely 6:45

a.m. and then his breakfast at 7:15 a.m. (eggs, light toast, crispy bacon, coffee two sugars), brush teeth and out the door to school. Eat lunch alone, chew up the hours of school, digest equations, dates, gerunds, and then drift home through the shortcut in the cemetery. Plod through homework, housework, a dinner eaten silently, and then bed. School was a gauntlet I walked alone, which occasioned a dozen teacher conferences and reports in grade school, all about "not interacting with peer group," and "causing distress" when accidental contact and no filter made me blurt out some kid's big secret. He wet the bed, she snuck into her sister's room and pinched her cheek until the baby cried. It was a slow boil every Sunday at Faith Fellowship, never mind the Tuesdays in the living room. Better to stay apart.

All that changed when I saw Mom's face in Mrs. Phelps' head.

Not a good time to be brooding on that, I thought as we passed the sign for City of Light Acres, the subdivision he'd built for the staff of his church, the faculty of Faith Fellowship Academy, College, and Seminary, and other worthies. Janitors and lunch ladies need not apply, they were relegated to the rundown section at the bottom of the hill. Once home, Dad as usual, retreated to his office to either work or read—the Bible, most likely, although sometimes he branched out to books published by Light of the World Publishing, also owned by the James family. He gave me a tight smile as he passed me in the hallway and then into his office, door closed, for once not giving me instruction to wash or clean or cook.

I hung a left into my own room and the next few hours were free to veg out on my bed with a book. He cleared his bookshelves of secular books. That was a battle I'd won, claiming I'd need them for school. I shuffled through my shelves 'til I found my worn, taped copy of *Watership Down* and tossed it on the bed while I changed into jeans and a t-shirt, then flopped down on the bed to lose myself in the story.

But I couldn't concentrate, thoughts of the past made me feel jumpy and jumbled. I shut the book, then my eyes, trying to focus. Instead, I fell asleep.

After my unscheduled nap, I felt better enough to focus on making dinner. A dinner Dad was less interested in than the expense reports, monthly revenue statements, or something of that ilk that made me yawn to think about. I wasn't allowed the luxury of reading material at the dinner table, but if I made my face a mask, I could think of a myriad of unapproved topics.

I cut my chicken silently, he didn't like the scrape of silver against plates or teeth. "It's distracting and impolite," he always said. Unlike, for instance, ignoring the only other person at the table. Still, I had mastered the art of silent eating years before. It no longer took all my attention to make sure that nothing precipitated the rattle of paper and the emergence of his cold blue stare.

There were reasons for this—the high bar I could never ever meet—I knew them all. The most intractable, stone-sunk reason was the development of my character, its shadow side, "Don't end up like your mother."

The pain of that thought sunk deep, instantly into my stomach and throat. I stared down at the remnants of dinner on my plate—a few bites of chicken, a forlorn leaf of romaine, scribbles of oil and balsamic vinegar—until I could be certain the mask was back in place. Thoughts of Mom could be saved for when I was alone.

Instead, I thought of Friday. Laine's cherub face and soft grin when he looked at Julian, who seemed all angles and other hard geometric lines until he smiled back at his boyfriend. And Chris, who watched me when he thought I wasn't paying attention, like the budding investigative reporter he was. Nothing cold or hard in any of them. I felt a smile emerge despite my best efforts, which unfortunately happened to coincide with my father looking up from his papers.

"Something funny?" The low light of the dining room and the downward tilt of his eyes over his reading glasses made them the only thing visible. I only ever saw bars when I looked at my father, I always thought they were for me.

I let the smile fade by degrees. "No, Dad. I was pleased the chicken turned out well."

Confusion flickered behind his eyes—no more than a flash—before the usual sternness reasserted itself in the downward pull of his mouth, the laddered creases in his forehead. "Yes, it was more than adequate. Nice work."

My eyes felt itchy, it took me a moment to realize I was near tears. I stared down at my plate, it doubled. "Thank you, Dad."

We sat in silence for the next few minutes until he stood up, gathering up his papers into a tidy pile. "Good night, Veronica."

I looked up, searching for any softness in his expression and hating myself for doing so. Of course, there was none, and he was already halfway to his office at the end of the hall before I could even respond with a "Good night" of my own. I gathered up the dishes and went to do my duty.

Once in my room, I let everything relax, starting with the sore muscles of my face. I rubbed my temples to ease the little headache brought on from trying not to cry at dinner and enjoyed the darkness of the room, broken only by the yellow streetlight in the alley behind our house. It cast everything into shadow, vaguely identifiable hunches in the dark, desk, chair, bed, vanity, and bookcase.

I turned on the light and they became themselves. While the rest of the house was undeniably Dad's—hard wood and straight-backed chairs—this was mine. The blue-painted vanity Mom had stenciled with flowers, the old desk with all its marks and scratches intact, and a picture I'd framed of the park near our old house in Denver, with its little grove of trees where the intense mountain sun was mellowed and refracted. I used to nip over there on hot days, a book in one hand, beaded glass of lemonade in reach of the other, and lay on the needles and leaves. I'd read and listen to the rattle of branches or roll on my back and stare up at the highest branches, the sky, a suggestion between the leaves. Mom had taken a picture and framed it, knowing how much I loved that place, how unreal it felt.

My earlier near-tears experience had not retreated far enough for me to look at that picture for long. I changed into my raggedy sweatpants and t-shirt, crawled into bed, and turned out the light, even though I wasn't really tired. Instead, I stared up at a ceiling I couldn't really see and that image recurred. In the dark, with no distractions, it was always more clear. Mom in a bed. A hospital, judging by the tubes I could see snaking up from the bed, like the IV I'd had when my tonsils came out and I got to spend a week eating pudding and ice cream. How? Why? As far as I knew, Mom had never been here and had never gone to Faith Fellowship. Did she come here and try to see me, only to have some kind of accident?

I leaned over, opened my eyes to the yellow glow of the streetlight in the alley behind our house. What I wanted more than anything was to ask Mom, to have her tell me everything was *okay*, even if it was a lie. No, it was worse than that. I wanted someone else to be the one to figure it out.

I rolled over on my back, tired but unable to sleep. The streetlight in the alley turned the star above my bed a sickly yellow. I knew what

I needed and no clue how to get it, someone to talk to, someone to trust. Someone who'd carry this with me, for once.

Chapter Four

Chris and Laine lay back in the carpet of leaves under the weeping willow in the park across from school. Here, with the weak, late, winter sun refracting through the denuded branches, the bone rattle of the wind, smoke rings drifting lazily upward toward the light, he could almost forget. He couldn't see the school, couldn't see his friend unless he turned his head, and Chris wasn't inclined to move much at that moment. Hell, he could've dozed off quite easily, with the quiet, soft mattress of leaves, and his battered leather jacket snug around him. Then he wouldn't have to think about the chilly reality of his situation. As it was, he could hardly think about anything else.

The bell rang, breaking the idyll. "Do we have to?" He heard the whine in his voice and cringed.

A smoke ring drifted upward. "No." Another pause, another smoke ring. "Well, probably. Aren't you supposed to be at the newspaper this period?"

"Yeah, the world's waiting for my deathless expose on the parking lot debate." Chris sat up and was momentarily discombobulated by the inevitable head rush. He shook it off and turned, saw that Laine was already standing, backpack slung over one shoulder. "What are you so fired up for?"

"Calculus test."

"Thrilling." Chris slowly unfolded upwards, his legs prickling slightly from being crossed. "It doesn't matter at this point, does it? We've already been accepted. For as much good as it does me right now."

Laine rolled his eyes, shifted from foot to foot, like his feet had fallen asleep, too. "Don't start. I told you already, you'll get there eventually. You need to make some money."

Chris shrugged and scooped up his satchel. "Whatever. I've got an interview after school."

Laine proceeded to dig in his backpack. "Shit. You got a pen?" Chris sighed and reached into his bag, feeling around until he felt a couple that had fallen to the bottom. He handed one to Laine. "Cool." Laine tossed it in his bag, "So, where's the interview?"

They had started back up the hill before Chris answered, "McClellan's Sporting Goods."

Laine stopped Chris' forward progress by grabbing his arm. When Chris turned, he could see barely suppressed laughter all over Laine's face. "Big Pat's McClellan's?"

"Is there another one?"

Then Laine did laugh, Chris could've hit him. "Following in your dad's footsteps? Is that what the cool kids are doing now? Maybe I should join the army like my dad."

"Shut up." Chris started, stomping back up the hill again and leaving Laine behind. "It doesn't matter anyhow. McClellans'll take almost anyone."

Undaunted, Laine jogged up next to him and grinned. "Screw it. You should think of happier things. Like that girl you picked up in the square last week."

Laine's optimism grated when he was all set to be crabby, but he couldn't deny the little lift somewhere in the vicinity of his gut. Chris didn't want to admit it, but his face didn't get the memo, before he could stop it, he smiled. He looked down and resumed his usual scowl with a great deal of effort, but not fast enough. Out of the corner of his eye he saw Laine jump, followed by a laugh. "I knew it! You like her."

He turned the scowl on his friend, but Laine was undaunted. "Want me to give her a message? We've got calc together."

"No!" He was surprised at his own vehemence. "I mean, there's nothing to say. If something is going to happen, it will."

Chris picked up the pace as the second bell rang, more to stop the conversation than out of any real desire to not be late.

Laine button-hooked around him and leaned against the door. "Don't you have a test?"

"Screw the test. I mean, I get the not-dating thing, you don't wanna get stuck here, but lately, you've an action problem. You let things happen and then bitch about how nothing turns out right. Grow up and do something."

A sharp ray of anger broke the grey clouds of the mood he'd been in since he'd found out there was no money for college. Laine was small and it took little effort to push him aside. "Fuck off."

Chris yanked open the door and stormed inside, not looking behind him to see if Laine followed.

By the time he'd reached the door of his history class, he was already regretting what he'd done. Being shoved around was nothing new to Laine and as Chris slumped into class and took a seat in the back, self-loathing lined his throat like puke. As he pulled out a notebook and pen, he realized he'd guilted himself into doing exactly what that wily little bastard suggested. Damn Catholic upbringing.

"Mulligan, huh? You Pat's son?"

Chris forced a smile. "That's right."

Art as his name tag proclaimed, gave him an exaggerated once-over. Chris could tell, in the laddered lines on Art's broad brow, in the light downturn of Art's lips, and in the wobble of Art's chin, that he was at a loss to see Big Pat's lineage in Chris' skinny black-clad frame. It wasn't exactly the first time he'd gotten that look.

"Your dad's a good man, hard worker. We'll all be happy to see him back here. You tell him that for me."

"Will do." Chris could hear the fake bonhomie in his own voice, but Art didn't seem to notice. He kept the building sigh inside, but the inhale brought with a hearty dose of eau de Art, a nauseating mixture of B.O. and cheap aftershave. He coughed before he could stop himself and Art looked up from the spreadsheet he'd been squinting at.

"Well, can use someone for the three to eleven shift on Saturdays."

"*A.m.* or p.m.?"

Art's smile verged on a sneer. "*A.m.*"

Chris was careful not to give Art the reaction he was sure Art was looking for. It was a test to weed out slackers, Chris was sure of it. "Sounds good. When can I start?"

Art's smile immediately warmed. "Next Saturday'll be fine."

Art stood, so Chris did likewise, dwarfing him by almost a foot. Art was almost all torso and bulging gut. "Welcome to the McClellan's family, son. I'm sure you'll do well."

"Thank you, sir."

"You want to get to shipping a little early your first time—paperwork, badge, you know. Give it an extra twenty minutes or so."

Chris nodded and gave Art another fake smile. At least he wasn't assigned to receiving. That was his father's domain, and he didn't think either of them could take the constant comparison. It was probably a legal thing—no shows of nepotism or favoritism—outside of Chris getting an interview in the first place. He'd lied to Laine, McClellan jobs weren't that easy to come by. He knew he should be grateful that he wasn't manning the fryer at one of the fast-food joints on Sunset. He'd traded on the Mulligan name and that queasy feeling he had would pass eventually, he supposed. McClellan's Sporting Goods was the biggest deal in town, outside Faith Fellowship Church, with good money, good benefits, and pensions. The only deal really, after the copper mines that boomed the town a century before had been stripped and abandoned, leaving nothing but scars on the landscape with some free toxic waste in the ground water. Chris knew he should be grateful to have that job but all he felt was a burn in his stomach, like he'd drunk a big glass of unfiltered Dalesville water.

Art handed him a stack of papers, shook his hand. "Fill these out and bring them with you on Saturday and good luck."

Chris picked up his beaten-up black cloth satchel from where it rested like a faithful old dog next to his chair, tucked the paperwork inside, and left. The relative freshness of the hallway after Art's haven of stinkiness, paper piles, and coffee-scummed mugs was a relief, but couldn't really touch that feeling in his gut.

McClellan's was the last place he wanted to be. Not only was his dad a legend there—fast rise through the ranks, a consistent rise in productivity since he'd become foreman, smart but could still relate to the guys on the floor—it was all mixed in with the disappointment of being stuck here on the threshold of escape.

He finally let out the sigh he'd been holding in as he pushed the door open and made his way through the parking lot to the wagon. He tried to let the bad feeling out with it but in that, he was less successful. All he could hear was Big Pat's voice telling him to suck it up and quit whining. He got in the wagon, slammed the door shut like it would cut that voice off, started the car and turned on the radio to block any other Big Pat-like thoughts out of his head. It wasn't really his parents' fault. Shit happened. His head knew that.

"It's a postponement, that's all," Mom had said, her eyes still traced with the red lines that bespoke a combo of crying and exhaustion. She'd been the one to break the news about it, for which Chris was grateful. Big Pat's bluff and walk-it-off brand of comfort would've pissed Chris off, ending with yelling and slammed doors, and honestly, he felt he was getting too old for that shit. Mom at least understood Chris' desire to get out, to a place where he wouldn't be eternally compared to Big Pat Mulligan and always found wanting. To elicit the badly concealed shock of the Arts of this town, that a specimen like his dad could produce a skinny-shanked malcontent like him. At the stoplight three blocks from home, Chris lit a cigarette and thought that it could be worse. He could be Laine, his father career army who made up for his short stature with constant weightlifting and a belligerence that shouted down any opposition. If Chris was a shock to his father, he wondered how Sgt. Melvin Gregory could produce a gay artist.

Chris grinned at the idea of some latent artistic strain in Laine's dad—some alternate reality where he sculpted male nudes—and decided that he should share that thought with Laine.

His mom's voice joined the chorus in his head, pointing out his particular offense to both biology and feminism in assuming that boys are only the products of their fathers and girls their mothers. He turned up the radio to just short of deafening, hoping to drown out both of them. Truth was, he *was* much more like his mother who was smart, quiet, and couldn't give a shit about sports. The only thing he'd gotten from his dad was the height. Megan was Dad's—she'd be tall like the rest of them, but even at ten, the broad shoulders were evident, and she'd have serious muscles when she grew up. She and Big Pat would sit watching sports regardless of season. Baseball in summer, football in the fall, basketball when the ground started to ice, and the wind got nasty. She'd curl up under his arm, mouth slightly open and eyes wide, asking questions about slotbacks and point guards while he pulled a braid and gave her a smile that would melt butter. In a low rumble, he'd explain or debate with her. He fought for her inclusion in various pee-wee baseball and football clubs in the neighborhood and would stand on the sidelines watching her with the same rapt attention she gave to their televised togetherness. The whole way home they'd discuss plays, blocking and other stuff that went right over Chris' head.

It bored Chris stiff, even overhearing it. He wasn't jealous, exactly, but he couldn't help but wish Big Pat ever looked at him with anything warmer than his frown of bemused confusion, when he saw his son curled up on the couch with a cup of black coffee and *Jude the Obscure*. Although his dad got plenty warm whenever they argued about gay marriage or legalizing pot. Red, really, with that one neck vein that throbbed whenever he got really worked up.

Chris pulled into the driveway, the truck was in the garage, which meant he could expect the whole family when he walked through the door. What joy.

He killed the engine, stubbed out his smoke in the ashtray, gathered the papers from the passenger side, and tried to mentally prepare for family time.

Big Pat took an aggressive bite of his pork chop as Chris made his announcement. "I got a job at McClellan's."

Big Pat choked and the next few minutes were a flurry of raised hands, coughing, and at least two glasses of water before he was given the all-clear. "My McClellan's?" His voice was a harsh rasp. Chris chalked it up to choking.

"Art assigned me to shipping."

It was odd to see his own relief mirrored on his father's face. He supposed it wouldn't be any easier to boss his own kid on the factory floor than at the dinner table. Chris knew it wasn't entirely fair to feel hurt that Big Pat didn't want him in his department, but there it was. Maybe he just wanted to know Big Pat would choose him for something. "Well, that shows some initiative, son."

Chris shrugged. "It pays better than anywhere else."

It was Big Pat's turn to look upset, and Chris felt his own bad mood lift fractionally.

"When do you start?" His mom, as usual, showed her ability to redirect such conversations out of the murkier waters.

"Saturday, three a.m. Oh, Dad, Art told me he sends his best."

"Art's a dick," he said around a mouthful of peas.

"Patrick!" Mom's outrage was almost drowned out by Chris and Megan's shared laughter.

"What? He is! Assigning *my son* to the graveyard shift? Who the hell does he think he is?"

Chris stopped laughing immediately and stared at his dad. For maybe the first time ever, he couldn't figure out where Big Pat was coming from. He waited until Megan's laughter tapered off and said, "It doesn't matter. I don't want any special favors."

Chris kept going over in his head, for the rest of the night, the look on Big Pat's face at that moment. As he sat doing trig, as he read *Return of the Native* for English, as he doodled feature topics for tomorrow's newspaper meeting, and as he brushed his teeth, his mind kept at it, like a recalcitrant screw that wouldn't loosen. Working the back molars, he finally realized that it almost looked like admiration. He spat out the idea with the toothpaste, he must have read it wrong. He knew full well how Big Pat felt about him, they had a history of arguments, misunderstandings, total confusion and no job was going to change that.

CHAPTER FIVE

M r. Pratt was droning on about ancient Greece, but I couldn't care less. Pratt, not unlike Reverend Ash at Faith Fellowship, could suck the life out of nearly any historical event. It was almost a talent.

Maybe I wasn't in the mood. It had been another nothing weekend. Dad had been home, so I couldn't sneak out, although he'd spent most of Saturday and Sunday with either expense reports or John's Apocalypse, so I might as well have been by myself. It was my goal to avoid him whenever he got apocalyptic, the end of the world scared me, or at least the lust for it I saw in his eyes and in the eyes of his Faith Fellows. I'd cornered Nancy after church to see if she wanted to get a coffee and catch up, but Jeremy Barnes was with her, and her refusal was distracted and not surprising.

I stared down at the blank page of my history notebook, trying to distract myself with doodling, copying snatches of lyrics that came into my head instead of notes on the Peloponnesian War, and it occurred to me that I was disappointed. I thought I'd see more of Chris—hoped, really, after that night at Sam's—but I guessed I hadn't made as much of an impression as I thought. Big shock there. I'd spent most of my time at Dalesville High School trying to be as invisible as possible.

I turned my attention to the bare-branched trees along the down path to the park, the sun played a futile peek-a-boo through the thick low clouds, and I tried to think of another plan to find out what happened to Mom. Or why I'd seen an image of her in the mind of someone at Faith Fellowship, a place I never thought she'd been. The few bucks I'd saved up and hidden in the pocket of Sparky, the stuffed overall-ed bear that I'd snuggled with in bed way past the age where that was cute, wouldn't be enough to hire a private investigator, even if I knew how to do such a thing.

The only real option left was the absolute last thing I wanted to do, take the gloves off and shake some hands at Faith Fellowship, to see if anybody else had images of Mom in their heads. The prospect made my stomach do high kicks. I never wanted them to know anything about me, never mind what *nobody* knew about me.

The bell rang across the gloomy drift of my thoughts, and Mr. Pratt's exhortations to *carefully* read chapter eight in *Pathways to History* and the day were over. I let the crowd thin as I put my books away at approximately the pace of a slug moving across a dry sidewalk. It was Tuesday after all, and Tuesdays bummed me out way more than Mondays. Mondays could potentially be the sparkling start to a wonderful week, even if it rarely was. But Tuesdays were the day all Dad's church buddies showed up to get pissed off and eat the food I had to make, without so much as a thank you. Nothing I wanted to rush home for. Even Mr. Pratt had departed by the time I pulled everything together and exited into the thankfully sparse after-school exodus.

Once out the main doors, I decided instead to keep on to the playground across the bridge. I was happy to see that the continued cold bite of the wind meant it was mostly deserted, except a jogging couple slowly making the circuit around its perimeter. I took a seat on one of the swings and let the wind push me from side to side.

Nancy and I would meet here sometimes, always at the end of summer without fail, when she'd get back from Bible camp—Dad never sent me, maybe he thought I'd run off—to share stories of our respective summers, while we tried to outdo each other in how high we could swing. At that moment, the recollection brought no warm glow of nostalgia or cold guilt that I hadn't talked to her much lately. Ever since she and Jeremy started dating, the distance between us—always there anyway, 'cause she was a true believer and I a reluctant participant—had only grown. Jeremy, the son of Robert James best bud Paul, only made it worse. Never mind that he was the perfect storm of pious and dull, but I didn't trust that anything I said or did around him wouldn't be reported to his dad. Then again, maybe it was always what happened when one friend started dating. Who could I even ask about that? A watery sigh escaped as I leaned my head against the chain of the swing and closed my eyes.

I don't know how long I sat there, half asleep, fingers numbing where I gripped the chains, when I heard the rattle and squeak of those on the swing to my left. I opened my eyes, not wanting to move forward and start home, but knowing I had no interest in sharing my time with a stranger.

"Hell of a place for a nap." Seated, swinging and with an insouciant grin, was Chris.

My words deserted me as I stared at his unexpected presence, his gangly legs dragging in the sand beneath the swing set.

"What, is there something on my face?" He ran his hands across his cheeks.

Embarrassed, I turned my attention to the joggers, who made a quick left into the grove of trees near the periphery of the park furthest from the school. "No, nothing. I was surprised to see you." In a lower tone, "And happy."

I glanced at him in time to catch the spark in his eyes that told me he'd heard those last two words. "Good. Good."

"What are you still doing here, anyway?" I could hear the echo of my recently departed bad mood in my voice and wondered if I'd ever manage not to act stupidly around other people.

Chris didn't seem to notice, he flashed me a grin as he adjusted his position on the swing, his long legs resting in the hollow. "Newspaper stuff. I'm working on a feature about plans to repave the parking lot. I'm sure the *Washington Post* will be banging down my door."

"I like your stuff. You always find some interesting angle. You're a good writer."

The tips of his ears turned red when I said that, and for a moment, he didn't seem to know what to do with himself. I thought I'd said the wrong thing and was seriously considering getting up and going home—cut my losses—when he smiled. "Sorry. I suck at taking compliments."

He took a deep breath and sat up straight, started pumping his legs and within a few moments he'd gotten a good height off the ground. Then he let go, and I gasped as I watched him fly through the air, as ungainly as an airplane taking off. He landed on both feet, no crash, and I released the breath I'd been holding in as a relieved sigh. He spun and faced me, raised his arms in triumph. "Come on, Veronica. Jump."

I shook my head. "No way. I lack your natural grace."

The grin quirked on. "Don't worry. I'll catch you."

"I'll knock you over."

He shrugged, his eyes still smiled. "I'll take that chance."

I smiled back. "It's your funeral." I stopped the sideways gentle sway and started to pump my legs, the wind biting my skin less painful, more exhilarating, and as I rose higher, I could feel that same abandon I saw in Chris as he leapt, not knowing how he'd land, not caring if he fell. That last of the pensive mood blew away as I went into the final high arc, let go, and flew toward where Chris was standing, ready to catch me.

I landed, and swayed with reaction to sudden gravity. Chris' hands gripped my arms, steadied me. We stood there as the wind blew around us, corkscrewing his hair around his face. He looked down at me, still holding my arms. For a moment, the wall cracked and let in an image of a slash of blue water, the sound of clinking cups, the smell of coffee. Not mine, but for once, I didn't mind. "Worth it?"

"Absolutely," I answered to both.

"Can I treat you to a coffee? You know, for your bravery?"

Reality would intrude, no matter how much I wished otherwise. "I can't. I have to get home and make dinner." I'd not yet apprised him of certain circumstances of my life. "Wanna walk me toward home through the cemetery?"

He grinned. "A morbid but fair trade. All right."

He dropped his hands and we both went back to the swings to gather our discarded bags. Chris got there first and handed me mine, our hands touched.

"Your hands are freezing. Don't you ever wear gloves?"

"Sorry. I lost them."

"Well, I'll have to keep them warm on the walk home." With that, he pulled off his gloves and threaded his right hand into my left one. The iciness began to thaw on contact—I felt warm all over. The image persisted, along with impressions of other things, an unwanted intimacy I didn't think Chris would appreciate. I took a deep breath to try and clear my mind, I wanted to be in this moment.

We crunched over the frozen grass. I was so focused on maintaining my wall that we were almost at the end of the park before I said a word. Finally, as we waited for the light to turn, so we could cross to the first cemetery gate, I turned to him.

"So, what have you been up to?" That seemed neutral but his eyes narrowed briefly, then smoothed so fast I could almost dismiss it. If I tried, I could probably find out, but it seemed wrong. I turned my attention to the flashing red hand, felt the shrug in the movement of his arm. The light changed and we crossed before he answered.

"Oh, you know, the usual." Chris let go of my hand and went ahead to push open the cemetery gate. I started to laugh, and he turned back, his lips curled in a wry twist. "What's funny?"

I swallowed the laugh, but I could feel the grin still on my face. "Well, I've hung out with you exactly once before today, so actually, I have no idea what your usual would be. You could be a male stripper for all I know."

The frown morphed back into a grin, he took my hand again to lead me down the few steps to the main path. "Oh, absolutely. Three nights a week at the Flamingo Lounge on Industrial. You should come tomorrow—Wednesday's Ladies' Night."

We both laughed, but mine only lasted until we turned right at the bend. I slowed my steps. I didn't want to go home. Ever again. Chris slowed with me, gave me a quizzical look. I smiled up at him, wanting nothing more than to take my free hand and rest it on that smooth, sharp cheek, which made him look serious even when he was laughing. Would my wall hold if I did? I'd worked so hard to keep it intact, there was a little thrill of fear down my spine at how quickly it cracked when he'd touched me. Instead, I said, "So, you work at the school paper but are a male stripper on the sly. Any other secrets I should know about?"

"Hmm," he said as we started walking again, so slowly I knew I'd be late getting home, but at that moment I didn't care. "Here's one, I used to want to be a priest when I grew up."

"Shut up! Really?"

The smile faded as he nodded. I stopped walking and stared at him. Seeing it, Chris holding the host, face alight with wonder. It suited that seriousness he exuded.

"You're staring again. That big a shock, is it?"

I jumped. "Sorry. I was imagining what that would've been like."

A crooked smile, then gone. I could almost see the wheels in his head grind as he looked for a way to steer the conversation in a more light-hearted direction. Maybe it was my earlier pensiveness, but I felt no need to be light-hearted. "Well," he finally said, "that whole celibacy thing's a real deal breaker. Makes a good outfit for The Flamingo, though."

I gave him the smile he seemed to want but I couldn't maintain it. I could feel it like it was my own pain and I shuddered. The wall shuddered and I was afraid. Still, I jumped. "It still hurts you, that loss of faith."

His own smile flicked off, his face reminded me of those sorrowing saints in that little book my grandma gave me for my first communion. I felt the bitter tang of self-loathing on my tongue. Would I ever learn not to blurt these things out?

He stood there staring down at me, face drawn, and I thought, this is it. He would avoid me. Maybe he should. After all, that was the reason I'd kept to myself all these years. I'd figure out another way to find out what happened to Mom. "You're a reader."

That was so far from the response I expected, all I managed to say was "Huh?"

He gripped my hand almost to the point of pain. "You read people very well."

I squeezed his hand with equal intensity. "But I don't need to blurt it all out. I'm sorry, Christopher."

He gave me a wan smile in return, and we resumed our amble down the path. "Nobody calls me that. I kind of like it."

"I'm glad."

"And you're right, it does still hurt. I miss the surety, the sense of purpose."

"That isn't always a positive." Robert James and his Faith Fellows had that in spades.

"True. I tell myself that sometimes." He cocked an eyebrow at me, a smile flickered briefly. "Maybe you already knew that."

"Very funny."

"So now it's your turn. Tell me one of your secrets."

"Just one?"

"You have to get home today, right?"

We were at the gate. I dropped his hand, went up the few steps, and pushed it open with a little more force than necessary. The rusty scream and scrape against sidewalk suited me at that moment. "My dad is a big wheel at Faith Fellowship. He made me do the born-again thing."

A single eyebrow went up, it was adorable. "You're a fundy?"

I grinned. "Technically. You know, in the 'no way in hell' sense of the word."

He laughed. "Is your mom one, too?"

I felt my grin disappear as I shook my head.

His laugh cut off. "I'm sorry. Divorce?"

I shook my head which seemed a bit untethered from my neck. This was the moment, to jump, to not care if I fell. Find her. As if from down a long hallway I could hear myself saying. "Not really. She hated Faith Fellowship. She…" That image of her lying in a bed, eyes distant, and sad overwhelmed me again. I couldn't say it, couldn't say it aloud to someone else. Couldn't make it real. "They kept her away. I don't know where she is."

I met Chris' eyes, could see what I fancied, hoped, was curiosity. "Veronica, that's…" was all he managed before trailing off.

I steeled myself. "You're a reporter. Maybe you could help me find her."

He didn't say anything, even if I concentrated—ignoring my earlier reservations—I could get nothing from inside his head either, like static on a TV. That was different. I dropped his hand. "I gotta go. Dad'll go nuts if dinner isn't ready when he gets home."

I left him standing at the foot of the stairs, his lips parted as if he was still trying to finish his earlier sentence, and ran, not stopping until I turned onto Sunset, pausing for a minute to catch my breath before making my way more slowly down the road. It was only when I reached the bottom of the hill where City of Light Acres sat in judgment that a car, all tinted windows and a bland beige paint job, had been in the corner of my eye during the whole trudge home. Before I had time to process that fact as more than a crawly feeling on my neck, the car made a U-turn and pulled up alongside of me. The window powered down to reveal a guy in a dark suit and equally dark glasses, like some paranoid stereotype of a CIA agent. It was only the pin on his lapel, with its two hands clasping a cross—the same one Dad wore to work every day—that told me if not who, what. "Veronica, we need to talk."

Chapter Six

After she'd run off in a swirl of hair and coat, Chris stayed in the cemetery, walked over to the gazebo, and sat down to enjoy a cigarette. No strong thought interrupted his reverie. It was all a merry-go-round of new revelations and Veronica's general weirdness. And hotness, if he was honest with himself.

The wind picked up, scattered old leaves, discarded candy wrappers, and he was kind of grossed out to see more than one used condom across the warped floorboards of the structure. He wrapped his thin leather jacket a little more tightly around himself, wondered idly what might have happened to Mrs. Simon and how he might help. Run off with the plumber? Took a wrong turn and got kidnapped by hillbillies? Joined a cult?

That last idea, according to the crawling skin on the back of his neck, seemed to have merit. Or maybe it was Faith Fellowship itself that gave him the creeps. Half the town seemed to be owned by the James family, or someone connected with them. Spreading out from their big church a shade north of downtown, with its college, attached seminary, and the k-12 school on the edge of Sunset before the big hill that led to the James-owned City of Light Acres housing development. If her dad was some kind of Faith Fellowship *VIP*, Chris wondered as he exhaled a series of smoke rings that broke apart in the cold air, how'd Veronica end up at Dalesville High? He could feel a smile tug at him, he bet there was a good story behind that.

As for her mom? Chris wouldn't be surprised if a man like Robert James had a retinue of lawyers at his fingertips, any custody situation wouldn't end well for the parent on the other side. There was something in Veronica's eyes when he'd mentioned her mom though, that hinted at something darker, like her mom had not left, but disappeared. He considered the problem like it was a story for the school paper, how did people disappear? There was always some sign, an abandoned car, a motel receipt. A body. Yeah, he wouldn't mention that last one to Veronica. The first thing to do, he'd tell her, was reconstruct the last time she'd seen her mom. Could be something there.

For all that, not a bad afternoon. Laine was right, damn him. Action did make him feel better. One last drag and he threw his cigarette butt into the little snowbank in the corner, slumped and melted into a shape that resembled a small gnome, stood and dusted ash off his jeans and started back through the cemetery toward home.

The station wagon was pulling into the driveway when he got there. It shuddered off and Mom got out, a plastic bag from the grocery store in one hand while she pushed the door closed with the other. The door did not go quietly, the rusty squeal was getting louder. She sighed. "The wagon is dying."

He ambled up the driveway. "She's been dying for five years."

Mom dropped the bag. "Chris! You scared the hell out of me!" She picked the bag up and peered in. "You're lucky that wasn't the bag with the eggs."

He grinned. "Sorry, Mom."

She raised an eyebrow before turning to walk toward the house. "Yeah, you look sorry. Bring in the rest, reprobate, and you're eating whichever apple you made me bruise."

"Always the nurturer."

Her laugh was the last thing he heard before she went in. He pried open the back of the wagon to another rusty yelp, gathered up the remaining bags, and slammed it shut again. Usually, the wagon was his to use, but Dad took the truck to physical therapy on Tuesdays and Chris walked to school. He followed her into the house and closed the front door with his foot.

Mom was standing at the fridge with the lone bag she'd carried, staring at its contents like a complex algebraic equation that she couldn't solve for x. "Counter."

He did as he was told.

"Can you unpack those? I'll have a better idea of how it'll fit if I can see it all."

"Slavedriver."

"Absolutely." Her head disappeared into the fridge again, emerging a minute later with a satisfied smile. "The solution is leftovers."

"Oh, happy day," he mumbled.

"I heard that."

"I meant you to."

He folded up the empty bags and stuffed them with the others in the broom closet. When he turned back everything had disappeared from the counter except the random leftovers in plastic containers.

Mom closed the door with a sigh and turned toward Chris. "You're home late."

He shrugged, they might get along, but she didn't need to know everything. "I had to finish some stuff at the paper, then took the scenic route home."

"Hmm." Her eyes narrowed slightly, then she shrugged and started to pry the lids off of the containers. "Well, go tell your sister dinner'll be ready in about half an hour."

Chris dutifully went upstairs, yelled through Megan's door and then went into his room and flopped down in his desk chair with a small sigh. Ms. Price, the journalism advisor and temporary senior history teacher, had mentioned that the *Dalesville Ledger* was running its annual feature contest, examining some aspect of the town's history, complete with a scholarship that would at least cover books if he ever made it to college. Half of him didn't see the point, the other half had already started turning over ideas. He'd checked out a few books from the school library and copied a few articles, which he started reading through to kill time until dinner, *Miners' strikes, McClellans' grand opening*. None of it spoke to him. He pushed them aside and picked up the illustrated children's town's history he'd checked out—*Dalesville: City of Light* (oh, yes, Chris thought, it's the Paris of the Midwest)—and started to read. He'd nearly finished it when he heard his mom calling up the stairs. He snapped the book shut and pushed back his chair, thinking about what wasn't included. He flipped the book over and saw it had been published locally, Light of the World Publishing. He knew them, that was the publishing house owned by Robert James, specializing in Christian fiction and non-fiction, and all manner of prayerbooks and tracts. Maybe it was the influence of his conversation with Veronica, but he thought he might have a subject after all.

"Chris! Now please!"

"On my way, Mom!" He scribbled a note to himself and went out to join his family.

Chapter Seven

I stared at the guy. Despite the suit and slicked-back hair, he didn't look much older than me. A nagging sense I'd seen him before was all I got, nothing as useful as a name. I considered, then discarded the idea of shaking his hand to see what I might see and gave him a big fake smile instead. "Sorry. I'm not stupid enough to talk to a stranger tailing me."

He pulled off his sunglasses and that familiar feeling increased. "I'm not a stranger."

I took a step back as he took one forward. "It doesn't matter. I have to get home. I'm already late."

His ramrod posture relaxed. "You don't trust me. That's smart. Still, there are things you need to know."

The urge to take his hand, to read him and know, was so strong I had to clasp my hands behind my back, my left clasping the right so hard it was red for the next half hour. "Like I said, now's not a great time. My father..."

He nodded. "Name a time and a place, and I'll meet you there."

I took a deep breath, trying to run through the possibilities as quickly as I could. Not Faith Fellowship, and I didn't want anyone associated with it in places I liked to go. "Food court at the mall. Saturday. I'll tell Dad I need highlighters or something."

"*Ok.*" An actual smile, before he slipped his sunglasses back on, started the car again, started to close the window.

"Wait!" The window stopped halfway up. "You didn't tell me your name."

"Theo Willis." The window closed and the car made a U-turn again and departed.

I ran the rest of the way home, not stopping until I was in the house, door closed and locked behind me. I slumped against it for a moment, catching my breath, noting as I did that I'd still managed to beat Dad home. The clock chimed once, 4:30. I trudged to the bathroom, splashed water on my sweaty face, dropped my backpack in my room, my mind still working on who the hell this Theo guy was, with his suit and car and fancy sunglasses.

That first year in Dalesville I'd walked in once or twice and saw Dad at the dining room table with one of the Faith Fellows. Like Theo, he wasn't one of the Tuesday crowd. Even then I knew the difference. I could smell money and power on this guy, from the trim suit to the peek-a-boo glint of gold on his wrist. All the Tuesday guys had that flop-sweat and cheap aftershave stink of defeat. Before Dad noted my presence by standing and steering me to my bedroom, I over-heard phrases like 'malicious abandonment' and 'forfeiture of parental rights.' It didn't take a lawyer to understand what that meant, but they were only words; there'd been nothing malicious about Mom.

I felt the familiar grief well up again and settle in my throat and a watery sigh escaped before I could stop it. I bit the inside of my cheek to stop the mental pain with physical discomfort—it was Tuesday, and I had snacks, sandwiches and mysteries to deal with—and less time to do it in than usual. Tuesday was not a day to think about any of it. I'd achieved one goal in bringing Chris on board and that was enough.

I went back through the house to the kitchen, pulling fruit, cheese, and crackers from fridge and cupboard and set them up on the long counter opposite the stove. I grabbed the large, flowered platter from the top of the fridge and set that there, too. Once that was all arranged, there was little keeping my mind on the task at hand, so I let it drift as I cubed cheese and tried to place Theo in any of the FF groups. He was an insider, judging by the pin, and way too young to be one of the Tuesday guys, they were all at least in their forties. I could ask Nancy, maybe he was a friend of Jeremy's. At least I'd know what to expect if that was the case.

Enough of that. I let my brain linger on the earlier part of the afternoon and the feel of Chris' hand in mine, the crunch of gravel under his boots, the cold that slapped color into his cheeks and made the green in his eyes snap. I popped a cube of cheese in my mouth as I dumped them on the tray, then turned to switch on the oven for the box of tater tots in the freezer.

As I cut up the apples, I thought about how he didn't smile much but when he did, well...I felt the heat in my own cheeks. Clearly, I was too close to the oven, cooking myself. Yup, that was it. Keep it professional, I reminded myself.

I arranged the apple slices around the platter of crackers. After years of monitoring, Dad allowed me the privilege of planning the Tuesday night food instead of telling me what to make. Progress, I guess. I stood back as I finished and admired my handiwork, all I needed was the cubed cheese and it was ready to go with an hour to spare. As I covered it up with plastic wrap I realized, with a grin, that it was a juice box and a nap away from kindergarten food. I slid the plate into the fridge and walked down the hall to my room, still smiling.

By 7:30 p.m. all the food had been served, and the men were deep
in a discussion of Godless Washington bureaucrats keeping prayer
out of schools and I could escape to my room. It was as bad as I
thought it would be, it really was the wrong day to be around all of
them. The thought of Mom made me vulnerable and the darkness
in the living room was so strong I was nearly blinded. I turned on
the overheard light, my desk light, and after a moment's thought, my
closet light for good measure. In the blaze of my room, I stared without
comprehension at my French homework, then gave it up as a bad job.
Instead, I pulled open my bottom desk drawer and yanked up the
false bottom to retrieve my journal. The newest was always on top
and beneath were nearly ten years' worth of older ones. They were less
journals of ideas for finding Mom and more records of all the weird
things I'd felt and seen, a way to get them out my head so I wouldn't
have to live with them anymore. The entries were less frequent now
that I figured out how to block most of it. Chris, though...

I wrote furiously for an hour, until I was interrupted by a knock
on my door. I slide the journal under my French notebook and went
across the room to open the door, feeling considerably calmer and able
to face Dad.

He stood there with his usual furrowed brow and downturned
mouth but the shadows around him were less than usual. "We're done
out there if you want to come and clean up."

I nodded and after shutting my door, followed him down the hall
to the living room to clear plates and glasses, fold chairs and return
them to their place in the garage. A place for everything. Right.

Half an hour later, with the living room returned to baseline, dishes washed, dried, put away, and Dad gone into his office, I went back to my room, which was still blazing with light.

I turned off the closet light, shut the door, and sat at my desk again. Now I could focus enough to get my homework done. I slipped the notebook back into its hiding place and worked steadily until 11 p.m., then crawled gratefully into bed and finally allowed myself to think about that last day with Mom.

I'd sat in the shifty lawn chair, sunk down in the large concavity in the middle, the product of at least two generations of butts. In my right hand, a beaded glass of tart lemonade, in my left *Bridge to Terabithia*, already three times read and starting to show its age in at least two spine cracks and a long crease in the cover. The sun was low in the sky, sending mellow light across the garden where Mom, clad in paint-spattered, worn jeans and durable gloves, both muddied from the spongy ground, pulled up weeds with an intensity that seemed out of proportion with the warm laziness of the afternoon. My stomach was a little queasy with guilt for not offering to help but the unobtrusive warmth of the sun was like a fire on a cold day, it made me lazy and sleepy. I put the glass on the little table next to the chair, closed my eyes on her industriousness and leaned back in the lawn chair.

In that state, that never-neverland between awake and asleep there was the sound of the phone, followed by the low murmuring of Mom's voice. Mom had a naturally calm voice, like a muted bell and I imagined when she was teaching, it kept her kids out of crying fits and other craziness. Dad was the lively one, in both voice and manner.

He was always enthusiastic about something, whether it was stoking the coals of the barbecue or scribbling notes in books or on articles. I'd pick those up later, most sailed high and wide above my head. "Colonization of the other?' or "PG again," although not all, I picked up one article praising former president Nixon full of margin notes reading "asshole" and "dipshit." Dad caught me with it and yanked it away, blushing. Then he gave a big booming laugh and ruffled my hair. "Your old man's got some strong opinions, kiddo."

"I don't mind." I pointed at the picture of Nixon in the center of the article. "He looks shifty."

He'd swept me up in his arms and planted a kiss on my forehead, the tickle of his beard made me giggle. "My kid's a friggin' genius."

Mom came in at that moment, a stack of papers in one hand, a gallon of milk in the other, and asked what we were laughing about. Dad told her, and then she kissed me, too, and told me I'd earned a special trip to the bookstore.

That was years ago. It was easy to see things were different. Mom's face seemed drawn, distant except when she looked at me. Dad got more severe, he'd shaved his beautiful brown beard and cut his hair short. There were no more big laughs and if I said something critical about the government or made a face when he was watching some TV church thing, he'd frown and go silent. If he was home at all. He started spending a lot of time with other frowning men, carrying worn bibles and a layer of sweetness when talking to me that couldn't quite cover the anger in their eyes. I learned fast to nod hello and get as far away from them as I could.

One day, they showed up right after I got home from school, Dad in tow, and formed a rough semi-circle I'd have to walk through to get to my room. I'd done my usual hello and tried to get past, but they closed ranks, towering over me and asking me question after question about what I liked to read, whether I went to church, and whether I knew if I wasn't saved I'd go to The Hot Place. I looked over at Dad, standing by the fireplace, but he stared down at the chipped brick mantelpiece, running his thumb over the jagged left corner he'd kept promising to fix. So, I responded with "I save. I've got almost five dollars in quarters in my piggy bank." At that, they shook their heads and gestured Dad over, told me to go sit on the couch. Dad looked like a kicked dog as they talked to him in hissing whispers. I had to strain to hear. I could only catch a few words, "pernicious interference," "secular humanist maternal influence," that made no sense to me. Finally, Dad nodded and came back to me. "Veronica."

I took his hand, squeezed. "Daddy, make them go away. They're scaring me."

He shook his head, disappointment in his eyes, in the downturn of his mouth. I wished he'd smile, he never smiled anymore. "They're helping you. You don't want to go to hell, do you?" His voice was almost a whisper.

I shook my head so hard my braids smacked my cheeks. I could feel the darkness in him, so thick I could choke. I wanted to drop his hand, but I didn't dare.

"Do you know what happens in hell?" I couldn't answer. Didn't want to. "You burn forever, with no water. And you'll never ever see your dad again."

I started to cry, big hitching sobs that felt like they were ripping me to pieces. "No, I don't want that," I finally gulped out.

In a louder voice, "So, do you accept Christ?"

Scared, I nodded.

Now, his voice got louder, his eyes dark and angry like his friends. "That's not good enough. Out loud."

The tears stopped and I felt cold. Cold and certain. It was a show, like TV, a show for these mean men in suits. I was furious, which felt good because at that moment looking up at my dad, his eyes looking down on me with no warmth, only chilly authority, as if he'd really stop loving me if I refused, it felt like my heart cracked into a million pieces, stabbing my lungs, my stomach, and all those soft bits inside.

I dropped his hand, my face a mask, and clasped mine behind my back, fingers crossed. He stepped out of my way, and I walked into that sneering circle of men, vowed inside that someday I'd get back at all of them for this and said, "I accept Jesus Christ as my personal savior," like they did on those programs Dad had started watching.

They pushed me out of the way to clasp Dad's hand, pat his back. I backed up, wanting to be far away from all of them. As I started to turn away, to run to my room, and wait for Mom to come home to find out if she was infected with this, too, the guy who seemed in charge turned to stare at me. He'd been handsome before he got all soft and jowly. He turned his round blue eyes on me and my knees went watery. When our eyes met again, I could see the flames Dad talked about, like a forest fire behind his eyes. I turned and ran into my room and locked the door.

After waking up screaming three nights in a row, Mom finally got it out of me what happened. As I told her everything except that last moment, the hand she'd rested on my forehead shook. She was angry. It boomed out from her like it did from those men, but I was old enough to know the difference. She was mad at them and for the first time since it happened, I felt safe. I smiled up at her. Those men didn't know what they were in for.

When I got home from school the next day Mom and Dad were head to head, yelling at each other. Dad's face was red, Mom's white. "There is no way in *hell* I'll let you expose her to that man again. I didn't fight..." is all I heard as I came in, she saw me then and stopped, gestured me out. I melted back out the door, sat on the front lawn far enough away not to make out any words, and yanked up dandelions, blowing seeds across the lawn. Later, Dad slammed out of the house with one icy look in my direction, got into his car, and peeled out. A few minutes later Mom followed, tears drying on her face, and sat down next to me, gathering me up in her arms. I leaned into her, listened to the steady beat of her heart as she smoothed my hair. "It'll be *okay*, honey. I promise." I accepted that, even though I knew differently. I could see, sure, but not well enough. Not then. It was off to Camp Serenity after that.

That had been more than a month ago, but I'd still wake up from bad dreams of the hell I saw in that man's eyes. That had been the only part I couldn't bring myself to tell Mom, I didn't know how to say it. Hadn't I always given her enough to worry about?

I didn't want to be thinking about any of that on a beautiful day in a Dad-free house but that grey zone between not-sleep and sleep was dangerous. I concentrated instead on the soothing sound of Mom's voice, the crack of her knees as she stood up, the pat of her hands against her jeans as she wiped off the first layer of dirt, the soft whisper of her gardening sneakers. She was still talking, quietly, like she knew I was trying to sleep. I only caught one sentence. "Can I come now?"

Silence, before I felt her hand on my forehead, soft touch despite the roughness of her skin. I opened my eyes. She was smiling down at me, her eyes crinkled at the corners, which did nothing to mask the film of what I thought were tears. Her allergies acted up when she gardened but she always said, "What kind of woman would I be if I let a few sneezes stop me?"

She leaned down and kissed each cheek. I giggled. "How cosmopolitan of you." I'd been dying to use that word since I learned what it meant the week before in school.

"Your old mom is full of surprises, hmm?"

"Of course."

She straightened up, the smiling fading a little as she laid her hand back on my forehead. "I need to run over to the Caros. I'll be back in less than an hour. You rest now, *okay*?"

I may have nodded but I didn't know, because the next thing I knew I was waking up, the sun almost down and Mom nowhere to be found. I sat up too fast, felt dizzy, and leaned back again. Everything was quiet, not even a neighbor's TV or a distant lawnmower broke the silence. I felt like I was the last person alive in the world.

I shivered at that thought, at the warmth from the sun gone, and at the certainty that I was still alone. I tried sitting up again, more slowly, put my feet on ground. The ice had melted in my lemonade and a fly and a bee had gone to their reward. My neck throbbed a little, cramped from sleep at an angle. Ignoring the silence that said clearly "no one's home" I stood up on still-shaky legs and wandered across the porch to the back door, feeling out of it.

I pushed open the back door and walked into a dark, empty kitchen. The clock above the stove read *5:10 p.m.*, and the house was so still, I could actually hear the little tick when it moved to *5:11*. Into the living room, dining room, down to the rec room. Nothing. The bathroom door was open, and it was dark, too. After a moment's hesitation at my parents' closed bedroom door, I turned the knob as silently as I could, so as not to wake her. I was so certain she was resting after all that work that it took almost a minute for my brain to register that the bed was undisturbed.

Despite the little rat-gnaw worry at the pit of my stomach, I concluded she'd lost track of time, like she sometimes did when she was with her best friend. I pushed all other thoughts away as I retreated back to the living room and sat on the couch in the dark, waiting.

It was there Dad found me the next morning, curled up with her picture pressed against my chest.

I woke up from that memory dream in the darkest acre of the night. My pillow was damp. I wasn't surprised. I could still feel her hand on my forehead, rough from gardening, gentle by nature. The idea that I'd never feel it again made me feel something close to despair, made me want to crawl under my comforter—Mom had picked out the cover—and never come out again.

Instead, I sat up. The streetlight cast enough light so I could see the picture of the park and thought again about how often I would doze off under those trees. I slept too damn much. Well, I was finally awake and I was doing what I needed to do. Malicious abandonment, my ass. I needed to know, one way or another, what happened on that last day.

Over breakfast Dad told me he had a dinner meeting with Reverend Ash—I could almost feel sorry for him—and that he trusted I would behave on my own. I gave him a smile and a nod while deciding to use this unexpected break to do whatever the hell I wanted. Maybe I couldn't sneak a trip downtown, but at least I didn't have to hurry home.

The day got even better when Chris caught up with me on my way out of history. We moved off to the side, by the windows, let the thundering herd pass as he caught his breath. I smiled. "Just happened to be passing by?"

A little half smile. "Right. I'm supposed to play it cool."

I shrugged, making my left backpack strap slip down my shoulder. Chris pushed it back into place, his hand lingering long enough to see that same image, a lake, a cup of coffee, the sound of water. My shoulder tingled where he'd touched it and I sounded a little breathless myself when I said, "Coolness is overrated."

His hand dropped away as he leaned against the wall, the afternoon sun bronzing his dark hair. So not cool was I. "Good. Then I'll embrace my dorkiness and as if you wanna go over to the Blue Moon after school and grab that coffee."

I said a silent thank you to Reverend Ash for scheduling that meeting. "I'm free. Should we walk?"

He shook his head as he stood up, linked his arm with mine. "As luck would have it, I'm wheeled today. I can transport us there—well, not in style, but marginally faster than walking."

I laughed. "Boy, you really know how to sell it."

He laughed, too, and we made our way through the mostly empty halls.

I did a quick scan of the coffee shop as we walked in and with a sigh of relief, noticed nobody I knew from Faith Fellowship. Chris raised a single eyebrow but said nothing as we scouted out a table near the bookshelf. I reached for my backpack and pulled out a few bucks from my wallet, but he waved it away. "Please. I think I can manage a couple bucks for coffee."

I settled in at the table, let my eyes wander over the contents of the Blue Moon's bookshelf, a delightful array of books customers left behind, from self-help books that had clearly been of no use to their readers, to battered Seuss board books and a few romances with fainting, busty women and dudes with surfer hair and washboard abs. I was contemplating grabbing one of the latter when Chris returned with the coffee and sat down across from me. Maybe I didn't need to read about romance, this had all the hallmarks of an actual date. Including my sudden inability to think of a word to say. I took a gulp of coffee instead, it burned my tongue enough to make talking even more of a problem.

I glanced at Chris, who was more prudent. He blew ripples across the surface before taking a drink, then set it back on the table, his face resolute. "I've been thinking about what you said in the cemetery the other day and if you want, I'd like to help you figure out what happened to your mom."

That twisty, nervous feeling in my stomach evaporated, replaced by a cold lump even the coffee couldn't melt. I stared down at my watery reflection in the dark surface of my drink, willing the words to come out of my mouth. They remained stubbornly locked in my head.

When I finally looked up, Chris's eyes were crinkled at the corners, a little slant-wise smile on his face and I realized I was being stupid. Date, not a date, it didn't matter. He could be a friend and that's what I needed. I laid out for him that last day—the phone call, the quick trip to her friend's house—wondering to myself if I'd managed to convey how eerie it was in that house by myself, how off-kilter everything felt. "Dad said she left, and then we left, and it all happened so fast. I never thought it would be..."

He ran his finger along the rim of his cup, a frown graven between his eyes. "You were what, twelve? You gotta cut yourself some slack."

"Not sure I deserve it." My hands ached, balled into fists so tight my knuckles had gone bloodless.

Chris's hand closed over my fist and for a moment I was distracted by a flash of trees and a nauseating brew of shame and anger. Not mine. I shook my head, trying to focus on being in the moment. On his voice, low, "Don't do that to yourself. We'll find out what happened, *okay*?"

I nodded, unclenched my fists, and tried a smile. "Maybe I can remember some names and reach out to some of my parents' friends in Colorado. Dad checks the bills, I'd have to use a payphone."

Chris let go of my hand, sat back in his chair. "That's a good idea. If you can find an address book, give me the names and I'll call."

"Sure. It's a...we'll do that." I finished off the now cool remains of my coffee and picked up my bag from the floor. "I should probably take off, I've got a bit of a hike home."

His right eyebrow shot up. "I can give you a ride, no problem."

I slipped on my backpack, shook my head. "Not a good idea. Nosy neighbors."

His face smoothed into a smile. "I get it."

I stood there at the table like I was waiting to take his order. Everything felt...unfinished. "Thanks for helping me with this, Christopher."

He full-on grinned, doing nothing for my resolution to go. "No prob. I've got to go the library in the next couple weeks for a thing I'm working on, I'll see what I can dig up."

"That means a lot." I gave him a little wave and departed for the long trudge home. Whatever might happen, whatever we might find out, at least things were moving forward. I just wasn't sure what the destination would be.

Chapter Eight

For once the white noise of the conveyor belt and forklifts was welcome. Chris didn't have to think of anything except pushing paper into boxes, pushing boxes into the tape machine, the burn of his feet after the first hour of standing there, and the arthritic ache of his arms that wouldn't go away until sometime the next day. He was so focused on it he didn't even hear the whistle blow signaling the break until Jim, one of the guys further down the belt, clamped a hand on his shoulder. "You trying to make us look bad, college boy?"

Chris grinned at him. "Ain't hard."

Jim laughed, hitched up his pants. They followed the rest of the crew into the smoker, a sad little lean-to of plywood and plastic sheeting, which felt refreshing for the first few minutes off the floor, until the itchy sweat cooled to a clammy singlet.

They lit and leaned. "So, I gotta ask you, are you one of them fags?"

Chris raised an eyebrow, Jim's cheeks went red even as he gestured to Chris' right hand, with last night's black polish still on, the earring in his eyebrow. "What, because of the polish and the hoop?"

Jim shrugged.

Chris dragged on the cigarette. "Nah, it drives my dad crazy. You should see what he does when I wear black eyeliner."

Jim let out a phlegmy laugh. "That sure as hell is one way to do it."

"I've got a million of 'em."

"Every kid does. Mine are always up to something." He tapped ash into the rusted-out ashtray by the door. "At least my oldest finally got his shit together, he's working for the sheriff's department."

Chris was amused at the way Jim's chest puffed out when he said that, only a little tempered by his own belief that Big Pat never bragged on him to his coworkers. They leaned in companionable silence for a few moments while Chris lit another off his first, listened to the wind rattle the plastic, the mumbles of the rest of the crew here and there. Jim had been the first person to actually talk to him since he'd started. Chris knew he should have told him not to use that word, but instinct told him this wasn't the time or the place.

"So, what's a college boy like you wasting your time in this shithole for?"

Chris shrugged, dragged. "Not in college. Still in high school and there's no money for anything else right now."

"Well, at least you're not sitting around whining about it like a big pussy."

Chris let out a smoke-filled laugh. "Tried that, but no one would pay me for it."

Jim's laugh was drowned out by the sound of the whistle calling them back to the line. They pitched their butts into the pitted coffee can by the door and shuffled back. Chris thought that he might ask Jim if his son could run a search on Veronica's mom, before a roar of the conveyor belt started up and once again drove out all his conscious thought.

"It's so dark, where's the moon?"

"Over there, son, coming out from behind that cloud."

"Chris."

His head snapped up and he realized he'd drifted off. The credits were rolling from the movie Big Pat rented, some action/adventure thing Chris couldn't recall. It was his second weekend shift at McClellan's, and he'd been up since 1:30 a.m. Chris thought that if he spent much more time working in that factory, he might die of exhaustion by thirty and felt a quickly suppressed surge of sympathy for his dad spending his life there. His mom smiled faintly from the other end of the couch. "If you can sleep through two explosions and three or four bloodbaths," she swatted Big Pat on the arm, "you can sleep through anything."

Chris tried and failed to stifle a yawn. "It was very soothing."

"Well, I get to pick the movie next time," she said.

Big Pat's laugh was a low rumble. "Then I'll fall asleep, too."

Chris could feel himself wanting to smile and fought it, stood up. "Been fun, but I've got stuff to do."

He saw his mom's face fall in the flickering TV light. "It's 11 p.m. at night. What do you need to do?"

"Things." He hooked his coat off the hall tree and walked out.

A cold and cloudless Saturday night, the stars hard, the moon far off. The sounds of the guns from the movie must have filtered through even while he slept. He'd dreamt about the one hunting trip his father had taken him on when he was eight and deemed old enough and strong enough to hold a gun. The good part was that first freezing night in the woods, where they sat with Big Pat's friends around a fire that threatened to blow out at any minute from wind that kept perversely changing directions. His father let him have coffee for the first time out of a tin mug that gave it a quicksilver taste, while Chris watched the moon, impossibly bright and huge, dart in and out of view. Kept calling Chris "my boy" and puffing out his chest.

The next day, though...

Chris shoved his hands in his pockets and walked, the grass crunching under his combat boots, no idea where he was going, except anywhere that would get that memory out of his head. Between the tiredness and that memory, he was in no good mood. He sighed, cast his gaze upward as if that would provide some escape route, but there was no harvest moon, or even full moon, only a thumbnail sliver high above that cast little light. Despite his promise to Veronica, either his weariness or his apparent stupidity had kept him from having any good ideas as to how to search for a missing person. So much for his vaunted investigative skills. Maybe he should just confess to her that his "yes" had been less about helping her find her mom and more about spending time with someone he found himself thinking about more often than a guy committed to no attachments and a quick ticket out of this dungeon of a town should. The fact that, in reality, he was going nowhere did nothing to cheer him up.

Even at this moment, he had nowhere to go, only a desire to be out of the house, out of any enclosed space, home, school, family. He kicked an empty beer can off the sidewalk as he turned down Cambridge Ave, considered briefly turning left and heading downtown, and as quickly dismissed it. He wasn't in the mood for Saturday crowds.

He didn't realize where he was going until he saw Julian sitting on his front stoop, sending smoke rings up into the sky. Julian looked down at the sound of the squeal of the gate latch when Chris pushed it back.

"Hey," was Julian's sole greeting. That was classic Julian. With the right stimulus, Chris supposed he could rival Laine in terms of talking.

Julian? Never. Julian would observe and when he talked, he was rarely ignored. Laine on the other hand, expressed every passing thought in his head and maybe one out of five was either germane or relevant. Chris smiled as he sat down and thought about how when he wanted to be cheered up, he went to Laine and when he wanted to be heard, he went to Julian. He wasn't sure which he wanted at that moment. Julian scooted over and made room for him on the step. Chris lit a cigarette and the two sat in companionable silence.

"You alone tonight?" Chris finally asked.

Julian nodded. "Mom and Dad went away for the weekend. Anniversary thing. You walked here?"

Chris took a drag and nodded as well. "Needed some air. What are you up to?"

Julian smiled. "I'm making a mental to-do list for the move to Chicago. What to take, what to leave, what has to be sent when."

Chris couldn't ignore the twist of envy in his stomach at Julian and Laine's plans. He knew the two of them were leaving in July—Julian to Northwestern, Laine to the School of the Art Institute—and getting an apartment in Wrigleyville, which was almost halfway between both. Chris was supposed to be there, too, but between his mom's recent promotion to professor and his dad's back surgery that put him out of commission for six months, Chris was out of the running for financial aid, without enough to cover the difference. It was one of those clusterfucks that seemed to run in the Mulligan branch of the family with sickening regularity, starting with his great-grandfather's broker forgetting to sell his stock when he was asked three days before the crash that started the Great Depression. Chris supposed that, in comparison, his own situation wasn't that bad, and he attempted to squelch any sour notes that might show up in his response. "Have you found a place yet?"

Julian crushed his cigarette on the step and shook his head. "Haven't looked. It's too early, I don't think anyplace is renting five months in advance."

"Guess not."

Silence fell again and Chris blew his own rings up to the distant stars. He felt Julian's eyes on him but continued to stare up at the sky, not wanting to whine about his own shit.

"You know, every time one of us brings up Chicago, you get this look."

"What look?" Damn, he should have known Julian of all people would notice.

"Don't bullshit me. You know. You're not going, are you?"

"Laine didn't tell you? That's a first." Julian's surprised face mirrored his own shock. Chris sighed and dropped his head from the stars to the scuffed toes of his boots. "Not this year. That's why I got the Saturday thing at McClellan's, I'll start full time in the summer."

He looked up at Julian, startled by the weight of Julian's arm around his shoulders. Neither of them said a word for a long time. Nothing could be said except useless "sorrys" or "that sucks." Chris returned his attention to his shoes, somewhat comforted by finally saying it out loud but not really in the mood to say anything else.

Julian abruptly pulled his arm back, scrambled off the step, and uncharacteristically paced back and forth in front of Chris. In the wan moonlight he could see Julian's eyes narrow and lips fold together, his thinking face. Finally, he stopped, flicked his butt toward the street, an orange streak of light disappearing into the darkness, and turned back to Chris. "What's more important, getting out of here or getting a degree right away?"

"They're kind of linked."

"Unlink them."

Chris did what he was told. "Probably getting out of here ranks a little higher."

Julian clasped his hands behind his head and gave Chris a little smile. "Do you want my advice?"

Chris gave him a smile in return. "Dude. I wouldn't have laid it out for you if I didn't."

Julian sat down again two steps below Chris, leaning back against the railing and stretching out along the bottom step.

"Comfy?"

"Strangely, yes. Anyway, I think you should definitely work through the summer and then come to Chicago in the fall."

Chris didn't know how to respond, so he said nothing for a long while, he opted instead to turn it over in his mind, looking for holes. Finally, "But then I take on rent and I don't know what job I could get there with a high school diploma that would cover that and let me save for school." The thought of working for minimum wage, scrapping pennies and nickels for train fair, rent eating a paycheck while he subsisted on ramen gave him shivers that had nothing to do with the icy wind numbing his fingers and cheeks.

"So, the three of us can share a place for a year while you establish residency. Maybe you won't be able to swing U of C, but you could do U of I. Any of them."

Chris' initial disappointment and anger, he realized, had muddied his mental waters enough that such a clear solution hadn't occurred to him. Or maybe he thought he had some fundamental flaw that propelled him toward a certain defeatist attitude. Which would most likely make it impossible to change. When he arrived at that thought, he couldn't suppress a laugh.

"What? Not a good idea?" Julian frowned up at him.

"No, it is. I was responding to internal stimuli." He let the laugh taper off. "It's a good idea. Let me think about it. You should talk to Laine and see if he's cool with it, too."

Julian shrugged and unfolded himself from the step, absently brushing ash off his pants that had drifted from Chris' cigarette. "You wanna go in and watch a movie?"

"What've you got?"

"Some action thing—lots of shooting and women in tight skirts."

Chris laughed again. "Sounds perfect."

It was after 1:00a.m. when he got home, the house was dark and quiet. They never did get around to watching the movie. Instead, Chris picked Julian's brain—Julian being a history buff and the kind of guy who'd track down footnotes and read all the supplementary material for fun—about how, in theory, one might track someone down. "What, you writing a mystery novel or something?"

Chris took a gulp of the soda Julian had tossed him and belched. "Sure. Gotta find some way to pay for college."

He narrowed his eyes at Chris for a moment, then shrugged. "You'd probably want someone with access to databases and police reports."

"Barring that?"

Julian settled on the couch with his own drink, staring at it rather than drinking it. When he finally answered, he'd said pretty much what Chris had suggested to Veronica, talking to friends, reconstructing the person's movements. "It's like a good research paper. You've got your central argument, hypothesis, whatever, and you sift through the material until the conclusion writes itself."

Thinking it over as he hung up his coat on the hall tree and made his way up the stairs in the dark, it was the conclusion that worried him. It was only when he got to the top that he noticed his bedroom light was on.

His mother was sitting on his bed. "Chris."

Chris crossed the room and let his bag slide off his shoulder into the space between the bed and desk, then slumped in the desk chair himself. "Mom. I'm tired."

"We need to talk." She looked exhausted but resolute.

"Talk all you want. I'm going to bed."

She straightened the pillows on his bed, looked around at the piles of papers on his desk, the discarded sock bombs, shirts, and drawers that hadn't made it into the hamper, and gave a small sigh before meeting his eyes again. "You can't be angry forever."

"I'm not angry." The words came out louder than he intended.

"Keep your voice down, you'll wake up your sister."

"I'm sorry, I'm sorry I left. I went over to Julian's." He didn't want to talk about what drove him out of the house, that memory of hunting with his dad.

Her smile was sad as she looked up at him and in that uncanny Mom-dar way, she seemed to know something of what he was thinking. "I wish things were better between you and your father, but he doesn't 'get' you. I could spend hours on the psychology of your father, Chris, but a big part of it is an act. He's acting," she stopped and sighed, "has always acted like he thinks a man should act. He doesn't always get that there are other ways to be a man."

He broke eye contact with her, stared down at the mess of papers on his desk, the outline for his feature article he'd sketched out before dinner. If only everything could be codified, set down with descending Roman numerals, a minimum of two sources and a thesis statement.

Like: "Big Pat is a pain in the ass." He had numerous sources to back that up and little interest in differing opinions on the subject at that moment. "I know, Mom."

"As to the other…" He looked up to see her grip her head with both hands like it would fly apart. "This isn't forever."

So tired, he'd been awake for nearly twenty-four hours. He flopped further down in his desk chair, felt as boneless as if someone pulled out his spine. Julian's idea tugged at his mind, but it seemed so intangible in the mild chaos of his room, in his mother's sad face. He didn't have to be psychic to see how strained things were, the new grey in her hair, the new lines in her face told him that she paid her own price. "Who knows? Maybe my destiny does lie in sporting goods."

She snorted a laugh. "Yeah, that'll be the day."

Chris managed a small one in return. "Yeah, well…"

She stood and came over to him, took him by the shoulders. Chris stared at the floor, drained. "What can I do to help you?"

He looked up at her, her face so much older than usual. "Nothing, Mom. I'm good."

She sighed and walked towards the door, opened it. "I know you are, Chris. And you need to know I'm always here, no matter what."

She shut the door behind her. Chris sat at his desk for a long time, contemplating how nice it would be to be alone, no one to worry or disappoint, to be responsible for only his own happiness.

CHAPTER NINE

Having successfully convinced Dad of my pressing need for a packet of clear folders, the one supply I'd assumed would not be available in his always-locked office, he dropped me off Saturday morning, on his way to Faith Fellowship, a good fifteen minutes before I was due to meet Theo in the food court.

"I'll be back in an hour, I expect you to be waiting by the doors." No smile, no warmth, but he did press a five dollar bill in my hand to cover the cost. One couldn't expect miracles.

"Thank you, Dad," I managed a smile and was surprised to get a fleeting one in return, "I will."

As I tracked down the clear-cover folders, paid, and pocketed the change and receipt to give to Dad, I supposed I should consider myself lucky he hadn't insisted on either buying them himself or coming with me. Absently dodging the crowds on my way to the food court, I thought about that divide between who Dad had been and who he was now. Back then, he'd always said how important it was to be independent, especially for girls; in that, he and Mom saw eye to eye. "Don't depend on anything external for your self-worth," one or the other had said. In essence, if not in those exact words. I turned the corner, saw Theo sitting hunched at a table by the pizza stand. No suit, no lapel pin, just a raggedy hoodie, like the dozens of other dudes milling around him.

Be independent, Dad said. Submit, Dad said. The sweet irony was enough to make my teeth ache.

I slid into the chair across the table from Theo, set my bag on top so I wouldn't forget it.

"Don't you want something to drink?"

I managed a tight smile. "Is this a date?"

He blushed, shook his head, the curls he hadn't slicked back jiggling as he did so. My smile became genuine out of relief at finally placing him. "Youth group, right?"

He sat up. "You remember?

"Sure." I pointed to his hair, he grinned. "You always used to talk about how Jesus is love. I thought you left."

His grin disappeared as quickly as it came, and he slumped back in his chair. "I wish," he said in a tone so low I had to lean in to hear it. That was encouraging and yet he wore the pin of an insider.

I kept my voice icy. "What is it you want, Theo?"

His answer, at first, seemed evasive. "Right after we started going to Faith Fellowship, my dad was laid off from his accounting job."

"So? Times are hard."

There was a bitterness on his face at odds with the sweet kid I'd had a minor crush on in those early days. "It was worse than that. He'd found some errors, stuff that didn't add up. Turns out one the head guys had been skimming. That guy got a big old severance package and Dad got blackballed. Robert James was the only person who'd give him a job. Told him he needed upstanding men like my dad around."

All the sarcasm I had to tamp down around Dad came out. "Wow. He's like the second coming, isn't he? The family messiah."

Theo went pale and I figured he must have thought I was being blasphemous. He leaned closer to me, close enough to see the spray of freckles on his nose, the pimple on his cheek. "That's what he does. Seeks you out when you're vulnerable."

I leaned back in my chair, I didn't like people in my personal space. The idea that I might touch him and see something was added incentive. "That's what every cult leader does. If that's what you came to tell me, I already know."

Theo sat up straighter, looking more like the version that had followed me home, except for the small smile. "*Okay*. You get it. I thought you might, but I had to be sure."

I kept my face impassive, not wanting him to know I was both annoyed and impressed. "A test?"

"It's hard to know who to trust. Mom, Dad, and me, all of us work there now." A sneer twisted his lip. "All their big ideals are gone. Dad does whatever Mr. James wants and all Mom cares about is getting one of those crap boxes in City of Light Acres."

I swallowed a laugh, but I could still hear it in my voice. "Trust me, they're not worth it."

Theo snorted and his face relaxed for a moment before he grew serious again. "Listen, there's more. I came across something. A name."

He stopped, his gaze darting around the food court, while his fingers tattooed an uneasy drumbeat on the table. I understood his anxiety but one glace at my watch told me I didn't have time to indulge it. "Theo. I have to get back to the office supply store before my dad shows up. Can you speed it up a bit?"

Theo took a shaky breath. "Matthew Simon. He's my dad's boss, you know?"

"Dude..."

"Sorry." He leaned in. "Dad asked me to file some papers since I've been shadowing him, an internship, I guess." The scowl returned. "More like go-fer. Anyway, I didn't know the place he told me to go, it wasn't any of the usual offices. They're all letters, you know?"

I swallowed a sigh. "No, I don't. I try not to get involved."

Theo shook his head. "That's my point. You are involved."

Ice all down my back. "What do you mean?"

His voice got lower. "The office? Office *m*? It's nowhere. "There's '*l*' and '*n*,' but no '*m*' in between. I asked some of the office workers and they didn't know either, so I ducked into the men's room and cracked open the folder, thinking if I knew what was in it—invoices or spreadsheets, I'd know at least who to ask."

I didn't want to ask. My mouth had a mind of its own. "And?"

"It was you. Report cards, teacher's notes, doctor visits." He blushed. "I didn't read them."

I felt welded to the chair, a block of ice. Whether anyone knew that Mrs. Freeman in third grade thought I had trouble socializing was the least of my worries. One question managed to emerge from my numb lips. "Does everyone have a file? Do you?"

Theo shook his head. "I've seen member lists and donor lists, but nothing like that. And when I came out of the men's room, Paul Barnes was waiting for me with a big smile, saying I'd been given the wrong file, and he would be happy to take care of it. Snatched it right out of my hands and took off. Anyway, I thought you should know."

Thanking him seemed stupid but I did it anyway.

His frown deepened. "There is one more thing."

Out of the corner of my eye I could see my own hand, lying flat on the sticky table, trembling like a douser scenting water. It wanted to take Theo's, wanted to be a conduit to whatever he may or may not be hiding. It wanted to be a fist. I pulled it off the table and stuck it in my pocket, where it couldn't do any damage. "Great. What is it?" My voice sounded strangled in my ears.

Theo blushed again. Some spy he was. "Another name. Marie Raynor. Does that name mean anything to you?"

I didn't trust my voice, didn't trust my mind. Certainly, didn't know to trust this boy. I opened my mouth, not sure what would come out.

"Veronica. You weren't waiting where I asked."

I closed my mouth so fast I bit the side of my tongue. My brain was a mad scramble of trying to think of a plausible excuse, when Theo spoke instead.

"I'm sorry, Mr. Simon. I ran into your daughter buying folders. She was quite patiently listening to me talk about how awesome the leadership program is at the college, and we lost track of time."

Dad's frown eased into the benevolent smile I hadn't seen in years. The hand still in my pocket made a fist as I seethed, staring at the table so Dad wouldn't notice. A few deep breaths and I was able to make my face a mask, able to mouth the words he'd require. "Yes, Dad, I'm sorry. I should've kept an eye on my watch."

He rested his hand on Theo's shoulder, the smile still beaming. "Well, I think I can overlook it this once. Theo here is going places, just like his father. You could learn a thing or two from him."

I caught Theo's glance as Dad turned to him, no doubt to inquire after his parents. "I already have," I said, too quiet for Dad to hear.

Theo, giving Dad a smile of his own, didn't seem to notice.

I was in no mood to talk on the way home, too many things to think about. Any other day in the past five years, that wouldn't be a problem, but Dad—in one more thing in the barrage of weird that threatened to push my brain into overload—had other ideas. "I can't say I wasn't disappointed I had to look for you but," he glanced at me with a smile I found even more unnerving, "that Theo is a nice young man."

Was he? I hadn't decided yet. I needed to be alone to figure it out, to piece together the info he gave—Mom's maiden name—and my impressions of him. The ease at which he lied to Dad, with no telltale blush, was troubling. Then again, I lied to him all the time. "It was weird running into him, I thought his family moved away or something," I finally managed to say as we approached the light on Main.

Dad hit the signal as he slowed. "They did spend a couple of years at the retreat center in Arkansas."

He said that as if I knew what he was talking about, although I had no recollection of Dad ever mentioning anything about Arkansas before. That could be because tuning Dad out when he talked about Faith Fellowship was practically my superpower at this point. "What did they do there?"

It seemed like a bland enough question, but Dad's smile disappeared and became the hard, unsmiling face that was more familiar. "That's their business. And Bob's."

The rest of the ride was silent and a status quo that was a relief for once. Only when we pulled into the garage and Dad killed the engine that a little of his earlier good mood surfaced. He pulled the keys out of the ignition and squeezed my arm. "I'm glad to see you making friends at Faith Fellowship. It can be a real community if you let it."

In that moment, I wanted to believe. The smile I gave him was genuine, even if it was gone—the smile and the feeling—by the time I followed him through the garage door and back into the house.

I watched him walk down the hall to his office without a glance back, shutting me out again. A sigh that seemed to originate from my feet emerged as I trudged down the hall and into the sanctuary of my room, flopped onto my bed and stared up at the cut-out star. I knew I wanted to believe because it made him happy. Stupid. It's not like it would last. All I could ever do consistently was disappoint him.

I heaved myself off the bed and went to my desk. For a moment, I toyed with the idea of pulling out one of my journals, but it was too risky with Dad in the house. My French notebook was still on my desk, so I turned to a clean page and scribbled down the messy tangle of hints and insinuations I'd gotten from Theo. For once, writing failed to make much clear. A file on me, Mom's name, retreat centers, Theo's motivation? I couldn't find a thread.

As I read what I wrote though, I realized there was a connection, Dad. Theo's father worked for him, there was a file on his daughter. My head gave a single, painful throb. The one person who could connect this was the one person I didn't dare ask.

He was disappointed in me? I scowled at the page. Well, Dad, the feeling was mutual.

Chapter Ten

L aine gave him the message, where he met up with him outside the cafeteria. "You don't mind eating alone?"

Laine shrugged. "Kind of, but I can manage this once. She sounded like it was urgent."

Chris opened the cafeteria door and breathed in the unmistakable smell of second-rate marinara. With a grin, he opened his satchel and handed his lunch bag to Laine. Laine peeked in, looked up at him with widened eyes. "You sure?"

"It's only PB & J, thrown together five minutes before I had to leave. Monday's menu is always gross."

"You are a good friend." Laine gave him a push. "Go meet your girlfriend."

Chris opened his mouth to protest but Laine was already through the door. Not that he would have listened anyway, Chris thought as he walked down the hall.

He didn't see her at first when he entered the library, but she'd picked a table in the back near the copy machine, still, except for her left hand tapping a beat on the table as she stared at the shelf in front of her. The nervousness—excitement? —was palpable as he got closer, she flinched when he said her name.

"I didn't mean to freak you out."

A smile twitched her lips and was gone. "Lost in my thoughts."

"Been there." He stood in front of her, unsure and feeling foolish. "Mind if I sit?"

The second smile lingered in her eyes. "Yes, sorry. And sorry for interrupting your lunch. It's just..."

He settled in the chair, noted the still-restless hand, the shadows under her eyes. "Something happened."

She nodded, taking a deep breath before laying it out for him. From being followed home after their meet-up in the cemetery, "Maybe they wanted to make sure I was behaving myself," she told him, to her dad's surprising information about Harrison. Chris wasn't sure what his face was doing but Veronica stopped talking, her hand twitching toward her mouth like she held a cigarette. "I don't know why I'm telling you all this, maybe...I think it's uglier than I thought."

He sat back in the chair, trying to get his thoughts into some kind of order, so the subtext of what Veronica had said took longer than usual to penetrate. He couldn't help himself, even though there was no call for it, he smiled. "You worried about me?"

She rolled her eyes, but Chris spied the faint blush in her cheeks. "I'm sure you can take care of yourself."

Almost he could laugh, at least *she* was sure of that. The jury in *his* head was still out. What was it Laine had said? He had an "action problem"? He sat up, leaned forward. "Could be. What can I do?"

The first bell rang before she could respond, making them both jump. The color had left her face again and she looked even more weary than before as she slowly stood up, holding onto the chair like it was the only thing keeping her upright. She stared at the table, her expression distant, before she let go and squared her shoulders. "There is one thing." The words were barely above a whisper.

"Name it."

Finally, a smile. She reached into her bag and grabbed a notebook, tore out a sheet, and scribbled something on it before handing it to him. "It's a long shot but could you dig around and see if you can find any info on that name? It's my mother's maiden name and I thought it might help. She might be trying to stay low-key." Her words were light but something dark flickered in her eyes.

He stared at the single name written there, Raynor, then caught her eye again. "What aren't you telling me, Veronica?"

She stuffed her notebook back in her backpack and slung it over her shoulder. To his shock, she winked. "Lots. Intrigued yet?"

He watched her long strides as she left the library, the second bell ringing, not moving even though he had to get to journalism class. Price wouldn't give him a hard time if he was a few minutes late.

He stuffed the little scrap of paper in his packet and grabbed his satchel, following her path out of the library and down the hall, dodging the last-minute runners, feeling buoyant.

As he opened the door to the journalism room, Price handed him his latest story with her edits, and he settled at one of the tables to look through it. His head though, wasn't in his story on new parking regulations, it was ideas and strategies and plans. The angry malaise he'd felt since the college plans crashed around him was burnt away. Intrigued? Hell yes. Whether by the mystery or the girl, he didn't know. After all—he shook his head, tried to focus—she was a mystery all on her own.

"It ain't for anything illegal, is it?" Jim asked as he tossed his back belt onto the seat of his truck.

Chris glanced over at the rest of the crew filing out of the doors, all looking as weary as he felt, before turning back to Jim. "I wouldn't do that to you. Or your son."

Jim seemed to consider it as he lumbered into the cab. "Yeah, I don't think you would. Still, you wanna tell me what this is about?"

Chris kept his sigh inside, reminding himself he was asking for a favor...and people always seemed to need reasons. "A friend of mine asked me what I could find out about that name. I'll vouch for her, she wouldn't use that info for anything bad."

"Her, huh?" Jim grinned. "All right, I'll give the name to Junior, have him run it for your girlfriend."

"She's not..."

Jim leaned out of the open window, winked. "Then why'd your ears go red when you mentioned her?"

With that, he gunned the engine and drove off. Chris couldn't decide whether to laugh or throw something. He went with the former, chuckling to himself as he made his way to the wagon.

Chris figured he'd have to wait until his next shift to hear from Jim, so he was more than a little surprised when Mom called him to the phone the following Tuesday as he was slogging his way through his physics homework. He figured it was either Laine or Julian—or maybe Veronica throwing caution to the wind—so he was shocked to hear Jim on the other line. "I figured your girl wouldn't want to wait."

Chris could hear the grin in Jim's voice and let it stand, taking the phone out to the back porch where they could talk in relative privacy. "He found something?"

"Yeah, somethin' weird. Hold on." He heard the muffled sound of Jim's voice and an even more muffled one answering him. "Right. So, there was a missing person's report filed for an M. Raynor in November of 1989, and dropped two days later."

That didn't sound weird to him—the person had been found, right? —so clearly Jim wasn't finished. "Any distinguishing info? Like a first name?"

"Nope." Chris heard the click of a lighter before Jim continued. "So that's weird thing number one, no first name, not even whether it was a guy or a girl. The really freaky thing is why it was dropped. You ready for this?"

If he learned nothing else from this conversation, the fact that Jim had a flair for the dramatic was an unexpected surprise. "So ready."

"The person who made the report wouldn't give their name, but it was the same number that called to say it wasn't needed. They said it was a prank, there wasn't nobody named Raynor."

"Nobody missing?"

"Nobody by that name at all in town. What?" A voice in the background, Junior maybe? "Right. Apparently Chief Farnsworth made a note in the file that there was a Raynor family in his neighborhood, but they'd moved away something like thirty years ago. Now it's my turn, what's all this about, anyway?"

Chris didn't say anything at first, the night around him was quiet as well. "Honestly?"

Jim gave a phlegmy chuckle. "That'd be nice."

He glanced back at the house, making sure nobody was eavesdropping. Especially Megan. "I have no fucking idea what I've gotten myself into."

Jim's chuckle turned into a full-on laugh. "Well, son, welcome to the club."

"Hell of a club."

"Got that right. See ya Saturday."

"You got it." He was about to hang up when he remembered. "Tell Jim Jr. thanks for me."

"Will do. I'd say, stay out of trouble but I'm pretty sure that ship's long out of the harbor."

As he said his goodbyes and went back into the dark kitchen, Chris had to admit that Jim was probably right about that.

Chapter Eleven

As annoying as a shopping list Saturday was—at least an hour of a precise inventory of kitchen, freezer, fridge, and laundry room before we sat at the kitchen table to write it all down—it meant a guaranteed hour alone in the house. Normally, I'd use that hour to sneak-watch some trashy TV, but I had other plans. Chris had Mom's maiden name. I was going to see if I could find anything of hers with information I could use.

I always felt better with a plan.

I watched from the living room window until Dad's car was out of sight, counted to one hundred, then went straight to his office. Locked, as usual. If I tried to lock my bedroom he'd rain fire, but obviously different rules applied to him. Back to my room, I grabbed my calculus notebook from my backpack and went to the living room where Mom's old grading desk stood, bare except for the slotted file where Dad sorted bills and wrote checks.

Dad had purged most of Mom's stuff, from clothes to books to old college binders, but I was hoping he hadn't gotten everything.

Chris had suggested calling her friends—even offered to help—but Dad had been extra present lately, this was the first chance I had to do an extensive search. I opened each door gently, lifting papers and pens exactly as they were placed, so it didn't look rifled through.

Nothing in the first three drawers except old bills and boring paperwork. Discouraged, I opened the bottom drawer, which stuck a little as I did, like something was blocking it. Inside, Dad had added a metal-frame filing system, all the folders labeled in his neat print, car, home and FF. I ran my hand across the underside of the drawer above, something was blocking it. I pulled, hearing the screech of tape as I did.

I stared at the object in my hands, my vision blurred. On the front, a picture of a beach at sunset, *Addresses* gold-stenciled across the top. It was a permanent resident in Mom's purse when I was a kid, hanging out with assorted coins and packages of tissues and pencil stubs at the bottom of her battered leather purse, the plastic cover scratched and worn at the edges. Opening it was worse, Mom's untidy handwriting, like on the notes she'd stick in my lunch bag when I was worried about a math test or sad because my Valentines box was empty. I turned the pages more slowly, reading the little notes paper-clipped on different pages—*buy cake for P's birthday* or *Call Dr. Shine ASAP. Reached.* I could see her, sitting at this desk, as if I'd just seen her off to the store instead of Dad, tapping a pen against her chin, a little wrinkle between her eyes before starting to write again.

My eyes itched and I absently swiped my arm across them. The little clock gave a single chime, alerting me that I only had—at best—half an hour before Dad came home. Names. Who had Mom said she was going to see that last afternoon, as I dozed and drifted? I went back to the A's, scanning the names to see if anything sparked a recollection. I hit paydirt on C, *Caro, Amanda and Len.* I scribbled the number in my notebook and kept going, but nothing else stood out. Until L.

I stared at a page with no numbers or names or notes. Instead, a small silver key taped dead center, no indication of what it might open. I worked a nail under the tape and pried it loose, sticking it in my pocket. Another mystery to solve. I sighed, pushed the drawer closed and it slid easily. Damn it. I wanted to keep the address book, as a memento if nothing else but Dad was sure to notice.

Tape in hand, I felt around for the sticky bits where it had been, unnoticed for who knew how long and secured it in place. Everything just as before, with ten minutes to spare. The key was a message, and I had the Caros' number. Progress, complete with a little thrill of an idea that maybe Mom was with them, had been there all this time. It was immediately followed by that image I'd gleaned of Mom in a hospital bed, curled up as if to make herself invisible. Maybe that was only my own fear, maybe this was the one time that special sense was wrong. I wavered between tending that seed or digging it up before it took root as I waited for Dad to come home.

The opportunity came faster than I'd anticipated. I knew I couldn't use the house phone because it would show on the bill, so I needed a pay phone and time where I wouldn't be interrupted. No easy task. Dad was going through another one of his monitor-my-every-move phases—calling by 4:15 p.m. every afternoon to make sure I was home from school—as I found out on Monday when I'd been slow getting home and got an earful, followed by being sent to my room without the supper I'd made. As I sat at my desk that Monday night, hunger and rage gnawing at my stomach, I wished that I could figure out what brought on these micro-managing fits. Did Mrs. Sneed, nosy neighbor extraordinaire, whisper some allusion in his ear? Had he come across that stupid "spare the rod" proverb in his millionth pass through the King James?

That little seed planted when I found the address book and the key had taken root despite me, making Dad's behavior all that much harder to take. I tried to logic myself, what if, I thought as I stared down at my calculus book without seeing it, by some remote possibility Dad was right and Mom had walked out and never looked back? Or had tried to see me, been rebuffed, and given up? I leaned back in my desk chair and pushed the book and the thought away at the same time. That was logical only if you didn't know Marie Simon at all. Walk away from a husband who'd become a stranger? Sure, but she wouldn't have left me behind.

By Saturday Dad's fit had passed, he even smiled at me at breakfast as I slid scrambled eggs onto his plate. I gave him a tentative one in return and went back into the kitchen to fill my own plate and join him. We ate in the usual silence, Dad flipping idly through the newspaper as he folded eggs and toast and bacon into his mouth. Finally, he folded the paper and cleared his throat. I looked up to another smile. Weird.

"Now, I've got to go into Faith Fellowship today, can I drop you anywhere?"

Yes, over the border of Dalesville, I can find my own way from there. "I was thinking of going to get some coffee downtown."

"Why don't you ask Nancy if she'd like to join you?"

I quelled a sigh. "Well, I was going to bring some homework with me, but I guess I could..."

He waved that away. "Just because you have an 'in' at Faith Fellowship College doesn't mean you should neglect your work. Go get your books and we'll go."

"Yes, sir." I took the plates into the kitchen, with a mixture of elation at getting out from under his thumb for a few hours and the clammy, queasy feeling I always got when he brought up that particular future, like it was a bad hotdog at the state fair. Tomorrow's problems though, I ran down the hall to my room to grab my backpack.

From my vantage point right inside the door of the Blue Moon, I watched Dad pull away, the blink of his turn signal as he turned left onto Sunset. When I was sure he was gone I walked right back out again, scooting past some entering patrons who tutted with annoyance, pulling my old black coat more tightly around me against the bite of the wind. I made a quick left of my own down the alley between Lou's Used Records and moldering wreck of the St. James Hotel. On the side of Lou's, facing the parking lot of the St James, was the world's grungiest payphone, where I knew I wouldn't be seen. I picked up the receiver with tweezed fingers, wondering briefly exactly how many diseases I was exposing myself to and dug the number I'd torn from my notebook out of my pocket. My hand shook as I dialed. I told myself it was the icy chill of the receiver cradled between my ear and shoulder, even as it metastasized to the rest of me as the phone started to ring.

"We're sorry. The number you are trying to reach has been disconnected. The new number is…"

Frantic, I dug a pen out of my bag in enough time for the second recitation and scribbled it above the original. I retrieved my quarter from the slot and tried again. "Hello?"

A child's voice. "I'm looking for Amanda Caro. Is she available?" My voice sounded alien even to me, it was hearty and business-like, like a telemarketer.

"Mom!" The pitch and volume were head-splitting, I held the phone away from my ear. "Phone!"

"Who is it, Lily?" I could barely hear the other voice over the static.

At a much more reasonable volume, Lily asked, "Who are you?"

"Lily!" The voice was more familiar at that pitch. I could remember that same inflection when her husband said something shocking. "How do we act on the phone again?"

"Sorry Mom!" Lily cleared her throat. "I'm sorry. Who may I say is calling?"

"Better." I heard the hint of a laugh in Amanda's voice.

Despite myself, I almost laughed, too. "Can you please tell her it's Veronica Simon? Marie's daughter," I added, in case she didn't remember me.

The phone clattered down, thankfully muffling Lily's next shout. "It's someone named Veronica, Mom. She says she's Marie's daughter."

"Oh, my God, Veronica." Amanda sounded out of breath when she picked up the phone. "Sweetheart, how are you?"

I knew there weren't enough quarters in the world to pay for the length of that answer, so I settled for, "I'm *okay*. Listen, I don't have much time. I need to ask you about my mom."

A long pause followed my words. Amanda's voice was nearly a whisper when she finally replied, "What do you need to know?"

I shuddered again, the phone heavy against my shoulder, my throat locked.

"Veronica? Are you still there?"

The dam broke and the words came rushing out. "Do you know where she is?"

Even through the crackle of distance and a dodgy pay phone I could hear her sigh. "I don't. I wish I did."

Disappointment robbed me of my voice again, made me aware how rooted the hope she'd been hiding out with her best friend, that Amanda would say, "Hold on, she's right here," had gotten. Stupid. "Okay, thanks anyway."

I started to hang up when I heard Amanda call out, "Veronica, wait!"

A flare too small to be hope sparked. "Yes?"

"She was with me briefly, about five years ago. I was...helping her out. She was planning to leave your dad, but it was...well, complicated."

"Yes." I could fill in some spaces at least. Len was an attorney, and Mom would have needed all the help she could get if Dad had Robert James on his side.

"She wasn't even here an hour. She told me she had something, something that would help you both. Your dad wanted to move to Dalesville, and he's got powerful friends there, so she'd need leverage, you understand. Len warned her to be careful, to make sure she didn't leave you in your dad's custody or he could claim abandonment. She gave me that little smile of hers and said she wouldn't."

"Did she explain what her leverage was?"

"No and she was so nervous when she even mentioned it, I didn't want to pry." I didn't know how to respond to that. I let the silence spin out, unmindful of the cost. "I'm sorry, Veronica. We tried to contact you but once you were in Dalesville, it was impossible. Your father blamed us for her leaving." Her voice was hoarse. "We should have kept trying."

For a second the urge to agree, to yell at her, ask what kind of best friend she was, overwhelmed me. To tell her that I knew something happened to Mom and she could have prevented it. My nails dug into my free palm, balled in a fist in my coat pocket for warmth, the cold air finding the gap between coat and scarf and rumpling my neck into gooseflesh. My throat seemed lodged with the same ice.

"Sweetie?" Her voice was so like Mom's at that moment I nearly dropped the phone. What would Mom have said? "It's okay to be angry, make sure it's at the right person."

I choked a laugh back. It bruised my throat. Should I fault this woman for what I did myself? "I'm here."

"Can I do anything to help you?"

I could hear the tears in her voice and that icy anger thawed a bit. I answered her as truthfully as I could. "I don't know."

It was her turn to be silent. The operator cut through. "Your time is up. Signal when through."

"Veronica," I heard her say as the operator stopped talking. Her voice had a little steel in it now. "I'm going to give you my address. If you need anything."

Stupidly, I nodded, like she could see me. "Do you have a pen?"

"I'm ready." I turned over the slip of paper with her number and scribbled down the address.

"You got it?"

"I do."

"I need you to know, Veronica, Marie loved you more than anything. If she's not there, it's because she can't be. Do you understand?"

This would be the time to tell her what I saw. Instead, I closed my eyes and mind. "Thank you," was all I managed to say and then I set the phone back on the cradle.

For a long time, I stood there staring at the phone, half-conscious of the shush of cars on Sunset, the wind rattling the chain link around the parking lot, my own shallow respiration and the fine sheen of sweat on my forehead.

The phone rang, I jumped, grabbed it, some wild certainty it was Mom warming me despite the nip of the wind, despite that cold reality inside.

"Two dollars, twenty-five cents, please."

The hard laugh I'd swallowed back returned in full force as I dug into my pocket for my change. The operator must have thought I was nuts, the operator may not have been wrong.

I was still laughing as I made my way back to the Blue Moon—another loon in Dalesville's darkening city center.

Chapter Twelve

H e didn't know what to say, how to approach her, with the information he'd gotten from Jim. No phone number, she hadn't given it to him and a quick check of the phonebook showed it wasn't listed. Given what she'd told him about her dad and place he worked, a call from an unknown guy would be more trouble for her than it was worth.

He speared the limp broccoli on his tray in frustration. Laine, who could be counted on to eat almost anything, pushed his own tray away. "You know, we're seniors. We could leave campus for lunch."

Chris sighed. "I don't have the car today and I'm sick of everything in walking distance."

Laine slumped in his chair. "Yeah." He pulled his tray back and took a half-hearted bite of an overcooked carrot and swallowed with a grimace. "Either this food sucks or my ennui is killing my appetite."

Chris snorted. "It's definitely the food, *mon frere*."

Laine balled up his napkins and threw them at Chris, laughing. "All I'm saying is that if it's salad for dinner, I'm writing the whole day off. So, what's up with you?"

"What're you talking about?"

Laine shrugged. "You looked tired and pensive before the veggie atrocity."

"Didn't sleep well, I guess." That was a vast understatement. He'd barely slept at all, his brain trying to make sense of all the things Jim had told him and how to tell her everything he'd found out. Too much to explain in the fifteen minutes left in lunch period.

Laine frowned. "I can help, you know."

"What? With my sleeping?" He tried to smile. "Got some pills in your bag or something?"

The frown turned into a scowl. "No, dumbass. With whatever is *actually* going on."

He stared at his friend, considering denying and telling Laine everything was fine. There was something inside that had always rebelled against asking for help, he had to figure shit out himself. A family trait, or some quirk uniquely his? He smiled at Laine, the least he could do was stop underestimating him. "I don't know how, but I promise I'll tell you when I do."

"Fair enough." Laine got up, picked up their trays. "I'll start by throwing this crap away and we can see if there's anything better in the machines."

"It's a deal."

Staring at the rows of snacks with a dollar in his hand, Laine finally shrugged and picked some corn chips before saying, "Oh, I've got something for you."

He stuffed the chips in his backpack and pulled out his sketchbook, flipping the pages before he showed it to Chris.

It was Veronica, caught in semi-profile as she looked down, brown hair pulled back in a ponytail, a crease between her eyes that, in conjunction with the downturn of her lips, gave an overall impression of sadness. He wondered how often she actually smiled. "It's really good," was all he managed to say.

Laine tore it out of his book and handed it to him. "It's yours. 'Portrait of a Young Woman in Calculus Class.' Hence the ennui."

"Is that your new word?" Chris folded it carefully and slid it in his satchel.

Laine grinned. "It will be, once I find a way to use it a third time."

Chris turned back to the machine and slid in his dollar, feeling the need not to be looking at his friend at that moment. "Sure you wanna part with it? You really captured her." The tips of his ears warmed.

Laine's stare was boring into him but his voice was casual. "I can recreate it—or borrow it from you for my eventual gallery show."

The bell rang over his words and the two of them made their way to their lockers in companionable silence, except for the crunch and crackle as they scarfed their chips. What he wouldn't give for Laine's confidence in his own work, or even the guts to pull out some of his own unfinished short stories and lame-ass verse to see if anything could be salvaged. He liked writing for the newspaper, but it didn't satisfy his writing hunger any more than the potato chips satisfied his physical hunger.

He crumpled the empty bag and stuffed it in his satchel but dismissing that thought wasn't as simple.

"I'm off to be bored stiff."

Chris grinned. "Enjoy."

He made his way to journalism class in a daze, preoccupied by what was and what might be.

He finally caught up with Veronica after school, she'd paused to adjust her backpack and sighed. The face she turned to him as he called her name also looked tired and drawn, brightening slowly as she picked him out of the crowd. He felt pretty good himself as he walked over.

"Been awhile, I was beginning to forget what you looked like." Her tone was light but that air of sadness that her slumped shoulders and dark circles gave off was in her voice as well. He flattered himself by thinking some of it was a sign she missed him. "This no shared classes is brutal."

"That and my dad's overwhelming need to know where I am every second has been a constant barrier to the whole making friends thing." The brittle bitterness in her voice though, was gone when she spoke again. "I do enjoy a challenge, though."

"I have no doubt." He smiled. "Listen, I've found out some things, but I need time to lay it all out. Are you free?"

She sighed. "Not today, but Dad's got his monthly budget meeting day after tomorrow and won't be home for dinner. We could meet in the park after school."

"It's a date." Under his hair, he could feel his ears go red, but he let it stand.

"*Okay*." Her face looked a little flushed, too, he was happy to note.

He rested a hand on her shoulder and the color drained from her face as she flinched, squeezed her eyes shut as if something hurt her. He yanked his hand away, mumbled an apology.

She shook her head, gave him a tired smile as she opened her eyes. "I banged the hell out of my shoulder getting groceries out of the car last weekend, it's still a little sore."

Her eyes looked strange, like there was too much blue, he dismissed it as a trick of the light. "Handle with care?"

A full-on grin blew all that away. "What'd be the fun in that?"

She turned and disappeared into the after school crowd. As Chris made his way to the parking lot, he realized he knew at least one thing about her, she liked having the last word.

She was sitting on the edge of the rusted-out death trap of a mer-ry-go-round, the weather was still cold enough so that the playground was empty. Not that it was used much when the weather warmed, and the specter of no-school and twenty-four/seven supervision convinced even the most overbearing parents to let their kids go free-range. Everything in the playground looked like the set of some post-nuclear movie, from the giant climbing giraffe sunk in asphalt and listing to the side like it was planning to nibble some leaves off the nearby oak to the creaky swing set and tetanus-shot-to-be warped metal on which Veronica sat.

She caught his eye, smiled. As he settled down next to her, she asked, her tone wry, "Was this place always this junked?"

He took his pack out of his jacket, offered her one. She took it and he lit both before answering. He pointed to the weathered climber and slide near the trees. "That was the last thing they built and I'm pretty sure it's been here longer than us."

She took a drag, tapped ash in the dead grass and sand. "Did you play here as a kid?"

"Most of us did until Mark Kemp—he moved away a few years ago—fell off this junker and got his leg caught underneath." Off her shocked expression, he amended. "He was fine. Tetanus shot and a big scar on his shin. After that, most of the parents warned us to stay away and the town magically found money to build that new one by Cambridge Estates."

"Right. In the nice part of town." Her smile and tone were cynical. "Did you play there?"

"Sometimes." He didn't mention Julian lived in Cambridge Estates. "But it was too new. Too shiny. We'd end up back here eventually." He dragged, tapped his ash again. "But you didn't want a lecture on Dalesville's civic duties. Julian would be a better person to ask anyway."

Her eyes crinkled at the corners. "I don't mind. I'm guessing it's better than what you wanted to tell me."

He raised an eyebrow. "You're a little spooky, you know that?"

"I do, actually." Her voice had gone flat.

That seemed as good a sign as any to tell her the disturbing stuff he'd found out. He stared down at the scuffed toes of his black boots and started from the beginning, only stopping when he heard her gasp about the missing person's report. When he looked up, her face seemed swallowed up by her shocked eyes, burning blue, her posture rigid, and vibe so electric he thought he touched her she'd fry him. He could feel the hair on his arms and the back of his neck rise and though he'd only admit it to himself later, it was kind of a turn on. A fleeting memory of her face when he saw her in the square that night rose and then was gone. "What," his voice came out hoarse, he cleared his throat and tried again. "What's wrong?"

A deep breath, a little shake and the moment passed. She looked like an ordinary—if tired—girl hugging herself as if she was cold. He thought about putting his arm around her—for comfort, for warmth—but hesitated. "Took me by surprise is all." A tentative smile before she relaxed, took a drag. "Didn't mean to interrupt."

"You sure?" If that's how she reacted to surprises he made a mental note to avoid any in the future, if possible.

"I need to know." He could hear the subtle underlining of "need" in her voice.

He finished by telling her about the retraction and the police chief's note. An echo of that earlier tension returned. "A prank?"

"Yeah, I didn't buy that either."

She shot up off the merry-go-round, her hands in fists, her body shaking. "Son of a bitch."

Chris stood up, knowing that if she turned, he'd see that same reaction as before, could feel it all along his nerve endings, that push-pull of "run" and "step closer." He stepped closer. Her shoulders slumped. His breath came out in a gusty sigh. The face she turned to him was pale, the eyes sad. "I shouldn't have dragged you into this, Chris. I don't think it's safe."

"I don't mind." He said the words without thinking, only realizing he meant them as they echoed in his ears. Head and gut were a bold brew of fear and confusion but underneath that was a bright silver core of excitement he didn't want to pick apart. Or end.

She took a step closer to him, her frown a crinkle between her eyes. "I don't want you hurt."

He stared at her, felt buoyant. "Oh? Why's that?"

Her lips twitched, her mouth open as if she was going to answer. Or kiss him. He would have been good with either option. Instead, she tensed, her posture like a deer scenting a predator...

Don't think about that.

She glanced to her right, narrowed her eyes, and muttered something under her breath. "I have to go."

Chris turned to see what she was looking at, but there was nothing but the bare trees of the grove on the edge of the playground. "Veronica."

Her hand twitched at her side as he came closer. A smile came and went. "Be careful. I think I might be trouble."

She turned and ran across the park before he could respond. He watched her go, thinking about trouble. Thinking that he hadn't felt this good in a long time.

Chapter Thirteen

I doubled back after Chris departed, my gut telling me exactly who I'd find there. Sure enough, Theo was emerging from the grove as I returned, his face red when he caught my eye. No suit, he looked more like the version I met up with at the mall, with a puffer coat over the same worn hoodie. I waited for him to come closer before I said anything. "Is this some kind of stalker thing? Is there a freaky 'me' wall in your bedroom closet?"

He shook his head, scowling. "You're not going to like the answer."

The urge to throttle him was strong, made worse by everything Chris told me. I crossed my arms to keep his safe. "There's no answer I'd like, if that helps."

He stared down at the carpet of dead leaves still frosted from the morning, the sun was too distant and weak to penetrate the canopy above. "It's my job."

The cold air of the grove found that sweet spot at the back of my neck and sent its ice down my back. "I thought you were learning leadership or investment stuff."

His head rose, curls bounding. One of my own memories surfaced, as overwhelming as the ones I'd get from others, of sitting in a circle in the small chapel at Faith Fellowship, the youth leader—Mr. Joe, he told us to call him—strumming his guitar as we sang "All for the Best," Theo's face lit up as he clapped along. He'd caught my eye and smiled, a smile that made me feet all mushy and blushy. My first crush. If I went home and dug through my old school notebooks, would I find his initials in a little heart in the margins, some sad, half-written poem composed when he'd disappeared from the group? Likely.

Those would be the only traces that remained. I never really knew him, and I didn't know him now. "It's my job? What, is that the Faith Fellowship version of 'I was just following orders'?"

He went even redder. "Be grateful it's me. You're supposed to be monitored and reported on. Anyone else would've ratted about your new friend by now."

I could feel the heat in my own face, felt my nails digging into my palms. "Is that a threat?"

The color drained from his face, and he took a shaky step back. "It's a warning. You think you know what that place is about. You don't."

The anger abated, left me worn out. I leaned against the oak tree behind me, the bark digging into my back. "Can you be straight with me? For once? All you're giving me is hints and insinuations."

He frowned. "You don't trust me."

Between the happy kid with the curls, I'd sighed over, and the pin-wearing intern was a vast grey space, true for anyone I hadn't seen in five years. Doubly true for anyone associated with Faith Fellowship. I didn't understand Dad's shift and I'd been there for all of it. "I don't know you. I don't know what you want."

He surprised me with a smile, so similar to the one from youth group, it was like time-traveling. "Isn't it obvious? I want to burn that place to the ground."

Singing my song. I wanted to join in, add a few verses, even, but that image of Mom in Mrs. Phelps' head, that weird missing persons' report with Mom's maiden name, stopped me. "Why?"

The smile disappeared as his eyes clouded over. "I can't tell you that right now."

My hand twitched at my side. I knew I could find out if I wanted to, likely whatever he wanted to hide would be right in the forefront of his mind. Knew I'd know I could trust him if I did. And if not? I would have revealed what I could do to someone connected to Paul Barnes and Robert James.

My breath seemed to stop, locked in my chest as I stared at the sad, distant expression on his face, the nervous way he tapped his fingers on his thighs like they were keyboards. Every time it had happened before was an accident—a knock on the shoulder as I cruised the halls at school, a surprise hug or head pat from one of my parents' friends at birthday or dinner parties back when Dad actually approved of such frivolity, or forgetting myself and shaking a hand, like Mrs. Phelps. The only intention I'd had was blocking as much as possible once I was old enough to understand. That, and keeping my distance.

Now, what? I was going to force myself into this guy's head to check if *I* could trust *him*?

My chest loosened its grip, and I let out a gusty sigh. "You want to take down Faith Fellowship, huh? Is there a plan?"

His hands went still, resting against his thighs. "Not really."

I lowered my voice, feeling beyond tired with the whole afternoon. "Are you going to report this? Tell them about who I was meeting?"

Theo, looking equally exhausted, shook his head. "Is he your boyfriend?"

I wanted to say yes, not just for the shock value. I'd had crushes before, but that went nowhere except my old diary. This was different. I was getting to know him as more than a fantasy, and the more I learned, the more I wanted to learn. And there were moments—a smile, the way he said my name or caught my eye—where I thought he might like me, too. And yet. "He's a friend who's a boy. So, what will you tell them?"

Theo shrugged, stood up straight. "What I usually say. 'She keeps herself to herself.' I should go. I'm supposed to be trailing you in the car as you walk home."

I tried to tamp down the sick feeling that produced, that the low-grade paranoia I'd always felt about this place had an actual reason for existing. That conspiracy shit was way too close to Dad's way of thinking about the world. "Why? Is someone watching you, too?"

Theo's usually soft features tightened, like a whole-face grimace, and I recoiled, thinking it was directed at me. "As far as I know, Veronica, you're the only one. Imagine that, a place like that dropping money to spy on a teenage girl. You think I need another reason not to like that place?"

He didn't wait for me to answer—not that I could form any words—before he turned and walked out of the grove.

I should have asked him what excuse his handlers gave for following me, but he'd taken off before I could gather the scattered bits of my mind to ask.

"Veronica? The derivative?"

I came back to reality with a mental thud and glanced over at Laine, who shrugged. "Have you tried looking under the couch cushions?"

Ms. Kelly frowned in disappointment, deepening at the sound of scattered laughs. After a parting pained look in my direction, she moved on to Sarah Tyler, who was practically levitating out of her chair in an effort to be called on. I was already gone again before Sarah started to speak, trying to solve the puzzle of how I was supposed to find Mom, hard enough already with this added bullshit. Thinking over what Amanda had told me and what direction I should try next. I doodled randomly in my notebook for a good five minutes as my mind wandered over possibilities before I realized that in fact, I'd written Chris' name in an elaborate, if poorly executed, bubble script. I could feel the heat rise from my neck up and after a glimpse around to see if anyone noticed, I saw Laine staring at me with a little grin. My ears burned and I quickly turned to a fresh page and directed my attention forward for the rest of the class, trying to ignore Laine's knowing stare.

Too many questions, the police report, Theo, secret files, paid st alking...I scribbled Nancy's name in my notebook. She was the one I needed to talk to, given that, if she got her way, Paul Barnes would be her father-in-law. She'd know things I wouldn't.

The bell rang, with me having paid exactly zero attention to calculus for the entire hour. Everybody started to move in masse toward the door. "Veronica, can you stay for a minute?"

A sympathetic look from Laine before he escaped cheered me enough to nod through Ms. Kelly's exhortations to work up to my potential. When she finally let me go after exacting a promise from me to make more of an effort, I walked out to see Laine waiting for me, with the slightest little quirk of his lips.

"Detention?" he said as he straightened up from his lean. We shared back-to-back classes, so we usually walked and chatted from calculus to history. It was a nice switch from doing the between-class slalom by myself.

"Nah. Work up to my potential."

"About time, you lazy cow."

I giggled and Laine full-on grinned. "You know, it's funny how the one time you didn't have the answer erases all the other times you did. Like one step is all it takes to sink you into the great morass of slackerdoom."

Laine took my arm. "Laziness is a gateway drug."

I laughed hard enough to turn heads. Unfortunately, we happened to be passing Billy Zacharias trying to set up a future date rape with a freshman cheerleader.

"Hey, fag, when did you get a girlfriend?" he shouted to the general amusement of the rest of his meathead friends. The girl, leaning against Billy's locker, looked dazed. It was Laine's face that killed me, the smile was gone, replaced with a taut look of resignation. That wall in my head cracked a bit, letting in all sorts of crazed signals I couldn't interpret. It frayed my temper and I felt my internal temperature rise, judging by the heat on my neck and cheeks, too fast to stop. "Fuck off, troglodyte."

Billy may not have understood the last word but he sure as hell knew the first two. "Bitch." He started toward me and I knew what was coming. Laine did, too, he dropped my arm and started to move in front of me to take the blow. I pushed him aside, not too hard, tried to communicate silently to him to let it happen. Language could merit a week's detention but if Billy Z actually hit me? He'd be off the team. I saw his fist draw back in slow motion, waited.

The blow never came. One of his friends grabbed his wrist, whispered something in his ear—most likely said consequences of hitting someone on school grounds—and surrounded him, bore him away down the hall as the first bell rang. Leaving me, Laine, and the hapless freshman girl, still leaning, wide-eyed, against Billy's locker. I gave her a smile, she didn't return it.

"A piece of advice?" She looked up at me, her face looked older than fifteen with blue eyeshadow and heavy foundation—but her eyes still looked like a little kid's. "Go for geeks. They're the ones who'll make money and treat you like a queen."

Laine gave a jagged laugh, and the girl skittered away, with one last confused look over her shoulder. I finally met Laine's eyes, he'd resumed slumping against the radiator under the windows. "I'm sorry I pushed you."

He shrugged. "It took me a second, but I figured out what you were doing."

"You aren't mad at me?"

His expression, usually open and sweet, was closed and hard. Stay separate, I'd told myself over and over. Apparently, I couldn't even keep promises to myself. Any of them. My stomach felt like a lead ball in the middle of my body as I stared down at the floor and waited for the inevitable. "How do you feel about blowing off history?"

I had no idea what my face did but a little of the humor and warmth had returned to Laine's expression when I looked up from my contemplation of the faded grey floor tiles, and I thought it worth the risk of detention, Dad's wrath, or Theo reporting me. "I feel really good about it, actually."

"Excellent." Laine took my arm again and steered me down the hall and out the door.

I continued to let him steer me down the hill to the park that faced the school, down to the empty playground where Chris and I had met yesterday. A glance at the grove revealed no one, which gave me one crucial bit of info that wouldn't bum me out until later, they didn't expect me to do anything as rebellious as cut school. Laine stopped at the giant wood slide and climber, pulled out a board and gestured me inside, then followed, replacing the board so neatly no one would have guessed we were there. It smelled of mildew and gone-over leaves, but enough air and light came through the warped boards so that it wasn't completely oppressive.

Laine sat down next to me, leaning against the loose board so it wouldn't fall open and give us away. I watched as he dug into his bag and came up with a piece of paper. He handed it to me, and I held it in one of the shafts of light. "It's an office pass! Where did you get this?"

He winked. "Swiped it from Gwinn's office. He's so spacey he never reads them, just puts them in a big file and goes back to scratching his ass."

I laughed, mostly from relief. I didn't know how I'd explain ditching if the school called my dad. Office passes meant that you were off campus with permission and Mr. Gwinn, one of the guidance counselors, had a habit of pre-signing them.

"Awesome," was all I could manage.

"I save them for special occasions. Don't want them to get too suspicious."

I folded the precious pass and put it in my bag. "Is this a special occasion?"

Laine didn't answer. Instead, he took what I first thought was a cigarette out of his bag and lit it. The first exhale proved me wrong as the sweet smoke drifted from his mouth. I hadn't smelled that since those long-ago parental parties, a memory that did nothing for my mood. He passed the joint to me. I toked and tried to at least let the immediate past drift away with the smoke. It didn't quite work, especially since Laine had never really answered my earlier question.

We passed it back and forth in silence until Laine took the last toke, crushed it on the sole of his boot and tucked it under the carpet of leaves. I coughed at both the smoke and the sour smell that drifted up when he disturbed the ground. That got his attention, and he stared at me, the chiaroscuro light from between the slats shading his face enough to make it hard to read. Or maybe I was too bleary-eyed. "I know."

"Huh?" was my intelligent reply.

"You're worried that you...what's the word?"

"Emasculated you."

"That's the one."

I let my head drift back until it was leaning against the slat. "Yeah. I am."

"Well, that's stupid. That's for assholes like Billy Z." Laine's lip curled, and he mumbled, "He should worry."

"Yeah?"

I felt rather than saw Laine's nod. "I'll tell you about that some other time. I know who I am. I know who you are."

I laughed, it hurt my scorched throat. "Oh, yeah? Glad one of us does."

"Friends defend each other. We're friends. You defended me. End of story."

The relief unknotted my shoulders, melted of the lead ball in my stomach, finally allowed the pot to work its calming magic. "I'm glad."

"Me, too."

All around and between us was quiet. I felt better than I had in years. I rested my head on Laine's shoulder, despite the discomfort in our disparate heights and what I might see, and enjoyed the moment.

We stumbled down Sunset to Sam's, I needed coffee and grease to be straight enough to face my father in a few hours. Over a plate of rubbery onion rings, Laine's smirk returned. "So."

I bit into a ring and sucked out the onion like a piece of spaghetti. "So?"

"I saw what you were doodling on your notebook."

I avoided looking at him by becoming intensely focused on the surface of my coffee. I liked Chris and it was a terrible idea.

Shirley, who clearly must have thought my laser focus on my coffee was a subtle clue for a refill, drifted by and topped off the cup, raising an eyebrow at the heavy silence between Laine and me. I gave her a little smile, and she shrugged and moved on to the hound-faced man at the next table, whose faded smile at her presence prompted an affectionate squeeze of his shoulder.

"Don't worry. I won't say anything."

More for something to do than out of any real desire, I grabbed the sugar and poured a generous amount into my cup. The first sip told me I'd been too liberal in the pouring, and I set the cup down and pushed it away. Only then did I meet Laine's still slightly bloodshot eyes. "I don't know if it matters if you did. We're not twelve, right? What's a little embarrassment?"

Laine picked up one of the rings, nibbled a bit, then set it back down with a sour face. "He likes you, too."

I felt a little flare in my stomach that must have shown in my face, Laine grinned. "How…" I stopped. How much is what I wanted to ask but I realized I didn't really want the answer. Instead, I shoved another ring in my mouth to ensure I couldn't say a word. It tasted terrible.

Laine turned and dug into his backpack, pulled out his worn sketchbook. He flipped through it, and I liked that he had a little smile on his face as if he was pleased with his own work. He stopped and passed the sketchbook to me.

It was me, my eyes looking down at a book, my hand tangled in my hair, a precise rendering even down to the little wrinkle over my nose I always felt when I was reading. I didn't know what to say at first. "You're really good," I finally managed.

"This one's better than the original, which is now in Chris' possession. That's how I know, *okay?*"

It should have made me happy, secure, that for the first time in all the flush-inducing, tingly-skinned crushes I'd had from the age of twelve, the boy in question felt the same way, or some species of it, anyway. I closed my eyes, blocking out the sticky table, the assorted crew idling behind the counter, the old man at the next table, Laine. Let the fantasy spin out, fingers twined, the friction between them some innocent precursor to later melding, head on the shoulder and the tickle of his hair on my cheek as we danced, a slow reveal of one button, two, and his hand cupping my breast. And then, unbidden and unwanted, an image of myself, adjusting a backpack more securely on my shoulders as I walked alone past motels and fast food joints. That image swallowed and nullified its more pleasant twin. I shivered, a shake that started inside and metastasized outward. I opened my eyes and took a burning gulp of the too-sweet coffee to counteract the ice in my stomach and the lump in my throat. Laine was staring at me, his normally baby-faced countenance marred by long sad lines. It was like a line to the future, I saw what he would look like as an old man. "I'm sorry."

That surprised me enough to be able to form words again. "For what?"

He shrugged. "I don't know. You looked all bummed out."

"I'm not." A lie. "I'm confused." Well, that part was true.

The crash of dishes from the kitchen startled us both, followed by "Way to go, dumb ass," in a deep tone. "Well, it could be worse. You could be that guy."

I smiled, not sure if Laine's remark was diversion or comfort. It didn't really matter either way. He reached across the table and took my hand, which had been lurking near my coffee cup. I tensed, but didn't pull away and for the second time felt nothing but comfort coming from him. Maybe he had nothing to hide. "You don't have to do anything, Action Girl."

I made a disgusted sound in my throat. I drifted through life, secure behind my wall, then when something actually happened, I was paralyzed and unsure. "I'm not."

Laine shook his head. "You are. What was that thing with Billy Z today? Maybe I haven't known you for long but really, it doesn't take much to see that about you."

I squeezed his hand. "Maybe not, but you're pretty smart."

He leaned in so close I could see his pinned pupils and said in almost a whisper. "Let it unfold. You never know how it'll turn out."

"Making the moves on my boyfriend, huh?" a deep voice whispered in my ear. Our hands flew apart and my face felt as red as Laine's looked. We couldn't have seemed more guilty if we'd tried.

Julian stood at the table, grinning while Chris was bent over, laughing so hard he was holding on to the opposite table for support.

Laine tossed his napkin at Julian. "You asshole! You scared the shit out of me!"

The hound-faced man gave a phlegmy cough of disapproval at Laine's language and signaled Shirley with a wavering hand that floated into the air like a tired bird. She rushed over and gave him his check and Laine a look that could fry eyeballs. Laine pleaded silent forgiveness with big eyes and a downturned mouth. After a parting stink-eye, she shrugged and moved on.

The boys' amusement tapered off while Laine surreptitiously folded up his sketchbook and slid it back into his bag. Once done, he said, "Are you two going to mock us or are you here for some reason?"

"Make some room, we'll sit," Julian said.

We dutifully scooted in, and Julian and Chris sat. Julian with Laine and Chris, doing nothing for my peace of mind, next to me.

Julian pulled a cigarette from Laine's pack. "You cut. What's up?"

Laine met my eyes. I nodded, trusted he'd omit the latter part of our conversation. I had to hand it to him, he was a great storyteller. He made the whole thing sound like some mythic battle between the evil homophobe and the badass girl superhero. I was both amused and embarrassed, even more so when I could feel Chris' staring at me. Steeling myself, I looked up from my hands I'd splayed on the table, the better to observe my ragged, chewed nails and knuckles rough and sore from winter, met his eyes before we both turned our attention to Laine. Something had passed between us in those few seconds, a flash of understanding. So much for keeping it professional, for keeping focused on what mattered. It confirmed for me what danger I was in. What danger I could put him in.

Too many variables, it was like the equation from hell.

Let it unfold, Laine said. I turned my attention to Laine's narrative but like an undertow, that final image of me walking away kept pulling my attention down, joined to that image of Mom in a hospital bed. I knew I couldn't. I folded the sweet fantasy into a dark corner of my mind and started to form a plan.

Chapter Fourteen

There was a fine dusting of salt on the dark cafeteria table due to Laine's caffeine-tremored hands' attempt to inject some flavor into the unappetizing mess dubbed "hot lunch." Chris doodled in the salt, having given up on his own food. On some level he knew Laine was talking to him, but he couldn't focus enough to form the most rudimentary thought, much less converse with any skill.

"Christopher Martin Mulligan!"

That did it. He twitched. His right hand hit his tray, it skidded halfway down the otherwise empty table and erased what he'd been writing in the salt. He scowled. "You sound like my mother."

Laine countered with a grin. "I like your mom. She's smart and she makes great pancakes."

Chris stared at Laine, surprised as always by his lack of bitterness. When Laine came out to his parents freshman year, they'd unceremoniously kicked him out by changing the locks while he was at school. Although Big Pat was less than thrilled with the idea, Mom had taken Laine in for almost a month. Chris never knew for certain, but he was pretty sure Mom convinced the Gregorys to let him back in. Laine would still show up for breakfast about once a month, like an anniversary or something.

"Where are you today, anyway? You've spent almost the whole lunch break in some private Chrisworld."

"Hungover."

Laine rolled his eyes. "Nope. You didn't even go out this weekend."

All he could do was shrug. His mom had made similar, if less aggressive, inquiries over breakfast the day before and he couldn't answer those either. "Just thinking."

"Well, stop it. It's boring for me to sit with you if all you're going to do is stare at your food and doodle."

"Sorry, dude. I'll warn you next time."

"Good. I'll bring my Walkman."

"Tell you what. If you abandon that pile of vomit on your plate, I'll spend the last twenty minutes of lunch having a smoke with you. I'll even give you one of mine."

"Cigarettes I don't pay for are my favorite brand."

"I know, you mooch. Let's go."

Laine picked up his tray, Chris dutifully retrieved his own and they were on their way.

Once they crossed the stone bridge that linked the school grounds to Point Park, they were officially out of the school's jurisdiction. Yet the way the school loomed—three floors, an uncountable amount of windows—they always looked for some place to go to earth. Chris favored the weeping willow about one hundred feet from the bridge and Laine generally didn't care, so they pushed through the denuded branches and sat side by side against the broad, serrated trunk, the icy ground slowly turning them to marble.

Chris ferreted his cigarettes out of his bag and handed one to Laine. They smoked for a bit in companionable silence, no sound but the crackle of burning paper and the clicking of the branches in the wind.

"Rattle the bones," Chris said, only tangentially aware he'd spoken out loud until Laine replied with a "Huh?" "Sorry. I was thinking that the branches sound like rattling bones."

Laine inhaled too fast and coughed. "That's cheerful."

"I'm a sunbeam."

Laine's cough turned into a laugh. "I always suspected."

Another silence. Laine broke it with, "Your new friend is nice."

"Veronica? Is she my friend now?"

Laine grinned. "She should be. Good-looking and she doesn't seem to dislike you. You took the sketch, and I bet I know where it's hanging. Besides, you picked her up."

Chris ignored the first part of the sentence. "Finders keepers?"

"Exactly."

"She's not a puppy."

Another grin. "Definitely not. You should ask her out. With us."

Chris shrugged, not wanting to talk about her. She hadn't told him the name she'd asked him to look up was a secret, but it didn't feel right bringing any of it up. Not that he knew much anyway. Beyond that, he didn't know what he thought about her exactly, only that he thought about her a lot. The laser look and the remoteness, the belly laugh and occasional confidences, that weird energy she gave off at times. She was an odd combination of warm and cold. Did she like him or was he just useful? He guessed he wouldn't mind puzzling it out, but...

"Dude. You're doing it again."

The cigarette in his hand was burned down to the filter and he'd only taken a couple of drags. He crushed it out in the dirt. "Sorry. Lot on my mind."

The bell rang for fifth period, distant and tinny. "I'll bet," Laine replied as he stood and brushed himself off.

Chris followed suit, swaying a bit with reaction from standing up too fast. "Let's motor. I'm dying to get to physics class, it's not-a-surprise surprise quiz Monday."

Laine held back the willow branches to let him through. "Aren't you lucky? I'm glad I picked chemistry, at least there's always a chance to blow something up."

Chris trudged a little behind Laine. "I know. I thought it was going to be more interesting than it was. I blame my junior high sci-fi kick."

Laine stopped so suddenly Chris almost ran into him. "God. I'd forgotten about that. You used to have that ten-foot long *Doctor Who* scarf."

"Put your brake lights on when you're going to do that." Chris steadied himself. "I still do. I save it for below-zero days. It's quite toasty."

They stopped at the door. Chris sighed. "Don't wanna."

Laine, still grinning, yanked open the door and pushed him inside. "Get your ass to class, whiner."

"Fuck you, shorty."

"Sticks and stones." Laine turned left to head up the stairs, then turned back. "I've got your new friend in calculus. I'm inviting her out for Friday. Wear something fetching."

With that parting shot, Laine ran up the stairs and was gone before Chris could say a word. He thought about chasing him down but instead, he turned the opposite direction and walked to class. Halfway there, he started to whistle.

Chris grabbed his well-worn leather jacket off the hall tree and jingled his keys in his hand. Sighed. He had the misfortune of being the designated driver that night, seeing as he was the only one who had to be at work by three. "Mom! I'm leaving!"

"Don't shout through the house, Chris. I'm in the dining room."

Another sigh and Chris fumbled into his coat and made his way through the living room to poke his head in to where Mom sat, papers spread in concentric circles where dinner had been cleared away, her brow furrowed as she picked up one pile. Without looking up she said to him, "Can you explain why I would've saved ten-year-old uncollected tests from students who dropped my class?"

"Hope?"

She tossed the tests on an ever-growing pile of paper to the left of her chair with a, "Begone, false hope!"

"Way to go, Mom." He zipped his jacket as he spoke.

"You know, I've been meaning to clean out my office for years, but I swear, every time I made a move to the filing cabinet a student would knock on my door." She grinned. "You'd be amazed how touchy the young get if they don't get your full attention."

Chris put on his sourest look for her. "I'd give my arm to be ignored. I don't know what kind of neurotics you teach bio to."

His mother gave him a wry smile after looking him up and down. "Yes, the black combat boots and nail polish scream ignore me."

Chris adjusted his satchel on his shoulders. "Are moms supposed to be sarcastic?"

She set the pile of paper in her hand back down on the table, got up, and stood on tiptoe to kiss his cheek. "Only after their children hit adolescence. Go have fun. Don't stay out too late. You've got a shift tomorrow."

"Yeah, yeah. Like I could forget that." He wiped off her kiss with a grin. "See ya, Mom. Don't get buried in all that paper."

He heard Big Pat's footsteps on the stairs and hurried through the darkened living room, not wanting to deal with his father when he was feeling pretty good. It wasn't like they hated each other, Chris thought as he slid into the wagon and started it, waiting for it to stop rattling and wheezing enough to pull out of the driveway. He knew that he baffled his dad, who'd been off the factory floor for a decade as a foreman, but still had the muscles from a lifetime of hard labor. As he pulled out of the driveway and started to make his way down the twisty roads to Sunset, Chris thought that the real question was how his parents even got together. Well, he knew how—they met on the factory floor where his mom had worked to pay for school (family tradition, apparently)—but what the hell attracted them to each other?

For that matter, he thought as he pulled into Julian's driveway long enough for the two of them to scramble into the back seat, what attracted anyone? He'd grown up with the two of them—playing war and shooting off illegal fireworks that caught Mrs. Nelson's prize lawn on fire, for which they were all possibly still grounded—and discerned nothing, really, until the day he caught them making out in the Thompson's abandoned shed they'd dubbed The Hideout. He'd known Laine was gay almost when Laine himself realized it, since Laine told him, but Julian was always quiet. He'd been in and out of the hospital when he was a kid after he had rheumatic fever, one of the million things he never talked about. Chris had shrugged it off, including the twinge of anger and hurt that they hadn't told him, hadn't trusted him, and the worry he'd barely admit that he'd be the third wheel, but the chemistry of attraction itself remained elusive.

"You know," Laine called from the backseat, "you're getting as bad as Stonehenge over here. Your mute button is stuck on 'on.'"

Chris hit the signal and turned back onto Sunset before answering. "I'm tracing the patterns of my inner consciousness. I was *this* close to enlightenment before you interrupted me. Thanks a lot, jackhole."

Laine laughed. "Fuck you, Siddhartha."

Chris met Julian's eyes in the rearview, saw him turn and look at Laine with widened eyes. "What? I read. I'm not just a pretty face." Julian raised an eyebrow. "Fine. Your brother Linus leant it to me before he left on his so-called 'soul journey.'"

Chris smiled to himself as he watched them. It soon faded and was replaced with the same restlessness he'd been afflicted with lately. It was like standing in front of the fridge, hungry, but nothing inside looked good.

He wished again he wasn't driving, alcohol sounded like the only cure. He pulled into *The* Club's parking lot and maneuvered into an empty space. As the three of them made their way to door, he noticed Laine looked secretive—a rare thing—and Julian vaguely embarrassed. He went to open the door, and Laine blocked his way for the second time that week. "Dude. What the hell?"

"Remember what I said I'd do? I did it."

Chris was in no mood to parse out the meaning of that sentence. "*Okay*, whatever. Can we go in now?"

Laine stared at him, opened and closed his mouth, then shrugged and moved aside, graciously holding open the door.

He saw her almost immediately, sitting at the bar, her scuffed black boots gently kicking the wood beneath, a cigarette in her right hand

and a drink in her left. She set the drink back on the bar and flipped a lacy black sleeve over her wrist to keep it from flopping into her glass. He looked back at Laine, who was grinning, and his meaning finally became clear. "You asked her here?"

Laine nodded. "And she didn't hesitate."

He wanted to be mad, to make his face into granite like he'd seen his dad do a million times, but he could feel it betray him in the twitch at the corners of his mouth. He looked back at Veronica, then to his friends but they were already gone, heading toward the melee near the stage.

As he walked toward her, dodging around lurkers and dancers and loiterers, he considered and dismissed half a dozen lines. Although he could hear Laine jeering at him in his head, he decided on the coward's choice, and slid into the vacant seat next to her. He lit a smoke and hoped she'd notice him. One heartbeat, maybe two, passed. She didn't look over. The music died down and she said: "Are you just going to sit there? I was promised conversation by Laine." She was still staring ahead at the untidy row of bottles behind the bar.

Chris busied himself searching for an ashtray. "I can go get him, if you want."

She laughed and swiveled to face him, an ashtray in her left hand. The drink was long gone. "Looking for this?" She set it between on the bar and rested her own in one of the slats.

He turned to face her. "Thanks. Buy you a drink?"

She grinned. "Sure, if you can get Mike's attention. Tell him it's for me. Vodka tonic."

He rolled his eyes. "Pretentious."

She stuck out her tongue. "Duh."

He laughed and futilely signaled Mike, finally giving up. "Save my seat."

She winked at him. "I'll do my level best, but I can make no promises."

"Cold as ice, you are."

"You know it."

He slid off the seat and headed down the bar. When he looked back, he saw she'd laid both her purse and one foot on the seat. When he returned with the drinks both had been spirited away. He kept his grin inside and handed her the vodka tonic and took a swig of flat cola. She sipped at hers, silent.

"How'd you manage to get out of the house?"

She set the drink back on the bar, smiled. "Dad had some team building prayer circle thing at Faith Fellowship and won't be back 'til tomorrow. You're lucky Laine's invite coincided." Her wink offset the arch tone.

"That I am." He gestured toward the drink she was ignoring. "You'd better drink faster than that."

She picked up her cigarette and took a drag, ignoring his advice. "Oh, why's that? Trying to get me drunk?"

The grin inside was lighting him up, making him feel a little bit drunk himself. "Cause I'm going to ask you to dance, and you can't take that with you."

She looked down at her bar, but not before he noticed the color in her cheeks. She took a long drink, taking it down almost to the ice cubes. "I...can't dance."

"Veronica." She looked up at him, her face still red, all poise gone. "That?" He gestured at the moshing dancers. "It takes no skill but enthusiasm."

He knew he'd timed it perfectly. He'd been coming to *The* Club for so long he knew how the DJs operated. Two fast songs followed by a slow one to recover. The second fast crashed to a halt of guitar feedback.

"But for now," he said, sliding off his stool and extending his hand, "we'll start slow."

She looked dazed from drinking so fast. Or, he thought, maybe not. She took his hand.

He took her in his arms as "Sadly Beautiful" by The Replacements began to play. She stiffened, breath-caught and wide-eyed, then relaxed against him. He could feel the crush of her breasts and her heart beating fast against his chest and realized he'd found what he'd wanted after all.

CHAPTER FIFTEEN

I took advantage of the burnt out streetlight over the alley to sneak back into my window unseen. Even though I knew Theo was done for the day there was always Mrs. Sneed, our across-the-alley neighbor, who got off on being nosy. Minding other people's business was a Faith Fellowship specialty too many did for free.

I banished Sneed as I stripped off my club clothes and slid into my robe, making my way through the dark house to the laundry room. I threw the smoky clothes in the washer and went to take a long shower and savor the hot water and my first dance. As the spray hit my neck and trickled down my shoulders, I thought of the feel of his hand right at the small of my back. I'd felt like I was tethered and floating, a balloon. A balloon with a heart beating all out of proportion to the exertion of the sway. At one point we'd danced past Laine and Julian, Laine winked and grinned.

Something was happening. Happened. I lathered up my hair and thought about the swooping feeling in my stomach whenever I saw him loping down the hall with his rangy scarecrow walk, the way my skin felt like warm wax when his eyes crinkled into a smile or lifted one eyebrow in shock or sarcasm. I backed into the spray and closed my eyes against the shampoo, and I saw it again, that vision of me with my raggedy backpack, walking away from everything here. Saw flashes of a tiny Chris looking lost among tall trees. Saw Mom abandoned in that sterile room.

I shut off the shower and clambered out into the steam, finding my towel by feel. I opened my eyes to my own blurred reflection in the mirror. The condensation drew lines across my image and for a moment I looked much older, a decade or more of bad road. I blinked and it was replaced by a vision of Chris and I sitting at some outdoor café, my head down, staring at my coffee, Chris' face drawn into its own hard lines. I squeezed my eyes shut and when I opened them a third time it was me, drippy hair and clad in a towel.

The giddy feeling was long gone as I made my way back to my room, dried and dressed, and got into bed. I wanted him. I wanted him and it was the granddaddy of all bad ideas to pursue it, to give in. I switched off my lamp and tried to settle but sleep obdurately refused to come. My brain insisted on serving up a variety of images, none of them good. Mom lying in bed like a carved image on a sarcophagus, a dying animal bleeding on a bed of leaves. I grabbed my pillow, beat it into a different shape, and laid on my back to stare up at the star above my bed and tried to figure out where to go from here.

I woke up early, which annoyed me to no end, shoved my clothes in the dryer, and shuffled, eyes at half-mast into the kitchen to make coffee while they dried. It was a lapse. If Dad had come home early, he would have surely questioned why I'd only washed two things and why they'd not been immediately dried. And that was only if he didn't look too closely at the clothes, which I'd bought with my own money from odd jobs I could pick up on the sly and kept hidden in the back of my closet. Although the look on his face if I'd said I'd forgotten because I was a teensy bit drunk after sneaking out and dancing with a boy would have almost been worth the punishment.

I poured a cup and stared blearily at the list of chores Dad had left on the fridge, his neat handwriting looked like a troop formation. Lightweight. I was to mop any mop-able floors and strip, wash, and make the beds. Enough time to make other plans. I got the bucket and mop from the kitchen utility closet, grabbed the cordless from the desk near the floor and called Nancy, guilted her into meeting me for coffee at 11 a.m. Sans Jeremy. At least I could get some answers to the million and one questions banging around my head.

By 10 a.m. I was done, dressed, and out the door. The sky was heavy with clouds, and I could feel my hair curl in the misty fog. I smiled, my kind of weather. Dad would be back by four in the afternoon (not 3:55 and not 4:05), but still, the rest of the day was mine. No car, even if Dad would teach me to drive, which he never did—I think he was afraid I'd drive off and never return and for once he was right to worry—but the town wasn't big enough to make walking a major inconvenience. I locked the door, turned on my tape player, and ambled toward downtown.

I sat for a bit on my favorite bench in the square to people watch, the oak tree cutting a little of the chilly late winter wind but downtown was mostly deserted except for mothers, faces flat with boredom, sitting in the Laundromat ignoring the squirrely little kids running riot over the wheeled baskets and jamming the coin ops, and a few skaters who kept wiping out trying to flip their boards. That was mildly diverting, particularly when they sprawled in a tangle of arms and legs, their little knit caps askew and elbows and knees netted with old scars and new blood.

I was restless after about twenty minutes and still had some time before I met Nancy, so I went into Lou's Used Records to see if he had any new tapes. He had an unwritten rule that he wouldn't sell you music if he didn't think you were cool enough to own it. Kind of a dictator for an aging hippie. I grinned to myself as I thought that maybe those weren't antithetical concepts and hoped, as always, that I'd make the grade.

Lou's was tiny and always infused with a combined bouquet of Lou's pot and B.O. funk and that musty mildew smell indigenous to Midwestern establishments in questionable repair. Any longer than ten minutes in Lou's induced the first nigglings of a headache behind my eyes. Not helpful, since Lou's unique approach to organization remained a mystery even to long-time customers. Ten minutes was never long enough to unearth what you wanted.

A wave to Lou and then I headed toward the stall by the window, where I'd had some luck the last time but after five minutes of digging, I realized what had been imports last week was now entirely disco. I let the tapes slide back into place and stretched, rubbed the back of my head where the headache had decided to get an early start, and turned to the window to see Nancy, and to my great annoyance, Jeremy, walk past. Never mind the seizure-inducing boredom Jeremy inevitably caused, I was going to have to high-wire it to get any useful info.

"Later, Lou."

He grunted from behind a dog-eared *Rolling Stone*, one of his friendlier good-byes.

I spied the two of them entering the Blue Moon and followed suit. Nancy and I had an odd friendship, full of weird undertones and conversational potholes I always drove right into. We'd become friends in sixth grade, my first year in town and my only year at Faith Fellowship Elementary. I was asked not to return at the end of the year, mostly because of a science class essay I'd written about evolution. At home and at school I'd been in disgrace, Mrs. Briel gave me a D and sent me to Principal Gray, who tried to impress upon me the importance of intelligent design as a viable alternative. When I refused to revise my paper, Dad was called in and shit really hit the fan. I wouldn't budge and neither would they.

"Veronica," Mr. Gray's cracked with weariness, "all we're asking is for a little extra effort here. Submit another paper."

I always felt a little guilty about that incident. I knew I was being deliberately provocative, I wanted to be kicked out. The morning prayers and the dress code were bad enough. Mom had been a teacher, I had a vague idea what constituted a sucky school and Faith Fellowship Elementary sucked. I was bored— "unchallenged" to use Mom's euphemism—and I didn't do well with bored. Looking back, I could finally admit they weren't mean about it, four years and countless Sundays at Faith Fellowship still couldn't convince me they weren't misguided. While it stung that Nancy refused to even offer sympathy—or talk about it, even now—the fact was that she remained my friend, even after I cast myself as the head heathen. That was something. She'd stayed there, transitioning to Faith Fellowship High School, I didn't doubt she'd do her undergraduate at the Faith Fellowship College. If Dad had his way, I'd be matriculating there, too.

Lost in the past, I almost didn't hear Nancy say my name before being enveloped in one of her stiff hugs.

"Hey! I'm glad you called." she said after finally releasing me. "I haven't seen you in forever."

I readjusted my bookbag on my shoulders. "Me, too. We can catch up."

She stifled a yawn and that's when I noticed the dark smudges under her eyes, rumpled khaki pants, and a shirt that looked slept in. She noticed me noticing and smiled. "Oh, we were doing the Life Chain last night outside of the Dalesville Central Clinic."

Lucas, the floppy-haired blond barista that was my favorite—funny and a little flirty—cleared his throat, saving me from saying anything about that. "Dude, are you going to order or do I have to cite you for inciting a caffeine-deprivation riot?"

Nancy faded back, gesturing to the table Jeremy had commandeered by the window. I nodded at her and turned back to Lucas, more grateful than he'd known for interrupting. "Not your best line ever. Large coffee."

He grabbed a cup and turned to fill it. "Oh, sure. Not only do you expect prompt service but four-star comic stylings?"

"Absolutely."

"Well, you're *sol* today."

"Obviously."

"$2.35."

"Price gouger."

"Yup."

I gave him three bucks and dumped the change in the tip jar. He scowled but his eyes still smiled. "That's it?"

I picked up my coffee. "Better quips, better tips."

"You suck."

I winked at him and turned to make my way to Nancy's table. I wended my way through the Saturday crowd, mulling over how to pick her brain about Theo without alerting Jeremy.

The two were in serious discussion mode when I arrived. "...turn from error," was the only phrase I caught before I took a cue from Lucas and cleared my throat to alert them to my presence. They both started, Nancy's face flamed. I kept my grin internal. There were *I-Can-Read* books more difficult to understand than her, and it was obvious they'd been talking about me.

I sat down into their awkward silence, sipped my coffee, and waited to see if Nancy would come clean about what they'd been talking about. I peeked out over the rim of my cup as I drank and saw some silent communication from Jeremy that terminated in a "come on" gesture.

"So, before we were interrupted," she threw a hard look at Lucas, who was too far away to notice and probably wouldn't have cared if he had, "I was going to ask why you missed last night. Don't you support the cause anymore?"

For a second, I considered honesty—that it was hurtful and use-less—for the relief of telling the unvarnished truth and maybe for the amusement of their collective shock and subsequent attempts to convert me. Reason intervened almost immediately, an intervention was not what I needed. "Oh, you know, schoolwork. They're really piling it on. I suppose it's to make sure we won't pine for high school once we've graduated."

Nancy's expression of relief meant she'd been neutralized but Jeremy narrowed his eyes in suspicion. My temper frayed as he said in his most holier-than thou tone, "Nothing should take precedence over the Lord's service, Veronica."

I wanted to smack the pious smile off his face. "And yet only God can determine what form that service will take. Who among us has the ability or right to determine that for another?"

Jeremy's face flamed and his eyes darkened. I could see the wheels spinning, turning my argument over in his mind. I'd bet my non-existent college fund that he thought he had both the ability and the right but wouldn't say it to me. His mouth opened, perhaps to ask me precisely what service I rendered, then, with a sideways look at Nancy, shut it again with a sharp click of his teeth.

Using what I hoped was a light, airy tone, I turned back to my friend. "Hey, remember our old youth group?" She smiled and nodded. "Guess who I ran into at the mall?"

"Mr. Miner?" she ventured.

It took me a second to remember that had been Mr. Jim's last name, with his battered guitar and love of *Godspell* and soft Christian rock. He'd been considered a hippie because his hair brushed his collar and hadn't been a Faith Fellowship regular, it seemed, for years. "No, Theo Willis. Remember him?"

She frowned, shaking her head. "What do you mean, remember? He never really left. Well, except for…"

"His dad works for your father, you know," Jeremy interrupted, shooting a scowl at Nancy, who visibly wilted in her chair. The urge to hit him resurfaced.

I drained coffee gone tepid. "I do know that, Jeremy. Thanks. Just thought it was funny I hadn't seen him around for a long time."

I turned back to Nancy, smiled and she seemed to perk up a bit. "I think they moved away for a bit, missionary work or something."

I pretended to drink from my almost-empty cup and saw Nancy look over at her boyfriend, as if for approval. He gave the briefest nod, the relief on her face broke my heart. I put the cup down, reached across the table, and squeezed her free hand. Light burst in a flare behind my eyes, with a crackle of electric energy that shuddered through me. My spine hit the back of my chair hard enough to rattle my teeth, and I wondered if I was having some kind of seizure.

When I opened them again a few minutes later, all I could see was blackness and all I could feel was my own shaking. Then, I saw not the coffee shop, but the green door and pale siding of a City of Light Acres house. In through the living room and the kitchen to the backyard I could see Nancy, a few years older, a line or two around her mouth, as she stared out at two peach trees growing riot by the fence. I walked across a seared lawn and saw little markers, five, between the trees. Each read "My Angel" each read. I looked back at her, eyes dry, her mouth a fine line, and knew.

Snail slow, the world returned, first in grey blues then smudges of color, finally the sharp outlines of tables, the mist of condensation on the window. The shaking subsided into a slight tremor in my hands, which caffeine intake could explain. "Oh, God, I'm sorry. So many stones, one for each one you lost and he looks at you like you've betrayed him." I felt my mouth moving but I couldn't hear my own voice.

When I could finally face Nancy, she was shaking, her eyes glazed, the black of the pupils threatening to overtake the brown. I looked over at Jeremy, who was still sitting back in his chair, arms crossed, and face furrowed as he looked out at the smeared view of the street.

I cleared my throat again. She didn't move. "Nancy?"

She jumped as if I'd hit her. Her eyes cleared and her face went pale except for two hectic spots of color dancing in her cheeks. She broke eye contact immediately and started gathering her coat and purse. "I…I have to go. Things. To Do. You know. Jeremy!" Her voice went up an octave on his name, sharp as the high keys on the piano. He jumped up and grabbed his coat.

"Oh, okay." My voice shook. If I'd scared Nancy, it was nothing to the way I'd terrified myself.

With a brief wave, Nancy practically ran out of the shop, Jeremy hurrying behind. I sat still, staring into the depths of my coffee and wondered what the hell happened.

Chapter Sixteen

The two of them slalomed between the incoming shift heading to the floor, as Chris rolled his own aching shoulders. The just-ended shift had seemed particularly endless and even Jim seemed worn out as he swallowed a yawn. "Hey, thanks again for the help."

Jim looked non-plussed for a second before busting out a grin that blew away some of the tiredness from his face. "No problem." He stopped at the doors, smacked himself on the forehead. "I've been meaning to tell you something else, too, I recognized the name myself. It didn't hit me right away, being ancient and all."

Chris snorted as he held open the outer door. "Whatever you say, Grandpa."

Jim's grin turned into a chuckle. "Anyway, I'm pretty sure there was a Raynor, back in the dark ages," he tipped Chris a wink, "the first couple years of school. Sweet girl but I think her family moved away. Does that help?"

He followed Jim out the door. "It does, yeah. I owe you a beer. Or coffee, if you don't wanna have to wait a few years 'til I'm twenty-one."

"I'll settle for a cigarette, I smoked my last during the break."

Chris dug the pack out of his pocket, passed it to Jim before taking one for himself. It was raining, that sullen drizzle particular to late winter in the Midwest. Still, it felt good against his face after the grind and heat of the shipping department. Jim gave him a pat on the shoulder and took off. Chris stood for a minute outside his own car, hand on the handle, and lifted his face up to the dark, heavy sky and let the water cool him off. It ran down his temples, converged on the itchy sweat on his neck. Better than coffee.

He opened the door and flopped down into the seat, sitting for a minute more to relish being off his feet for the first time in hours, stretched them and winced at the burn in his soles. Then he turned on the car, let it warm up, cracked the window, and blew out a series of smoke rings. Only when he'd flipped on the radio and set it to the local college station did he pull out.

It was a ritual. He liked rituals, he supposed it was the Catholic upbringing. Not routine, the pointless repetition of every day same as the last but certain prescriptions that he guessed probably verged on superstitious behavior.

He took a drag off the cigarette while he waited for the traffic on Sunset to thin so he could pull out of the parking lot and thought about when he'd snuck downstairs when his parents had rented *The Exorcist*—waited until he could hear Big Pat's thunderous snoring and then crept into the den and sat close to the TV so he could keep the volume low. It scared the shit out of him, gave him screaming nightmares for a month and made him institute one of his first rituals to ward off any potential demonic invasion. What scared him the most, aside from the green vomit and the cold and the stabbings was that his five-year-old self could pinpoint no objective moments when the little girl invited it to happen. Which meant it could happen to him. So, he lay in bed night after night, the dark no longer peaceful but alive with potential devils waiting to take him over, and said four prayers, in descending order according to length—the Act of Contrition, the Our Father, the Hail Mary, and the Glory Be—then he slept, secure.

A space opened when a truck paused to let him in, and Chris pulled into the street with a wave to the driver. The Cure played softly from the radio as the clouds made everything dusk, he wondered when that terror stopped. Robert Smith sang about how the spider man came to his window but Chris no longer worried about what was abroad in the dark. He couldn't decide whether that was a gain or a loss. After eight hours of packing sporting equipment and pushing boxes through an automated tape machine, his mood lowering like the clouds above, the liveliness of mortal terror would be a welcome break.

Chris stubbed out of his cigarette with a little thrill of fear, quickly suppressed. Maybe not all the superstition was gone, he wondered whether he should tempt fate in such a cavalier fashion. He smiled to himself, he knew it was perverse to be relieved, but he couldn't help it—he was no lost boy, but he didn't want to be so inured to adulthood that everything was sucked dry of emotion. Although a permanent stint at McClellan's might take care of that.

He was at Lime and Sunset, ready to go home, when he decided that wasn't where he wanted to be yet. He kept going toward downtown. Some coffee, a sit under the big spreading catalpa in the square might wash the McClellan part of the day off a little better and make him more fit for family interaction. He parked on the street and dashed into the Blue Moon.

He was about to place his order when he felt an odd tingle that raised the hairs on his neck. It was somewhere between the sensation when someone was staring at him and that electric moment right before a thunderstorm. He turned around but the guy behind him was turned to the side, checking out the ass of a passing patron. He looked toward the door and saw a girl hurrying out with a buttoned-up guy following behind. A brief glimpse of her face reflected in the door gave Chris the fleeting impression of fear. He turned back to Lucas. "Large black, please."

"No prob."

Chris dug out a few bucks out and had it ready to hand him when Lucas slipped it into his hands. He was out the door again moments later. The girl who'd run out was still scurrying through the mist, with a death grip on the guy's hand, practically dragging him across the slick pavement.

"What wrong with you? You're the one who wanted me to come with you!"

"I know...I know, I don't... Let's go, *okay*?"

They were in their car as Chris passed by, and he couldn't help but look inside. The girl had her head down and hands crossed, a worn leather-bound book gripped in her hands. Her lips were moving and Chris realized she was praying.

He kept walking, mostly to suppress a cold shudder of fear. The bible beaters did occasionally freak him out but this time he had an irrational conviction something strange had happened right behind him in the coffee shop and he'd missed it.

The tree in the square seemed to float in the mist and he walked toward it slowly, suddenly uncertain. He thought about going back to the Blue Moon and...doing what, exactly? He sat down on the damp bench, sipped his coffee, and after a moment's thought, dug out his pack and lighter and lit a cigarette. The prosaic act reasserted rationality. She probably saw two guys holding hands and had to go pray about it. If he craned his neck, he could see the giant stone cross of the Faith Fellowship headquarters from where he was sitting. The highways in and out of town sprouted billboards instead of trees, announcing that homosexuality was a sin, or festooned with lurid pictures of aborted fetuses. The town was full of those types. Instead, he stared half-lidded at the soaped windows of the store in front of him, trying to cleanse his brain of those images. The paint had mostly chipped off the sign on the brick front, but Chris knew it read Happy Family Chinese. They'd had kickass eggrolls, he remembered. Stupid mall.

At moments like that, staring at one of any number of abandoned building in his immediate vicinity, there was a twinge—not even strong enough to properly be called a feeling—that there was something wrong with the town. Not the abandoned downtown or the mall on the edge of the city selling cheap crap—that could be any town in the middle of the country, where chain stores started on the border and drew tighter and tighter, strangling out all the local color. It eluded him, the precise weirdness of the place.

He shivered again and wrapped his hands tighter around the cup, tried to focus on happier things—the night before at *The* Club with Veronica—but the uneasiness deepened even as she came into his mind. Deepened and sharpened into almost fear. Fear of her? Fear for her? So many questions he had to ask her, if he had the guts. Why had she been followed? What had she seen in the grove that made her take off?

He took another drink of coffee, watched the mist condense on the restaurant's windows and creep downward. That moment in the coffee shop had reminded him of something and as he lit a second cig off his first, stubbed the butt, and tossed it in the trashcan to his right, he finally nailed what it was. It was that same sensation he'd felt when Veronica and he were at the park, like she was generating electricity that could spark and burn anyone in her path. He blew smoke rings into the drizzle. Who the hell gave off that kind of energy, that made him feel like a bug too close to a zapper?

That was another question that needed answering. And the one he'd never ask.

The clouds lowered and he heard the sonorous tones of the clock tower at the college, muffled by mist and distance, peel out twelve times. Time to go home, take a shower, eat a snack, and listen to his parents argue politics over roast beef. No weird girls with weird vibes, no endless, unanswered questions. The reassurance of the everyday.

He swallowed the last of his rapidly cooling coffee and dumped the cup, walking fast toward his car. He told himself it was to get home but the flesh of his neck crawled with a newly reawakened fear of the dark.

"If I hear one laugh out of any of you, you're in detention for a week." Mrs. Jones looked more stern than usual, which Chris thought was a feat in and of itself. She was a tiny woman who managed, with her granny glasses and upswept hair that looked straight out of a 50s sitcom, to look as tall as Julian at moments like that. She was showing them a film lecture by some British scholar supposedly famous for his analysis of Oedipus the King, but apparently his pronunciation was a bit different. Jones' warning had the tone of one that had been issued for decades, weary and no bullshit all at once.

"Paula, please get the lights." Paula did and Jones started the film.

"Eat-a-pus the King—a lecture by..." Chris looked down at his notebook, let a grin escape in the safety of the dark. He turned his attention back to the screen, to a guy who looked like he'd not laughed for decades, and Chris' attention flagged. The room was a little too warm, the only light was the small lamp from the projector and the black and white film in front of him, and he could feel his blinks getting longer and longer. He shifted in his seat, pinched the skin between thumb and index finger on his left hand, and tried to focus. But the monotone voice of the lecture, the darkened room were against him. When the lights went on half an hour later, he jumped, his eyes flying open and temporarily blinded from the sudden light, and he knew he'd lost the battle.

"We'll be discussing his analysis tomorrow, so review your notes and be ready," Mrs. Jones said as the bell rang. Maybe he could borrow Julian's notes, if he could decipher Julian's handwriting.

Chris' sigh turned into a yawn as he tossed his notebook—empty—into his satchel and shuffled out into the hallway. The mellow afternoon sunlight through the bank of windows was warm but not stultifying, like it was in late August and September, the school a greenhouse that wilted students and teachers alike.

That and the sight of Veronica in the distance, woke him up a bit.

The other night at *The* Club, he told her that even if he hadn't noticed her before, now he could always pick her out of a crowd, at *The* Club, Sam's, or at school. He watched her at the other end of the hall, black shirt and dark brown hair, picking her way through the crowd, slaloming around knots of people talking with her head down. He thought about calling out to her. Didn't. Instead, he watched, wondering for the first time why he hadn't noticed her in the years before. They didn't share any classes, but they were both in the college track, and she had two classes with one of his best friends. She was taller than average and with the mellow amber of the afternoon sun turning marble to bronze, kinda beautiful. He grinned to himself, he liked tall girls with strong features, and she was his type. So, why?

She was close enough now for him to see the cramp of annoyance on her face as she ghosted around a particularly large cluster that took up about seventy-five percent of the available walking space. She was slick, she managed to get past the group without touching anyone. Funny how she could slip past anyone without contact, no small thing when it was as packed as it was. She spun around another group and that's when she met his eyes and smiled, strolled over to where he leaned and leaned next to him. "You're gonna be late to class."

"I'm going to the library. Price wrote me a pass. What about you?"

"English with Mrs. Jones."

Chris laughed. "You're watching a film that you're forbidden to laugh about. Consider yourself warned."

A smile. "Well, crap, that means I won't be able to stop. So, what's so funny about it?"

Chris grinned. "And ruin the surprise? No way."

"Mean."

"Yup." He straightened up and turned to face her. "I gotta ask, how do you do it?"

Her scowl was a little wrinkle between her eyes, like the one in Laine's drawing he'd hung in his closet. "Do what?"

"You made it all the way down the hall without bumping or touching anyone else. How do you do that?"

He watched her face smooth out, and she stared down at the grey-tiled floor but not before he saw a distant, sad look in her eyes. "I don't know. I just do."

In for a penny. "Veronica."

She looked up at him, her eyes narrowed. "Fine. When we first got here, Dad used to make me pass out tracts at the mall, he'd go with me to make sure I did it, particularly the food court. When I went to Dalesville Junior High in seventh grade, they remembered me."

"Who?"

Her expression was all rolled eyes and pursed lips, like he'd said something stupid. "The kids who hang out at the mall—Billy Z, Tiffany the Amazing Wonder Gymnast—you know. That first year sucked."

She drew the last word out to three syllables, it made him smile, and he squeezed her shoulder. "So, what did you do?"

"Took my mom's old advice and ignored them. Didn't help much, it was a year of stupid shit, crossing themselves when I walked by yelling 'Uh-oh, I'm going to hell, Jesus' best friend heard me swear.'" Her lips curled, half smile, half sneer. "I'm disappointed they didn't make more of an effort. Kids today."

He took her hand and felt a level of that energy from that day in the park. A low thrumming though, not a live wire. "Then what?"

"Summer came. I spent most of it in my room. Got a haircut. Got some cheap clothes Dad didn't pick out. When school started again, they'd moved on to someone else. I kept my head down since then."

The second bell rang, he had time, but she didn't. Never mind that disproportionate tension in her arm that made him pretty sure she wasn't telling him everything. No time. "It's kind of cool, you're like a ghost."

He was surprised to see her frown. She shook her head. "It's weak."

"What do you mean?"

She adjusted her bag. "I don't know. It's complicated. I gotta get to class. I'll see you, *okay*?"

She turned away, head down, and walked fast down the hall to class, leaving Chris to wonder what he was missing.

The Dalesville Ledger only went back ten years in the school library. Chris sighed, wondered, between McClellan's and school, how he'd get any time to get to the main library. The town council had cut the two libraries' hours, claiming budget issues. Julian, who followed local, state, and national politics with more enthusiasm than Chris had ever felt for anything, was cynical about it. "Of course, they cut them, the treasurer owns the book franchise at the mall. Can't have all those ideas be free, can we?"

Either way, the libraries were closed by three during the week, 12:30 p.m. on Saturdays.

"You want them anyway?" Mr. Backer, the pint-sized librarian, always sounded annoyed.

"Yeah, thanks."

Backer sighed and disappeared into the stacks behind the desk. He returned about five minutes later, slogging the weight of five hard-bound, oversized books. He slammed them on the desk in front of Chris and squinted at him. "No highlighting, no pen, photocopy machine is by the door. You're welcome."

Chris gathered up the volumes and took them over to the table closest to the copier and got to work.

Half an hour later he straightened up, back cracking a bit, bored out of his skull. So far, the only insight he had was that he might live in the most boring town in the country. At least the paper wasn't big, he'd managed to flip through most of the past decade. Council meetings, local fundraisers, and a hot scoop on the mayor's wife's "Super-Duper Yum Cookies." Woodward and Bernstein were in agony over missing that one.

Chris bent down again over his notebook at the few things he'd jotted down, hidden among the ephemera. A little squib about Light of the World Inc becoming majority owner of the local station, KLON, another about selling the *Ledger* back to the town. That was odd, wouldn't he want both? Maybe he would ask Price, she might know. Another was a puff piece about Paul Barnes, Robert James' "right hand man", Chris photocopied that one, including a picture of the two of them—Bob and Paul—with arms linked, part of a chain of po-faced people blocking the entrance to the Dalesville Central Clinic.

He closed the final book, picked up the article, staring at the grainy faces of those two men. Even the poor reproduction couldn't hide the smug self-satisfaction of their smiles. These dicks weren't avoiding trouble, he supposed. They had conviction and weren't afraid to act on it. And what did they do with it? Bullied women. Bullied everybody.

He scribbled a note on the photocopy, he was certain now that his entry for the *Ledger* contest was going to focus on Robert James' little mini empire, but it was still amorphous. His arms still ached from work. He set down the pen and rubbed his right wrist, let his mind drift as he stared at the two men. In the end, it was always about money. Money and power. What if...

He picked up the pen again, turned to a fresh page in his notebook and scribbled a question. One, his gut told him, had less to do with his article and more to do with what Veronica had told him. "What would they do to someone who stood in their way?"

The first bell rang, and Chris gathered up his books, threw his notebook in his bag, and returned the volumes to the desk. Backer was nowhere to be found, thankfully.

She was already on his mind, so he let his thoughts land on that moment in the hall with Veronica. She's a close one, one of Grandpa Martin's pet sayings, one of the only things Chris remembered about him. That was how he'd always described politicians he thought smiled too much and said too little. Veronica was no politician, but

Chris wondered how deep he'd have to dig to figure her out. He felt lighter than he had in a long time, a little mental spelunking of an enigmatic girl sounded like the thing to break the boredom. He grinned to himself as he joined the between-class melee.

CHAPTER SEVENTEEN

I made my way slowly down the aisle of church, Dad's bald spot at the crown of his head was two people ahead of me. I had no energy to walk faster. I'd caught Nancy's eye as I stood up, sketched a little wave and was about to cross the aisle to talk to her when she skittered off after her parents. Same as last Sunday. In the brief moments we'd seen each other, she'd looked almost terrified.

I sighed. Another unquantifiable moment in a life where confusion seemed to be the baseline condition, although it had given me an idea. Dad was at the door, and I saw him turn, then frown when he realized I was not there. I waved from my position behind Mrs. Phelps, over her green-clad shoulder, and the lines of his forehead smoothed. He moved aside, holding open the door for exiting churchgoers until Reverend Ash gestured him over.

My steps got even slower, I heard the disgruntled sighs behind me as I slowed to a crawl, followed almost immediately by a long string of people button-hooking around me with sour looks. I could not have cared less if I'd tried, their annoyance was nothing compared to my desire to avoid conversations with Ash. His cadaverous voice could make Happy Birthday a dirge, and worse, he was always going on about the signs of the impending Apocalypse. That is, when he wasn't having a go at gays, liberals, and feminists. I felt too shaky and tired for that scene.

I let my heavy head drop and managed to bounce off Mrs. Phelps' shoulder pad and stagger backwards, nearly causing a domino effect in the people still egressing down the aisle. I grabbed her green-clad arm. "Excuse me." I felt her arm yank away, opened my eyes to see her mouth pooched in an annoyed smirk.

"I'm sorry, I should look where I'm going." My voice started out shaky, but returned to normal as I continued. "I'm such a klutz."

Her face relaxed and she patted my shoulder. "It's all right, dear."

We started walking again, my brain trying to find a tricky way to ask her where she worked. "Mrs. Phelps?"

She turned back from giving a wave to her husband, who was currently talking to a knot of other guys in khakis and didn't seem to notice. "Yes?"

"I was wondering. I'm close to graduating high school and thinking about college but I've no idea what to major in. I've been picking people's brains about what they do to see if something jumps out at me." The truth in that last part made it easier to lie.

She gave me a funny look I couldn't interpret until she replied, "Well, I'm a nurse at Dalesville Community Hospital but I don't think Faith Fellowship College has a nursing program."

The words almost escaped before I could stop them— "why the hell would you think I'm going there?"—before the caution that used to be second nature finally intervened. I was slipping, I never used to need a reminder about where I was and who I was talking to. "I guess I better re-check the catalogue then. Thanks, Mrs. Phelps."

A fleeting smile and she departed to join her husband.

At long last I was at the back entryway. Dad was still deep in conversation, so I sunk into one of the chairs reserved for the greeters, even more exhausted than before. I should have asked what part of the hospital, but this type of stuff was new to me. I rubbed my temples, watched the last few stragglers, perhaps hoping for a moment of the Reverend's time, file out with looks ranging from disappointment to barely concealed hostility at the man taking up so much precious time. One of them straightened his golf shirt, hitched up his chinos with a decided air, and marched over to where Dad and Ash stood talking. Under the guise of prayerful reflection, I observed their interaction. It was too far away to hear more than baritone rumblings, but it was interesting to see the furrowed brow of frustration pass from the congregant to the Reverend—quickly suppressed. The guy's shoulders dropped and then he said only a few words. Ash squeezed the man's shoulder, made a writing motion with his left hand, and the man seemed satisfied enough to leave them alone.

I sighed from the depths. My life seemed to be nothing but waiting for instructions, for other people, for anything to happen that would break the monotony. I felt perpetually at the threshold, always frustrated in my quest to move forward. Chris, bless him, exacerbated rather than relieved that discontent. Those few weeks—not only with him but his friends as well—were a window to something new. And that night at *The* Club…I could feel my ears redden and brushed my hair over them. The knowledge they were having me followed, even if Theo didn't tattle, put it all at risk. Put them at risk. Was there nothing they couldn't take from me?

I felt the sharp pain of my own nails digging into the backs of my hands and realized how hard I was gripping them together. Too many questions. What happened with Nancy? What would happen with Chris? What was wrong with me? What happened to Mom?

"Veronica! We're going!"

I relaxed my hands, the tension transferred itself into an iron band around my forehead and temples. I followed Dad out of the church.

Dad was silent in the car, silent as we went into the house. I tried to gauge what his silence was about but the headache that started as I left church jammed all signals. It didn't seem like an angry silence, nor particularly peaceful. He looked straight ahead at the long stretch of asphalt scrolling out in front of the car, hands at two and ten, his jaw as straight as the line as the road. Usually, the ride home rendered me a captive audience for a steady stream of critiques of my behavior, as if all his prayer time at church was spent cataloguing them. I focused instead on how I might share this new information with Chris, to give him an area to look in, but I couldn't figure out how to do it without revealing my weirdness.

Once inside the house, he went straight into his office with no "be sure to hang up your dress" or "defrost some chicken," or any other such instructions. What had Ash said to him?

My head gave a throb, as if to indicate that it would not take one more question without exploding. I shuffled down the hall in search of an aspirin and a change of clothes instead.

Dad hadn't emerged by the time I made my way into the kitchen, so I pulled out two pork chops from the freezer, grabbed a ginger ale from the fridge, and took myself and a book onto the back porch. The cold air was fresh and dispelled the last vestiges of my headache. I curled myself into one of the lawn chair recliners and proceeded to lose myself in *Pride and Prejudice*.

Some unknown time later, I heard Dad calling for me. I slammed the book shut and scrambled up, girded for a delayed (but never avoided) critique. Glass in hand, I was heading for the door when I saw Dad was coming out. He gave me a start. "Oh, there you are."

I tensed, waited to hear what I'd left undone.

"I was just wondering." His tone was strange but in a familiar way. "Thanks for taking out the pork chops without being asked."

The glass nearly dropped from my hands, but I managed to catch the lip between my fingers before it hit the ground, an act that would've shattered the moment along with the glass. I set it on the table next to the door in case any more shocks were on the way and answered, "You're welcome."

He smiled and I was glad I'd put the glass down. Gratitude and a smile? Forget all the other questions swirling around me. Clearly the important one was figuring out exactly what went down with Reverend Ash. "Anyway."

I waited for the rest of the sentence, but it didn't come, and I realized my father, possibly for the first time we'd moved here, was at a loss for what to say. He stood there, shoulders slightly slumped and I, too, had no idea how to proceed.

Finally, he said, "Schoolwork?" indicating my book.

I shook my head, and answered without thinking. "No, for fun."

I winced immediately after I said the words. Reading was fine to increase knowledge or faith (ideally both), but for amusement? A slippery slope of idleness that would allow one's soul to become the devil's playground.

"Oh, well, I'll let you get back to it then."

He had already slid open the back door and had one foot in the house by the time I recovered enough to speak. "Dad?"

He turned his head.

"Is there anything I can do?"

For a second, I could see the smallest crack open behind his eyes. The bars were gone and inside was a storm of grief and confusion and fear. The confusion and fear were fleeting but the grief remained. I thought maybe it had something to do with Mom. I wanted to tell him what I saw, what Theo had told me. I wanted not to be going through this alone. He opened and closed his mouth, as if he didn't know whether to speak, and I didn't move, didn't say a word, knowing for once that this was a chance we wouldn't get again. "Veronica, I..."

Deep in the house, the phone rang, sharp enough to break the moment. Dad's hand dropped from the door handle, and he completed his turn inside. I heard the hurried whisper of his loafers across the linoleum as he scrambled to get the phone before the machine picked up.

Then I moved. Stifling the urge to throw the glass in frustration, I moved closer to the door to see if I could hear anything. While the logical part of my mind agreed it was probably a sales call, there was a little twist in my stomach, an echo of that nightmare-inducing fear from my twelfth year. That part of me had a pretty good idea who was on the other end of the line.

There was little to interpret, Dad's part of the conversation was a collection of fragments—yeses, noes, buts. Finally, "I understand. Half an hour."

I scrambled back to my chair and opened the book. I couldn't read a word, I was too focused on pretending I was reading to comprehend anything. When Dad slid open the door, I looked up, saw how pale he was under his natural ruddiness, saw in the shadows under and in his eyes that my suspicions were correct. "Everything okay?" I tried to keep my tone neutral.

"I have to go out. I'll be back for dinner." His voice, too, was careful and distant.

"All right." For the first time in years, I wanted to hug him but not like when I was little for my own comfort, for once it was for his. I didn't, couldn't cross that divide yet, not with the distance back again in his expression, the stiff way he stood in the doorway. I settled for a "Be safe."

He gave me an odd look that reflected my own confusion as to why I chose those words. Still, I didn't take them back. With one parting confused look he strode through the house. I heard the garage door open and close, and he was gone. I dropped the book in my lap and my head into my hands, my throat tight, knowing that we'd lost the only chance, for once knowing what I had to do next.

Chapter Eighteen

Chris looked up from the bound book of old *Dalesville Ledgers* and pinched the bridge of his nose. Something—inhaled silverfish, dust—was giving him a wicked headache. That wasn't the only thing that hurt. He'd dropped off the car at home after his shift and walked to the main library, his feet still tingling, his arms and shoulders still holding the ache of endless stuffing and sliding. He leaned across the deserted library table and pulled his satchel toward himself, ferreting around its interior until he felt the smooth bend of the aspirin bottle he'd thrown in on a whim before he'd left the house that morning. He'd been getting headaches more and more often, at school or while studying and thought, with a small sigh, that he probably needed glasses. He stood and stretched, slipped the bottle into his jeans' pocket, told the library assistant, who was oozing boredom as she played solitaire on an ancient PC that he'd be right back—she barely nodded in response—and slipped into the hallway in search of the water fountain. He found a children-sized one squatting between the doors of the bathrooms and had to bend double to reach it, his head pounded with reaction. Still, once the water hit his lips, he could feel the pain ease.

As he straightened and started back down the hall and into the reading room, he wondered if part of the headache was caused by the uglier parts of his hometown. He might hate it, but shame was a whole other thing. A lynching of four black men in the town square where he'd first seen Veronica, smoking and staring up at the sky. An end days cult on the outskirts of town where the mall and big box stores now brooded and stretched over the landscape committed mass suicide, Jonestown style, in the 1950s. Not to mention fiddling preachers, money scams, and every other kind of peccadillo the human animal engaged in.

Chris sighed as he sat back down at the table and realized he really didn't want to know anymore. He was only up to the early 1970s and already felt sick. He knew there were dark parts of every town's history and maybe he was naïve, but he supposed he didn't expect to find quite that much. Was every small town like that, or was there something about this place that made it particularly ugly?

It wasn't like he hadn't noticed—he wasn't old enough to vote, or a history buff like Julian—but he'd grown up in the 80s and knew things had taken a sharp right turn politically, despite who was in the White House. America wasn't the friendliest place to be different, despite what the Constitution and stump speeches said, but it seemed like Dalesville had never been anything but a tight sphincter of conform or else. Can something be rotten if it had never been fresh?

No more, he decided. He scratched the date where he'd left off in his notebook and slammed the bounded one shut. A flurry of dust rose like disturbed bees, and he sneezed three times in quick succession, his headache flared for a minute more and then subsided again.

He was stacking the bound copies when he came across 1989-1990, and on a whim, sat back down at the table and flipped through the pages, looking for the police blotter. He felt stupid for not thinking of it before, the *Ledger*, back when the James family still owned it, had a police blotter column. All the better to shame one's neighbors.

He skimmed past August, September, and October—the usual stolen bikes or kids caught tagging downtown—to November. Pay-dirt. An escaped patient from Dalesville Community Hospital's psych ward was apprehended on Sunset. The fascinating part, Chris thought as he stared at the small print long enough to make his eyes throb again, was that someone had deliberately marked through the name with a Sharpie. He flipped back through the binder and found no other entry similarly defaced. The timing aligned with what Jim Jr found out. He dug a dime out from the bottom of his satchel and went to photocopy the page.

That done, he stuffed his notebook and the photocopy in his bag, zipped up his coat, and turned in the bound volumes to the bored library assistant, who actually looked up and nodded before going back to computer solitaire. A veritable triumph of social interaction, Chris thought and smiled to himself as he exited the library and lit a cigarette before starting the few blocks to home.

Despite the bite of the wind, lifting his hair and weaseling its way down his back, he was glad he'd walked instead, it gave him time to think about what he'd read. He wondered if it wasn't much too big for the feature contest, or if they'd even publish it if he won. As for the other, he thought he might know where to look for an unexpurgated version of that blotter.

He took a drag off his cigarette as he came to Sunset Street and waited for the light to change. He should talk to Julian about some of this, he was annoyed with himself that he hadn't thought of it before.

Julian, who studied history for fun, doodled timelines during their occasional political debates and earned the praise of Ms. Price, doing double duty as the journalism and honors history teacher, with even the implied depth of his answers in class.

The light changed and Chris crossed, his headache easing in the cool March freshness of the air, the near warmth of the early spring sun. Not a day to be curled up with Dalesville's dark past, the first one in God knows how long where the grey wool blanket of clouds had finally been pulled back to reveal that cool, dazzling blue above.

He turned onto Lime and broke into a faster walk. He'd call Julian and see if he wanted to meet at the Blue Moon after Chris finished with his Sunday morning family bondage and then he'd sit in the backyard with a cup of coffee and a cigarette and enjoy the day.

Julian was already seated at a window table, coffee cup folded in his hands, staring up and out at the grey sky, back for an encore. That was problem with March in Chris' opinion, it taunted you with a handful of sunny days, only to knock you on your ass with wind or rain or snow the next. He got his coffee and joined his friend. Julian turned and smiled. "So, you want to pick my brain, huh?"

Chris shot him a grin as he pulled out the chair opposite and sat down, sliding his notebook out of his bag as he did so. "Absolutely. Do you feel used?"

"Totally." He winked. "I'm gonna need a shower after this."

The smiled faded by degrees from Julian's face, as if he'd heard his own words.

Chris felt his own good humor fade as well and nodded. "I already do, and I've just started."

Julian sighed as he slid a cigarette out of the pack and lit it, his eyes again drifting toward the window. Chris followed Julian's gaze and saw what he was staring at—a bus stop bench inscribed with the town's motto: "City of Light"—still visible through the blur of condensation on the window. When he looked back at Julian, he saw a cynical smile curl Julian's lips. "Oh, the irony. You've read about the lynchings, I take it? The bound copies, not the microfilm?"

Chris nodded, sipped his coffee. "The reader gives me a headache."

"Good, 'cause you won't find that story there, it's been redacted."

Chris almost dropped his cup. "By whom?"

Now Julian turned toward him, his normally affable face full of hard planes, his pupils wide with anger. "Robert James. Who else?"

"But why..." he stopped and flipped open his notebook and read through his scrawls. No mention of Robert James. He closed his eyes, tried to visualize the article itself.

"He's not in the article, he's in the picture. Robert James, Sr, lead businessman, newspaper owner, mayor of the fine city of Dalesville."

"How did you..." Chris stopped again when he saw the look on Julian's face.

Julian closed his eyes against the smoke from his cigarette. When he opened them again his eyes were stony with barely suppressed rage. "Dad said it's important to know your family's history."

For a long time, Chris stared at his friend, his brain taking its time to catch up to the sick, swooping feeling in his gut. "Your grandfather?" he finally managed through numb-dumb lips.

Julian barely moved his head in response, a bitter smile graven on his face. "They were all workers at the old paper mill, where McClellan's factory is now. All they wanted was a union that included all the workers, blacks, and women, not just the men. So, what did the management do? They got one of the female workers to claim that she was assaulted by the four men who happened to be the loudest voices for unionizing among the black workers and bang! Not even a trial."

Of course, none of that would be in the newspaper, Chris thought, Robert James Sr owned it, and Junior would have redacted it when it was no longer politically feasible to be proud of what they'd done. That sick feeling intensified and Chris took a burning gulp of his coffee, then fumbled out another cigarette and took his time lighting it. He felt Julian's stare. He didn't want to meet it, afraid of what judgment he might read there. Sack up, he thought.

The hard lines were gone and a little smile that was a shade lighter than sarcastic—gently ironic, maybe—played around Julian's lips and eyes. "You didn't do it Chris, so you can go ahead and let go of that white liberal guilt. For that, anyway."

His brain took a minute to catch up to what those last three words meant and when he realized what Julian was saying, he felt his ears heat up. In his quiet way, Julian was telling him not to make Julian's family tragedy—or hell, what he dealt with every day in this crap town—about Chris' reaction. "Can I ask you a question? You don't have to answer it."

Julian shrugged. "Shoot."

"Why come back? I mean, I'm glad you're here, but..."

For a second the anger flashed again in Julian's eyes. "Because it was our home, too, damn it!"

Chris saw the woman at the table behind them jump when Julian smacked the table, then get up and move a few tables away. Some things never changed. He met Julian's eyes and watched as Julian sagged a little in his chair, as if exhausted by the whole thing. Chris felt a new flavor of guilt rise up again as Julian dragged on his cigarette and sighed out smoke, a guilt he was fairly sure he'd earned. "Dad said that his father always told him that what's right and what's easy are usually two different things. After the lynching, pretty much every black person in town cleared out. And most of the women quit the factory."

"Why?"

Julian gave him a look that clearly said "dumbass." "The ones who didn't believe their coworkers were disgusted with what happened and those who did were afraid. The owners got exactly what they wanted. Anyway, Grandma moved the family back to Georgia, where her parents still lived. Dad moved to Chicago to go to med school, met mom, who was in the nursing program and when they got married decided to settle here, her family lived only a couple towns over. Dad said it was a challenge. Thompsons don't back down from a challenge."

Chris grinned. "Hell, no they don't."

They high-fived across the table.

Julian leaned back in his chair, seemingly calm except for the slight furrow above his nose. "So, it's my turn to ask you a question, how much of this are you actually going to use?"

Chris shrugged. "All of it, with your permission."

Julian smiled and nodded, as if he hadn't expected any other answer. "You know you won't win, right?"

"So? We Mulligans are used to failure."

Julian laughed hard enough to make people turn and stare, before he got serious. "Be careful, *okay*?"

"Dude. It's a high school journalism contest."

Julian shook his head. "You know what I mean."

Chris opened his mouth to disagree, to make Julian clarify what the hell he was talking about, then shut it so fast he heard his teeth click together. Thought about that cold feeling he got every time he passed by the Faith Fellowship Church, that mysterious, low-rent redaction in the blotter. Thought about Veronica's warning. Thought maybe he knew what Julian was talking about after all.

CHAPTER NINETEEN

Two calls. The first to Dalesville Community Hospital, which accomplished little beyond confirming that there was no patient named Marie, Raynor or Simon, currently there. They wouldn't tell me anything else, no matter what line I gave them. The second I wasn't sure would be any more successful. I sat at the dining room table with the phone in my hand, frozen with indecision. Nancy was another call I needed to make—to talk with her without Jeremy present—but the idea that she would hang up on me or have her mother give me some kind of excuse was a rejection I could definitely live without. But it was a dangling thread, and I always had a habit of pulling and unraveling, maybe it was better to tie it off before the whole thing was a pile of yarn.

I dialed. It rang twice and then, "Hello?"

It was Nancy and for a moment, I couldn't say a word.

"Hello?" Two syllables, thick with annoyance.

Speak, damn it! "Nancy, it's Veronica."

"Oh." Then silence and for a moment I thought she'd hung up. "How are you?"

I sighed in relief. "I'm *okay*. How are you?" Banal but safe.

"Fine. Been real busy, you know, school and stuff."

"I know how that is."

Another silence, excruciating in length. My brain seemed to shut down and I could not think of a thing to say. Finally, Nancy said," Well, if that's it, I gotta go. Mom needs my help with dinner."

"Oh, sure." Then, quick as a slap, my brain re-fired. "No, wait. I called because we need to talk about the other day."

"No, we don't." Her voice had a sharp note. "I mean," she paused and when she spoke again, her voice was calm but refrigerated. "I don't know what you mean."

My neck ached where I was balancing the phone, and I wondered why I thought it was a good idea to push this rock up the hill again. One last push and then I would let the damn thing roll down. "Oh, good, then you won't mind coming over after church tomorrow. I'll make coffee."

Nancy was the only person I could have over without checking with Dad first, hell, she was the only one I could have over, period.

"Hold on. I have to check with Mom."

"Sure. I'll wait."

I tucked the phone more securely between shoulder and neck and stood and went into the kitchen. I turned the oven on to pre-heat. I'd already finished making the salad by the time Nancy returned.

"Okay. I'll see you around 10:30 a.m." She hung up.

I hung up, too, and set the phone on the counter, rolling my neck and shoulders to work out the stiffness. What a bitch, I thought, startling myself with the vehemence of that thought. Once that thought banged through, others followed, as noisy and as demanding of my attention. Exactly why was I trying so hard with her? She wasn't even that great of a friend even when I hadn't accidentally freaked her out.

Maybe you need everyone to love you.

I slid the salad back into the fridge next to the coffee cake I'd picked up earlier in case she did say yes to coming over, then slammed the door and slumped against it. If that was the case, I'd already failed miserably. I needed to be realistic. Nancy was involved with the son of Robert James' second-in-command. Isn't that something I could use?

And that makes you better than him, how?

I banished that question, went back into the living room, and flopped down on the couch, at loose ends. Dinner was ready to cook, but for whom? Ever since that day Dad got that phone call he'd been coming home later and later, taking his meals in his office—if he took them at all—and shutting the door. Dad being in my face wasn't something I liked, but I sure as hell had gotten used to it. Five years of same old, same old, and then everything goes topsy-turvy on me.

The sun was sending its last feeble rays into the kitchen, it was already dusk in the living room. I reached over and flipped on the little table lamp, which did little to alleviate the darkness, but at least drove the shadows away from my immediate vicinity. I shook my head at my own perverse reaction. Now that Dad was leaving me alone all I could do was worry, and not be able to do a damn thing about it.

Action Girl, Laine had called me and maybe he was right. Maybe it wasn't always the right action but at least I felt better when I could do something.

The clock rang five times, and I supposed there was one action I could take, I hefted myself off the couch and went into the kitchen to cook dinner.

By the time I had pulled the chicken out of the oven an hour later, there was still no sign of Dad. So, I prepared him a plate, covered it, and left it in the kitchen, taking mine into the dining room with a book. A small rebellion but I still got a little thrill doing it. I suppose I could have gone all out and eaten in the living room while watching television but it was hard to break years of training. Afterward, I washed up everything except his plate, left a brief note at his place at the table, and retreated to my room.

The clock was striking nine when I heard the garage door open, followed by the rattle of his keys in the lock, and by force of habit I found myself in the hallway, to be at hand if he needed anything.

I watched him walk slump-shouldered through the shadows of the living room into the dining room, where my note was a dull white gleam. He reached over to turn on the light to read it better. When he saw me in the doorway he jumped, the color draining out of his face.

I rushed toward him, he stared at me like I was a phantom, and I stopped dead. "Dad, are you alright?"

That seemed to bring him back to himself and he drew a shaky hand over his forehead and sat down at the table. "Veronica, I thought you..."

"I'm sorry, Dad. I came to see if you wanted me to heat up dinner for you."

"Dinner." Again, he gave me that look of incomprehension. "Dinner, yes please."

"*Okay.*" I moved into the kitchen faster than I really needed to, shaken, my little seed of worry now grown into a great flowering fear. For a blessedly brief moment I was grateful for the years of training Dad had spent making me into a household drudge, at least I could do things like heat food on autopilot, while my mind gnawed over what had happened.

I brought him his dinner, my mind still far away, and took my place at the table. I folded my hands over where my plate would have been and stared down at them, sneaking a look every so often at Dad. The thousand-yard stare that seemed permanently affixed to his face made me break five years of hard training. "Dad. What's wrong?"

The face he turned toward me looked younger than I'd ever seen it, all those laddered, frowning lines smoothed out. The fear that dilated his eyes, that was like a child, too, one who can't explain away that slumped shape in the corner of his room, and too scared to leave the bed and turn on a light to be sure. As the moment lapsed into minutes, him staring at me like an unknown shape in a dark room, I thought again of the bars I almost always saw when I looked at him, and for the first time I wondered if they weren't in fact to keep me out, but to keep himself in.

He came back to himself slowly, like a footprint filling with water. Finally, "Nothing." His voice shook on that word and he took a deep breath. "Nothing's wrong."

This time, the tone held more of his old firmness and then it was my turn to sigh. I braced myself for a reprimand at my presumption.

I resumed staring at my hands, waiting, but the only thing I heard was the small clink of his knife and fork. I looked up in time to see him rest them crisscrossed on his plate. "Thank you for dinner." He dabbed his perfectly clean face with his napkin, folded it carefully, and set it next to his plate, then stood up and was halfway down the hall to his office when he turned and came back to the table, his hands gripping the back of his chair as he stood behind it.

"Veronica." As I looked at him, I saw the same harsh-drawn face I'd been seeing for so long, but the unreadable brew of emotion in his eyes was strikingly similar to that day the week before, when he'd seemed so close to telling me something, anything, that wasn't an order, until the phone rang and shattered the moment. Maybe I'd been wrong about it being the last chance.

When he did speak, it was the same kind of thing I'd been hearing for years. "I'm going to have to be gone a great deal over the coming weeks. I trust you'll continue to behave in the ways I've taught you. What I don't see, God does." The words were the same, but the tone was wrong, it crackled with something unspoken, something that couldn't be said. The knuckles that gripped the chair were white. "Do you understand?"

Was he talking about Theo following me? The file that mentioned my name and Mom's? I answered without thinking, to the substance of the question. "I'm trying to, Dad."

His hands dropped to his sides and he came around to my chair, laid his right hand on my shoulder. I looked up at him, knowing that I hadn't kept the surprise off my face. He paled as he looked down at me, his face again devoid of lines, and his eyes bright with what, if I didn't know better, were tears. "Keep...keep trying." His voice was no more than a hoarse rumble I felt more than heard.

I laid my hand over his and saw not bars but a wall, remarkably similar to the mental one I'd built for myself. I knew what I was hiding but what was he? "I promise."

When I woke up on Sunday morning, the sun was already streaming through my window and that's how I knew he was gone again. I rolled over to look at the clock, 9:30 a.m. Church had started half an hour earlier. I rolled over on my back and stared up at the ceiling, relishing a Faith Fellowship-free Sunday.

Finally, I sat up, slung my feet over the bed and into my slippers, grabbed my robe from the back of the door and shuffled down the hall into the dining room, empty except for Dad's plain white coffee cup. I picked it up and turned left into the kitchen, straight to the refrigerator where he left his notes.

Under the Faith Fellowship Church magnet was a folded note. That was weird. His notes were usually a list of chores on a small sheet of paper. I pulled it out and opened it, two twenties fluttered to the floor.

"Veronica, I've gone to the retreat center in Harrison. I will (the word "will" was underlined twice, which flummoxed me) be back on Saturday night. My apologies for the short notice. Please take care (also underlined)."

I bent over to pick up the money, then slumped against the counter. What in the name of hell was going on? I stared at the note for a long time, like it was in code, then folded it in a small square and dropped it into the pocket of my robe.

The coffee pot was still on, which meant he hadn't been gone for long. I poured myself a cup, took it to the living room, and flopped onto the couch. I considered turning on the TV but the only things on Sunday morning television were holy rollers and news shows, and I needed to think.

I took a long drink of coffee, polishing off half the cup in one go. This was the second time I'd seen him change so drastically and it was no more comprehensible to me at eighteen than it had been at twelve. I'd seen the pictures of Mom and Dad, grim-mouthed and holding "No More Nukes" signs at Rocky Flats, the parties of my childhood, overflowing with beer and wine and pot and the importance of the social contract. As I sipped the rest of my coffee, I thought about how that group of friends got smaller through the years. When I'd asked

Dad why I hadn't seen my friend Tina for a while, the daughter of their friends the Billings, Dad called them "sellouts, more focused on social climbing than social justice," with an ugly scowl on his face that precluded further inquiry. When I'd asked Mom to explain, she'd told me, "It's hard for your dad. He sets high standards for himself and everyone else. Very few people can live up to that."

Maybe the Dalesville version was the flip side of the same coin. So, what caused this new turn? He was scared of something, that was clear. There was only one thing I could think of that scared me, Robert James. Even thinking of his name made me shudder and I wondered if Dad finally got a taste of that.

The clock struck ten, making me jump. Nancy was due in half an hour. I shot off the couch and hurried down the hall to get dressed.

I was ready when the doorbell rang precisely at 10:30 a.m. Of course. I'd managed to pull myself together, dressed in comfy jeans and a plain blouse. I'd considered, then discarded the idea of wearing my "Bite Me" t-shirt, complete with a lurid picture of bloody fangs, but figured that wouldn't put Nancy in a good frame of mind. The coffee was still hot and the cake out on a nice plate.

I answered the door with a smile and a wave to Nancy's mom, who tooted her horn and drove off.

I opened the door wider and gestured Nancy inside. She gave me a brief smile that didn't touch her eyes. "Where were you this morning?"

I knew she would ask that, and I'd already prepared my answer. "I was sick last night, Dad agreed to let me sleep in. Would you like some coffee?"

"Yes, thank you."

"Go ahead and have a seat on the couch, I'll bring it out to you."

She nodded and turned toward the living room. I watched her out of the corner of my eye—she took the easy chair instead, perhaps in some species of defiance—before retreating to the kitchen. I shook my head and turned to go into the kitchen.

She was still sitting straight-backed in the chair when I came in with the tray, with her cream-and-sugared coffee and two slices of cake. I suppressed a smile as I settled on the couch at the thought of how deliciously suburban the moment was, two ladies with coffee and cake, sitting in a decently appointed living room. The next moment, I found the same thought depressing.

We nibbled and sipped in silence for what seemed like an eternity. I finally resorted to the most banal of conversation openers. "How's the coffee cake?"

Nancy polished off her last bite. "Very good, thank you."

"Would you like some more?"

She gave me a plastic smile. "Maybe later."

I put my plate on the table, with half my piece still left. "Nancy."

She placed both plate and cup on the table and if possible, became even stiffer. "Yes."

"I don't know what happened the other day but if I inadvertently upset you, I'm sorry."

I took a sip of coffee and watched her over the rim. She relaxed, the shoulders went down a bit, she crossed her ankles, and the pinched look around her mouth smoothed out.

I, too, leaned back on the couch, surprised at the depth of my relief. While the apology still felt wrong, I had been as disturbed and as disinclined to examine what happened at the Blue Moon. This ability—curse—was getting stronger the more I used it, the wall harder to rebuild.

"Veronica?"

I pulled myself back to the moment with no small effort, simultaneously resentful and grateful for Nancy's (invited!) presence. I was giving myself emotional whiplash, a sensation I'd been happy to leave behind years ago. "Sorry. Woolgathering. I guess I'm still feeling the lack of sleep last night." I searched for a safe conversational harbor. "How's Jeremy?"

Nancy actually grinned, if it was any more smug it would have to be fined. "He got the word, he's been accepted into the Faith Fellowship Seminary."

"Really? That's wonderful." For perhaps the first time ever, with regards to the future most Reverend Jeremy Barnes, I was completely sincere. I didn't know precisely what or why I needed to know about the inner workings of Robert James' money machine, but the calculating part of my mind jumped on the idea of having a connection to an insider, to offer help, however unwillingly or unknowingly.

Nancy lifted her chin up with an air of decided haughtiness that sat strangely with her mousy, demure appearance. She seemed to be born to be a minister's wife, even regular features, enhanced by a small amount of make-up, pretty enough, but not striking, so as not to be an occasion to sin. Not unlike Nancy's mom, come to think of it. "Well, it's hardly a surprise, really, with Mr. James personal recommendation."

I dropped my cup from a hand that went completely nerveless. I bent fast to pick it up, hoping Nancy hadn't noticed but she was far away in contemplation of her future husband's bright future. I said a quick thank you under my breath that the cup was empty, set it back on the table, and after a deep breath, leaned over to my plate to take a bite of cake. "Well, that's impressive."

"He's a good man, Mr. James."

The cake lodged in my throat, and I cursed silently that my cup was empty. I swallowed hard and it seemed to move far enough down so I could talk. "Oh, you've met him?"

I pushed the plate far away, knowing any answer she might give could lead to choking.

Her look shifted from haughty to nearly disdainful. "More than once. He's told both of us that he thinks Jeremy has great future with Faith Fellowship, like his father."

Before I could stop and remind myself who I was talking to, I burst out with, "What about your future?"

Now the expression shifted from haughty to dreamy, she was in no position to notice my tone. "I'm to help any way I can."

It was either laugh or cry, but I knew I needed to get out of the room before either one erupted. "More cake?"

"Sure." She was already far away.

I barely made it to the kitchen before I began to shake with a laughter that bordered on hysterical, in intensity if not noise. Still, I was glad it was laughter. Red eyes might be harder to explain.

I got myself under some degree of control by splashing water on my face and sliced the cake with a hand that shook only a little. Why would she want to throw her life away? She of course, would deny any such thing, having been given her purpose directly from the man himself.

As I slid a generous slice of coffee cake onto her plate, I tried to think objectively about the situation. There was a certain degree of comfort, even relief, in knowing one's purpose, of being told exactly what you have to sacrifice—autonomy, career—in order to achieve it. But was anybody really ever aware of how big their sacrifice would be? The thought of those stones between peach trees welled up behind my eyes and I felt simultaneously cold and nauseated.

Or even if they knew they were making it?

I set the cake on the table in front of a still-distracted Nancy, my own thoughts still whirling, Nancy and Mom all mixed up in my head. *She doesn't even know she's being used.* A deep breath as I tried and finally succeeded in maintaining a calm façade in voice and manner. Dad's training proved useful for a second time in twenty-four hours, that must be some kind of record.

"So, what happens now? Are you still planning on going to school?" I was pleased at the lack of judgment in my tone.

Nancy snapped out of her reverie and her eyes narrowed, so maybe I hadn't been as successful as I thought. "Of course, I am! Education is important, regardless."

I didn't pursue the regardless. "Have you decided where, yet?"

Nancy took a bite of cake before answering but her eyes remained focused on the plate long after she'd swallowed. "At Faith Fellowship," she finally said, so low I had to lean in to hear her. Then she did meet my eyes, and her expression registered first surprise, her mouth slightly ajar, and then a smooth relief. I knew she'd expected disappointment or annoyance—maybe even a futile argument—but I'd known for awhile that she wasn't leaving. What surprised me was the hard lump of sad in my stomach and throat. It was as if our friendship was narrowing to a distant point on the horizon, a few more miles, and we wouldn't even be able to see it anymore. It was the simplest thing, she wanted in, and I wanted out. We happened to briefly meet in the doorway. I took several deep, watery breaths, swallowed the last dregs of coffee in my cup, and the tears retreated, waiting.

Nancy leaned back in the chair, content, or at least full of cake. "What about you?"

I gave her what I knew was a weak smile and shrugged. I hadn't applied anywhere, much to my guidance counselor's chagrin. Ms. Penobo kept trying to convince me to apply somewhere, but how could I tell her I couldn't afford the application fees, or that Dad wouldn't pay them unless they were for Faith Fellowship Evangelical College? I held onto my pride like it was my last dollar. "I don't know yet. Depends on where I get in, I suppose. I'll keep you posted. So, you think Jeremy'll start working at Faith Fellowship when he's done?"

"Probably." For the first time that morning, there was a crack in her demeanor, a shaky little frown she quickly turned into a weak smile. "He's been spending an awful lot of time in Harrison. It's nice, I guess, but I'd rather stay here."

For the first time—and hopefully the last—I wished I'd paid more attention to Dad's talk about work, to Reverend Ash's droning sermons and announcements. Three times, three different people and situations had brought up the retreat center in Harrison. That sense that this was bigger than what happened to Mom, so strong when I talked to Chris at the playground, was back. "Maybe they're building another church down there?"

Nancy shrugged, shook her head. "Could be. Jeremy won't say anything about it except 'we're building the future'."

Maybe my ears were deceiving me but there was a note of annoyance, almost mockery, in Nancy's tone. Trouble in her Faith Fellowship paradise seemed too much to hope for, but still. I thought it best not to comment. "If I run into Theo again, I'll ask him. He said something about it, too."

Nancy leaned forward, a sly grin on her face. "You like him!"

"Sure, he's *okay*." My brain caught up only when Nancy's face brightened. "Not like that, I saw him for all of ten minutes in the pen and highlighter aisle."

"If you say so." She ran her finger over the plate for the last few cake crumbs. "I just thought maybe you two could double date with Jeremy and I."

Only a supreme act of will kept me from either laughing or gagging. I didn't think she'd take either response well. I settled on the noncommittal. "Who knows?"

She reached out and took my hand, what I saw in the coffee shop flashed in my mind. A deep breath to clear my head and I squeezed back. Nancy smile lit her face again and I could feel, like a low, pleasant hum, the motive behind the clumsy matchmaking. She missed me, she wanted me to be happy. I smiled back, my throat a little scratchy, wanting the same for her, and knowing what I couldn't ever tell her, neither Jeremy nor Faith Fellowship would bring her anything but grief.

"Good." A horn beeped outside—her mom was there, right on time, on so many levels. Nancy stood, brushing off the few crumbs that had migrated to her lap. I stood, too.

To my surprise, she pulled me into a tight hug and said, "I know it's selfish, but I hope you stick around."

I couldn't answer, the tears were too close to speak.

She let me go, sketched a little wave, and was out the door without me asking any of the real questions I'd meant to.

I shut it behind her, locked it, turned and slumped against it, sliding all the way to the ground as I sobbed.

Chapter Twenty

C hris arrived at Sam's not long after school let out for the day. He was already backing out of his space and speeding across the parking lot by the time the heaviest flow of students started streaming out the front doors. He'd already smoked half a cigarette before he arrived at the stop light at the school crossing.

It hadn't been a good day. Not a terrible one and maybe even typical for a Monday, but he still wanted to stick a fork in the school half of the day and move fast to something else. The light changed and he was off, making every light between school and Sam's. "It's my destiny," he said aloud as he pitched his butt out the window and laughed. Finally, something was going right.

He walked through the door a mere ten minutes after the last bell rang and scanned the diner for any familiar faces. He didn't really expect any—who could have beaten him there? —so his shock was genuine where he spied Veronica at a table near the center of the restaurant, staring morosely into her coffee.

He slid in across from her with a "hey" that made her look up. She smiled, warm, but it didn't touch the sad expression that darkened her eyes. He pulled his cigarettes out of his coat pocket and offered her one, thinking he'd seen precious little of her since that night at *The Club* and for a moment entertained the notion that his absence was the reason for her sadness. As flattering as that idea was, he dismissed it. If that were the case, Mr. God's Gift, he chided himself, wouldn't your presence have dispelled the gloom?

She took the offered smoke with another sad little smile. "Thanks."

Chris shrugged. "Sure. So, I gotta know, how did you get here so fast? I mean, I sped, but you don't even have a car."

She set the unlit cigarette on the ashtray, and she dug into her bag, pulled out a small white piece of paper. An office pass. "Ms. Penobo wanted me to check out Dalesville College. Again."

Chris frowned. DC was *okay*—his mom worked there—but tiny and more importantly, in Dalesville. He'd supposed Veronica would want to get the hell out as much as he did. He slid the pass back to her.

Veronica absently put it back in her bag. "She's trying to get me to change my mind about applying."

Chris nearly dropped his cigarette. "You haven't? Why the hell not?"

She flinched a bit, and Chris realized how loud he'd spoken. "Sorry."

She handwaved. "Don't worry about it."

She had that marble statue look again but Chris couldn't let it go. "But seriously, Veronica. Why?"

Color melted the stone a fraction. "Chris, can we please talk about anything else?"

So much she never said. He met her eyes and saw for the first time something he'd never seen in her, desperation. He bit back his question. "Okay. I'll drop it. For now."

She took a drink of her coffee, grimaced, and pushed it away. "I am glad to see you, you know." He raised an eyebrow at her. The dark cloud receded a bit and she gave him a stronger smile. "No, really. I was much more bummed out before you got here."

That thought alone was enough to make Chris feel some inkling of her mood, if this was more cheerful, she must have been in the depths before. "Do you want to talk about that instead?"

Then she laughed. "You sound like a therapist."

Chris gave her a smile, stroked an imaginary beard and put on a fake German accent. "Yes, tell me about your father."

That cut her laugh right off and the cloud descended again.

Shirley appeared at that moment to refill Veronica's cup, sparing Chris from saying anything but "Can I get a coffee, please?" in the awkward silence that followed. She nodded, refilled Veronica's cup, and by the time she'd retreated, Veronica looked okay again.

"I'm sorry," Chris said again, although he wasn't sure what for. She flapped her hand again, making little curlicues in the air.

"Don't mind me. I just get sad sometimes." She took a long drink and finally lit the cigarette he'd offered her. "How are you doing? I feel like I haven't seen you in ages."

Shirley floated by and deposited a cup of coffee for him, and he took a drink, understood Veronica's grimace. It was one of the wall-paper-stripping strength days. "I'm working the graveyard shift at McClellan's on Saturdays. It's kicking my ass."

"Dude. That sucks."

He grinned, it turned into a yawn. "You know, I can stay up 'til three a.m.—but without a drink? That ain't right."

"Can't they give you a better slot or something?"

"It's a test. They want to prove they don't play favorites." She gave him a quizzical look. "My dad's a foreman there."

She took another drag. "That's gotta be…challenging. Expectations and all that."

Her tone resonated with unspoken understanding, prompting Chris to ask, "What does your dad do at Faith Fellowship?"

She smiled, but it was dark and cynical and full of teeth. "The books, among other things. Or, as he says, 'God's work', which also includes teaching me to be a proper, obedient girl, born again to serve men."

"Oh." He tried to visualize the girl in front of him with a cigarette jutting from the corner of her mouth as the scion to a Faith Fellowship insider, the juxtaposition amused him. Then he thought of her facing Robert James and all the humor hissed out of the situation. "Oh!"

She twitched and dropped her cigarette. "What?"

"Well, I've been researching the James family and Faith Fellowship for the *Ledger* contest." She gave him a quizzical look as she retrieved her smoke from the table. "Scholarship thing. Anyway," he stopped, dug into his satchel and pulled out the photocopy of the police blotter and handed it to her, "I found this and wondered what you might make of it."

He watched her skim it and then look up, something flickered in her eyes that he couldn't quite interpret, but it seemed like fear. "What?"

She absently put out her cigarette as she continued to stare in his general direction, silent.

"What?" As if louder would help.

She shook her head as if she was coming back to herself, gave him an apologetic smile and the photocopy. "It feels important, but I don't know what it means. Do you think you could find out the redacted name? Other copies maybe?"

He folded the paper and put it back in his satchel. "Tried. It was redacted from the bound copies at the school library, too. When I called the *Ledger* offices, they said they'd try to see if they still had a copy of that issue. That was three weeks ago. It…"

It was his turn to go silent, he swore he could actually hear his brain trying to make a connection that was just out of reach. His words came slowly, like a tape in his Walkman when the batteries were dying. "A lot of things are converging on one thing."

"Which is?"

Chris couldn't repress a shudder. "Robert James. He owned the *Ledger*. He could have ordered it redacted, but why?" When he looked at Veronica, she was smiling. "What's that for?"

Her smile grew broader. "I've realized that I can tell the people I can trust by the physical reaction to hearing his name."

He returned the smile. "Did I pass?"

"With flying colors."

Her smile faded by almost imperceptible degrees, the second clicks of a clock. First it left her eyes, then the tick-tick of the curve of her lips retreating into a straight line. It wasn't a complete return to the morose baseline of earlier, but it was in walking distance of the neighborhood. He lit another cigarette and decided to be forthright. "So, who didn't?"

She jumped a little. "What do you mean?"

Playing stupid clearly wasn't her strong suit, Chris thought, and he loaded his tone with disappointment, all focused on a single word. Tricks from Mom and Dad. "Veronica."

She blushed, then busied herself lighting another smoke from his pack. "My friend Nancy."

"Is that why you were so bummed out when I got here?"

She nodded. "One reason, anyway. Her boyfriend, Jeremy Barnes, is tight with Mr. James."

The name pinged something in Chris' brain, Barnes. That was in his article file, a profile of Paul Barnes from the late 80s, when he'd been named deacon of Faith Fellowship. "Is he related to Paul Barnes?"

The pensive droop to her eyes disappeared as they widened, then crinkled into a smile. "Impressive, Christopher."

Chris bowed his head in mock modesty.

"Yes, Jeremy's his son. That, and…"

The line was back between her eyes. "I don't know how safe it is for you to be looking into this stuff."

Chris felt a spark of irritation, he was tired of hearing that. Like he needed to be protected. He tried to keep his voice level. "It's what I do. Hell, some of it is what you asked me to do."

Her eyes narrowed, then brightened, crinkling at the corners. "I know." Somber again. "Then again, all those weeks ago I hadn't been followed or known about weird police reports. Or being…"

She stopped, her lips a thin, white line, like she was sealing herself off. A taste was on his tongue, of possibilities, of something new. He tapped the ash, tried to figure an angle that might unlock what she was hiding. He leaned back in the booth, took a drag. "You could tell me why you get so jumpy sometimes."

A cynical smile curled her lips. "I owe you that much, do I?"

He shook his head. "You don't owe me anything."

Her face smoothing into a pale blank before settling on a frown, her cheeks red as she stared down at the surface of her coffee. "You're right. That was a shitty thing to say." She took a sip, grimaced, and pushed the cup away. A contrite smile. "It feels like I'm surrounded by liars and assholes. Not you. Or your friends."

He never did know how to respond to compliments, so he settled for, "I try to be neither of those things."

A real smile. "I know. And you've helped me without prying, you deserve something. Some truth, anyway." She took a drag, sat up and leaned closer, her voice low. "I still think it's dangerous, but...I think there's something weird going on in Harrison. It could be an avenue you could explore. Maybe long-term."

Not what he expected her to say. "Does this have to do with your mom?"

She shrugged. "Honestly? I don't know. Dad spent last weekend there, and Nancy told me Jeremy goes there, too, and all he'll tell her is that they're 'building the future.' That sounds ominous, don't you think?"

"Like the beginning of every sci-fi movie ever." His own words echoed in his ears, made the skin on the back of his neck crawl. That same feeling he got when a random remark in an interview put him onto something bigger, like when Mr. Peterson bragged on his students' "unbelievable" progress and his gut told him something was off.

With a little quirk of a smile, she reached out, took his forgotten cigarette from between his fingers, dragged, and placed it in the ashtray. She laced her fingers with his now empty ones. That all of this—the info, the contact—might be a distraction, didn't occur to him until later.

That electric feeling jolted him, he barely noticed her pulling her hand away. "I have to go."

Her eyes narrowed as she glanced to her right, a gesture that seemed familiar. Before he could place it, she was sliding out of the booth, backpack in hand. "Veronica, wait..."

A fleeting smile and she nearly ran out of the diner. He was about to follow her when a curly-haired guy blew past him and out the door. Coincidence? He slid out of the booth and went to the window. Sure enough, he saw her in the parking lot, her face red as she argued with the guy he'd first seen dressed in baggy jeans and a sweatshirt standing there like he was in uniform. Finally, she stormed off, and the guy finally relaxed.

When he turned back toward the diner Chris moved, went back to the booth and grabbed his stuff, leaving a few bucks on the table for Shirley.

He looked for her as he drove home, but she was long gone. Things got weirder and weirder with that girl. Who was that guy? Some ex? That thought brought an ugly feeling in his gut he realized might be jealousy. He flipped on the radio to drown it out as he slowed for the light near home. He could examine what that meant later, but the interaction he'd witnessed didn't give off that vibe, as far as he could tell.

You could ask her.

He caught himself smiling as he glanced in the rearview, flipped on the turn signal. Right, 'cause she's so forthcoming. Who knew, though? Maybe this time it would be different.

Hope? Delusion? He found he didn't care which.

Chapter Twenty-One

It was well past five when I finally made it home, the soles of my feet burning from the walk, thinking of Chris and why I couldn't come clean about that vision of Mom, continually foxed by my inability to think of a non-weird way I'd come by that information. Thinking about what Theo said. "You're putting him in danger. You don't even know what they're capable of."

Forgetting for a minute his earlier reaction in the grove, I'd hit him with, "Oh, and you do?"

He looked like I'd slapped him, guilt made me even angrier. "Yeah, I do."

"Then tell me! Stop fucking around and tell me."

"I can't." Barely a whisper.

I'd stomped off, not looking back, trying not to think about how I did the same thing to Chris as Theo did to me.

I half expected Dad to be home, breathing fire at my late arrival, but true to his word, the house was dark and empty. I flicked on the living room light and wandered into the kitchen in search of something to eat. I settled for a cold chicken drumstick and gnawed on it while I watched TV. There was a certain pleasure in even watching crappy sitcoms, it had been ages since I'd watched TV and even the stalest, see-them-coming-a-mile-away gags seemed at least vaguely amusing. Still, I couldn't sit still. My gloominess seemed to have been replaced with a weird kind of twitchy restlessness, I kept bouncing off the couch and wandering around, looking for I didn't know what, only to collapse back into the couch again with a sigh. The last time I got up only to switch off the TV and sit quietly in the low-light pool created by the lamp, thinking over the paired threads of everything I'd learned so far. Nancy and Jeremy's connection to Robert James, Chris' article. The lingering question of what Reverend Ash had said and what the hell was going on in Harrison. And of course, the perennial one, what happened Mom? I dug out from my backpack the photocopy Chris gave me, held it under the lamp's light and read it again. Something about it seemed meaningful in a way that made me feel cold inside.

The person in the blotter had to be Mom. The problem with that theory of course, was that Mom wasn't crazy, so why would she have been in a psych ward? Why had she been here at all?

I jumped off the couch and ran down the hall, stopping at the door to Dad's study. If there were answers to be had, that's where they'd be.

Dad had always issued stern warnings that I did not belong there. He needn't have bothered— up until the last few weeks, I'd zero interest in anything he might be hiding. His need to warn me against financial reports from Faith Fellowship, his bills, or whatever other paperwork he might have, business or personal, seemed part of his desire to be in control and nothing more.

It should have been locked but the door sprang open into darkness. My vision doubled and I realized I was near tears. He'd trusted that I would obey him, he who never seemed to trust anything I might do without his guiding hand.

I recognized familiar shapes even in the dark, the big light wood desk that used to be in the living room at our old house, where Mom would sit writing letters or grading papers under the small yellow square of light from the green glass lamp, which still held its place on the desk. The end table I'd spilled nail polisher remover on at eight years old during a pink nail polish experiment gone terribly wrong. A still life of a bowl of fruit that had hung in our old living room was on the wall behind the desk. It was like a time capsule of the time before here.

I slid into the desk chair that was new, smooth leather decorated with rivets on the arms and back that rested comfortably against my back. I wondered how comfortable it would be after a few hours of sitting. A hair shirt in chair form. I flipped the lamp on, it spilled its low light over an empty desk blotter. I ran my fingers over the grooves and scribbles that marked it, let my mind wander over ideas of where to look first.

I slid open the top drawer. Nothing but pencils, paper clips, and other assorted office ephemera. It was repellently tidy, as was everything Dad touched. I missed the days of books stacked by his chair, dog-eared magazines littering the coffee table.

Except there was a torn corner of paper, slid halfway under the pencil well in the desk. I slid one of the pens under the tray and got it loose. I held it under the light, it had two words in the same neat printing as his chore note, Project m. It ended in a question mark.

That rang a bell. I traced the words with my fingers, trying to fit it into the ever-increasing puzzle of info I'd gotten. Project m. I closed my eyes, saw Theo dressed in a sweatshirt, sitting at the mall, in the parking lot at Sam's. "They have a file on you."

My hand closed involuntarily over the paper as I opened my eyes again. That was it. He told me he'd been asked to deliver the file to an office he couldn't find. Office *m*.

Another question but at least I had a place to start.

At the moment, I could at least see what Dad knew. I moved my hand over to the side drawer, pulling at it hard enough to bend my nails back. I hissed in pain, stuck my index and middle finger in my mouth.

I leaned back into the chair, letting the steel rivets dig into my back. Now I knew why the door was unlocked, everything important must be in the locked drawer. So much for trust, I thought, all the more sour for my earlier tears. He locked the drawer, he locked up all the things that reminded us of Mom—the desk, the end table, the lamp, the painting—in this room. How was I supposed to trust he didn't have anything to do with all the other weird things?

I closed the door behind me, the pure rebellion I'd been nurturing for the past five years, untainted by any of the recent grey areas Dad's behavior had introduced, back for good. I still had most of the forty dollars Dad left for the week, I made a quick left into my room to change into my club clothes.

As I slid out my window into the pitch-black alley, I thought that the advantage of wearing black was not only that it pissed Dad off but also because I could get through dark streets virtually unnoticed. The streetlights in our subdivision were numerous—spaced every fifty feet or so—but over the past few years I'd been pleased to see a marked deterioration in the bulb replacement. At least a quarter of them were burnt out, allowing large, gap-toothed pockets of darkness I could slip into unnoticed by neighbors. I pulled up the hood of my coat and ghosted down the alley until I reached Sunset.

Chris frowned when I told him about my little shadow jaunts, finally saying, "Aren't you afraid of getting, well..." Red danced in his cheeks, his mouth closed over the unsaid word so hard I heard his teeth click together.

I'd squeezed his arm in reassurance. "I'm careful Christopher, I promise. Can't live my life afraid, right?"

He raised an eyebrow, the wary look in the eye below seemed to suggest that he could think of a few arguments against that idea, but he didn't press the point.

I pushed open the door of *The* Club—safe and sound again—and looked over the sparse Monday night population.

There was a grand total of six people on the dance floor, making the world's smallest mosh pit to the Clash's "White Riot," clearly Dalesville could boast few fans of early British punk. Most of the couple dozen patrons were either seated at the bar or scattered at the various tables at the edge of the pit or the booths against the back and side walls.

I ambled over to the bar, ordered my usual from Mike and took a booth in the corner. I slid in, lit a cigarette, and rested my head against the high back of the booth. Some species of tired made me feel heavy-boned and -lidded. It wasn't the walk. I'd made that walk so much it seemed like nothing, it must be mental.

I lifted the cigarette to my mouth and took a drag, squinting against the smoke. Why not? The last few days had been a morass of unanswered questions and whipsaw emotions. Despite the jacked-up bass of the music, I could have stretched out in the booth and slept the night through.

"Mind if I join you?" The sound of a voice so close to my ear made me start out of my half-doze, my cigarette landing in my lap in a brief shower of sparks immediately extinguished in the air. I stood up, brushed the few live ones off my pants and retrieved the cigarette from the seat before it could burn another hole in the pockmarked faux leather.

I looked up to see Julian wearing an expression equal parts sheepish and amused. The amusement won out and he grinned at me. "Sorry about that."

"Hmm." I did my best to look severe, but as his grin didn't falter and I clearly failed. I finally gave into an answering smile and gestured to the seat across from me. We both slid in.

We sat in silence for a bit while I took a drink of my neglected vodka tonic. Finally, Julian broke it. "So, what brings you here on a Monday?"

I shrugged, not in the mood to talk about that feeling of rebellion that rose up so strongly outside Dad's office with all its locked-up secrets, or the need to drown all the unanswerable questions in the miasma of noise and alcohol *The* Club offered. "Needed to get out of the house. You know."

Julian's brow laddered up. "By association, mostly."

I puzzled over that remark as I stubbed out my cigarette. Really, I knew next to nothing about Julian or his family. Laine of course, shared everything, and I knew Chris and his father didn't really get along, mostly from the way he called his dad "Big Pat," which always sounded like a swear word when he said it. "Let me guess," I said at long last, "you're of that rare genus of *famillius normalicus*."

Julian's laugh was a lovely sound, a sonorous ring like a large bell. "Pretty much."

"So, what brings *you* here on a Monday night?"

He winked. "Escape from normality."

I winked back. "Mission accomplished."

We sat in a good silence, finishing our drinks.

"So, no Laine tonight?"

Julian's mouth twisted, a lemony look on his face. "We don't go *everywhere* together, you know."

I stared down at the table feeling the heat in my ears and neck. "Sorry, I assumed..."

Julian squeezed my hand briefly—whether by luck or habit my wall stayed in place and I saw nothing—a slow smile spreading across his face. "It's true. We're together most of the time. He's one of the few people outside my family that I don't have to watch what I say with. Everybody needs someone or a few someones even that they can be who they are with. Remember Aaron Hemings?"

I nodded. Aaron had been the same year as us, although I hadn't known him really well, he was part of the group that was hyper-involved with school stuff, student council, yearbook. He'd shot himself in his parents' basement the year before. No note, so gossip had circulated around school about why—bad grades? home stuff? —with most people settling on the idea that it was over a girl. I mentioned this to Julian and his smile morphed into a wry, cynical grimace. "You might say it was a girl, in that he wasn't attracted to them."

"Oh." I hadn't considered that. Then again, I'd had very little interaction with him. We'd shared a couple of classes throughout the years and the occasional "hey", not enough interaction to either wonder about or determine his sexual preferences. "I take it that wasn't...acceptable to him."

Julian's grimace seemed frozen on. "You might say that. My guess is that was uglier than that. You know, not only expose him but someone else—and he didn't have anyone he felt he could be honest with."

No, I hadn't known him, but the tragedy of it hit me like a stomach punch. "What a fucking waste."

Julian nodded, his eyes soft and sad. "I knew what he was hiding. I even tried to talk to him, but he avoided me."

I thought about how I'd sat through the memorial assembly, trying to figure it out why it pissed me off so much, why so much of the tears and kind words seemed fake, with the overwrought dabbing at eyes and leaving the podium in tears. It took on a new context in light of Julian's revelations, better dead and preserved as who they thought he was, then alive and gay. I stared down at the table, my feelings finding expression finally in, "I hate this town."

Julian chuckled, making me look up from the scarred and warped table. "That was pretty much my reaction."

"Thanks for telling me. It..." I didn't know quite how to express what I was feeling without sounding like a stupid greeting card, one of those ones with watercolor abstractions and end-stopped prose faking a poem.

Julian smiled, then took a long drink, leaning back against the seat. "Well, you're kinda weird, too. I mean, you come out to party and then thank me for telling you suicide stories." He winked at me.

The music had shifted, after a long run of downbeat songs that seemed to reflect the DJ's increasing depression that absolutely no one was dancing, he suddenly switched to the Cure's "Friday I'm in Love." Julian gave me another slow smile. "What do you say to bailing on this conversation and making a spectacle of ourselves on the dance floor?"

"You know I'm a spaz."

He slid out of the booth and extended his hand to me. "Don't worry, I'll lead."

A sweaty half-hour later we sank into two vacated chairs on the edge of the dance floor, now marginally crowded. The DJ, seemingly thrilled by this development, focused on dance-y goth and punk.

I fanned myself ineffectually with my hand and grinned at Julian. "You really are a good dancer."

We'd twirled, dipped, and spun. Or rather, Julian twirled, dipped, and spun me like I was weightless. I felt weightless, actually, he guided me with a gentle hand when it looked like I'd take a wrong turn, knowing exactly what step to take without seeming to be concentrating at all.

Julian took my hand again. "Let's go get a drink."

I nodded and followed him, thinking about dancing. Once seated at the bar, drinks in hand, Julian said, "What are you so deep in thought about?"

I took a sip before answering, trying to formulate my line of thinking. "I was wondering what you could read about a person by how they dance."

Julian frowned in consideration. "Quite a bit, I guess. Laine always throws himself into the pit, which is kind of his approach to everything."

"I'd say based on your dancing, you're confident and knowledgeable."

He nodded. "Not bad. I always figure what I don't know I can learn. It's worked so far."

I was warming to this idea, although I wasn't keen on an assessment of my lack of skill. "And Chris, you can see the wheels turning, like he's planning every step."

Julian took a drink of beer. "Just wait."

"What?"

His grin was almost a leer. "There's a lot going on below."

I felt completely nonplussed, until I connected the words with Julian's expression. I felt the heat rise from my neck up, as I thought about Chris and I dancing, my head against his chest and the rapid beat of his heart. I felt that same flutter in my stomach, as if it was happening again at that moment, and I wondered exactly how red my face was, because it felt like I might burst into flames. I stared down at my drink on the bar, picked it up, and polished it off in three swallows.

Julian's laugh was a low rumble in my left ear. I looked at him and gave him a smile and a shrug, then signaled Mike for another drink.

"So, what are you going to do about it?"

I stared at Julian, his own smile gone, despite the natural curve of his mouth that made him look like he was always smiling, the frown line between his eyes, and something pinged in my brain, this was no idle question. Underneath was that perennial parental inquiry: What are your intentions?

I opened my mouth to answer but what came out was a hitching gasp, almost like a sob. In that moment, I knew myself utterly. The girl who hated where she was but didn't leave. Who wanted to find her mom but didn't exhaust every resource to find out what happened, including being honest with Chris about who I was and what I could do. Who was attempting to use both him and Nancy for info under the bullshit of my ends being totally justified. Who kept avoiding the reality, I needed to step up and find Mom myself. I felt myself contract like a slug in the bitter brine of self-loathing.

Julian slid off his stool and enfolded me in his arms, offering me a comfort I didn't deserve. I leaned against his chest, as I had Chris, my hitching breathing finally slowing to match the rhythm of his heart. I took a deep breath, smelling cigarettes and soap and clean sweat, with a slight undernote of barley and hops from the beer he'd been drinking, and relaxed, the constriction in my throat lessening. I straightened up finally, and Julian loosened his arms but still holding me. I gave him a smile, I wanted to give him something more. "You'll be a great dad someday."

Julian dropped his arms in shock, a flicker of hurt deep in his eyes.

I took his right hand, let the wall crumble. "No, you will be—you'll adopt—you and Laine." The picture unfolded in my mind. "He'll drive you crazy because Laine will always make you be the disciplinarian of course, he's a big kid himself. Both of them all covered in paint, and Laine shrugs— 'we were in the moment'—with a gorgeous mountain scene painted on the east wall facing the lake. The landlord…"

I came back to the present moment when I felt Julian yank his hand away. I blinked and focused on the man standing in front of me, his face almost comically slack with shock. He stared at me, his mouth working soundlessly. He stumbled to the left and slumped back onto the bar stool, gripping his bottle of beer with pale knuckles as he lifted it and downed the remaining half. He took a deep, shuddering sigh and finally faced me again. "Veronica, what are you? Your eyes…"

"My eyes?" It was my head that felt untethered, floating.

"They were all blue, no pupil at all. It…" He slumped even further down, splayed his hands on the bar, and stared at them, as if the right words to describe them might be fine printed across the broad expanse of the back of his hand.

It was then I realized what I'd done—I hadn't been imagining—I'd been predicting. That must have been what happened with Nancy, too. All those weird little vibes I'd always gotten—that made school some species of hell. I always knew who hated whom, what lay beneath toothy smiles and backslaps. Little mind pictures of secrets and shame before I learned to protect myself, notes sent home when I couldn't help myself and blurted something out. So, I'd held myself above it all and called it smart. That was bad enough, but this? It felt like being digested. It wasn't just the past I could see now, it was the future.

"Oh, God." I spun toward the bar, the fresh drink I'd requested waiting for me, and I picked it up and downed the entire thing, then slid off the stool, swaying. "I have to go. Julian, I'm sorry." I wanted to take his hand again, reassure him that I wasn't a freak but now we both knew that wasn't true, and I didn't want to see him flinch away. Instead, I thrust my hand in my pocket, pulled out a few crumpled bills and threw them on the bar, and started toward the door.

"Veronica, wait," I heard him call after me, but I slammed my weight against the door bar and ran.

Chapter Twenty-Two

He was at the mall, the absolute last place he ever wanted to be, particularly after a McClellan's morning. It seemed masochistic to follow that up with a mall trip on a Saturday. But his mom's birthday was that night and Big Pat had asked him to take Meg and pick out "something nice" more than a week ago and time was up.

Meg looked like he felt, she was tugging hard at her left braid, her eyes glazed with a boredom that Chris could see was a scrim over her annoyance. He rested his right hand on her head and grinned down at her. "You want an ice cream or something?"

She twitched under his hand, her eyes narrowed at a large group of middle-aged, middle-weight shoppers who'd stopped in the center of the walk to have a lengthy conversation about where to go next. "Well, George definitely needs athletic socks, and I could use some…"

They button-hooked around the group and resumed walking fast, missing the rest of the scintillating discussion. Meg turned her face up to his and smiled. "Yes, *please*."

Five minutes later they'd found a tiny table in the corner of the food court, far enough from the main thoroughfare so that the wall of noise—screaming babies, sugar-hyped kids, parents shouting to be heard—faded to a dull-edged roar. They sunk into the hard plastic chairs and Chris was amused to hear an identical sigh of relief to his own from his little sister.

He watched Meg pick up her plastic spoon with a determined grin and attack the banana split he'd bought her. "That is the biggest freakin' one I've ever seen."

Meg looked up from her ice-cream spelunking, chocolate smeared on her chin. "I know. You're the best brother ever."

"Yeah, well, you better be able to eat dinner or Mom'll kill me."

"Don't worry. I will.

Chris leaned back in his chair, flipped the lid off his chocolate shake and took a gulp. He believed her—that kid could put it away. Besides, Mom probably wouldn't notice what Meg ate tonight.

She took a breather, setting down her spoon in the wreckage of the ice cream and looked around at the rest of the food court, he followed her gaze to two white-baseball capped guys leaning on opposite sides of the trashcan by the McDonald's, one let out a piercing whistle at a girl in line wearing a short white skirt. A kid not much younger than Megan but tiny and twitchy, jumped at the sound and tipped his soda into his lap. With a casualness that made Chris' stomach turn, the boy's mother reached out and slapped the boy with one meaty paw. The boy didn't even cry, he picked up his now-empty cup and trudged to the trashcan.

Chris met Meg's eyes and saw his own disgust mirrored in her expression. "I hate the mall," she finally said, her eyes gone slate-grey with anger.

He gave her a little smile. "It's a boil on the butt of humanity."

That made her giggle, and she picked up her spoon again, mixed the remaining whipped cream, sauce, and ice cream into a disgusting sludge and started to eat again, pausing only to say, "I think Mom'll like her presents, though, don't you?"

Chris nodded. Mom always like her presents, whether it was a macaroni picture or a diamond ring. The two of them had pooled their money to get Mom a fountain pen and some gloves, they found a nice silver bracelet with a Celtic design for Big Pat to give her. All in less than an hour. Big Pat, on the other hand, was the biggest pain in the ass to buy for, a gruff "thanks" was about as emotional as he got.

Megan surprised him with the fact that her thoughts were following the same lines. "Way easier than Dad."

"Next year I'm gonna get him a gift certificate to McClellan's and call it good." Meg interrupted her ice-cream inhalation and gave him the same narrow-eyed look the mall loiterers received. "What?"

"You always sound weird when you talk about Dad."

Chris shrugged. He couldn't deny it, but he wasn't going to go into it with his ten-year-old sister, who was, he saw over the rim of his milkshake glass, glaring at him in a remarkable imitation of Big Pat. "You don't like Dad?"

Chris sighed and lied. "Sure, I do."

She lifted an eyebrow.

"Dude. Just because Dad and I don't get along like you two doesn't mean I hate him." Well, he amended mentally, not always.

"Good, 'cause that would suck." She turned back to devouring the remains of her banana split and Chris concentrated on his milk shake, taking a deep, headache-inducing swallow to freeze the bad taste he always seemed to get when he thought about their dad. It had a metallic taste, it was the taste of coffee in a tin mug around a campfire.

He closed his eyes against Megan, against the darts and flashes of food court patrons, against the dull throb of the cold headache, twice now in the past month that memory had risen up to taunt him. It was as fresh as his disappointment in his dad. He'd stupidly thought that the McClellan's job would at least give them something to talk about, but except for that dinner where he'd announced it, Big Pat had not only shown no interest, he seemed to go out of his way to avoid interacting with Chris at all. Maybe he was an employee now, instead of a son.

Megan belched loudly. He opened his eyes to see her lean back in her chair, arms crossed over her stomach. "I'm so full."

He grinned at her, letting the bitter train of his thoughts derail. "C'mon. We'll walk it off on the way to the car."

He gathered up the bags and Meg picked up the remains and threw them in the trash as they started off, taking the long way to the parking lot. He adjusted the bags more firmly in his left hand and took Meg's with his right.

By 9 p.m., Meg was crashed out on the couch, and the party had already divided along gender lines. Chris slumped in the Barcalounger in the corner, the morning at the factory and mall making him feel like someone had pulled out his spine and left him a boneless chicken. Seen through the grimy film of his exhaustion, everything looked tired, the sag in the sparkly *Happy 40th Bea!* sign and pink streamers Mom's best friend Marcia had bustled in and hung up an hour before the guests arrived, the balloons sinking to the carpet, the abandoned plate of food on the end table with two pieces of lettuce limp in a sea of ranch dressing.

From his vantage point, he could see the split. The men were gathered by the liquor cabinet, talking sports and telling jokes that would have earned them a withering look or a shouted "Richard!" or "Jim!" from their wives. The women were around the dining room table, where Mom's gifts were spread in an untidy pile and two pitchers of sangria were down to a few pieces of drowned fruit. He couldn't hear what they were saying but judging from the shocked crescendo of their laughter, he thought they might be telling a few off-color jokes of their own.

He wondered if anyone would notice if he slipped out.

The thought gave him enough energy to get up and he started edging toward the kitchen, where he could slip up the back stairs to his room. He made it to the couch where Megan was passed out when his dad caught his eye.

"Chris! Where you goin'?" A beer-induced grin made Big Pat's face a topographic map of cheerful creases.

He thought fast and returned the grin with one of his own, imitating Big Pat's bluff gruff tone. "Thought I'd take Meg upstairs and sling 'er into bed."

"Sure, you can manage? She's all muscle." He looked blearily but fondly at his daughter, but Chris caught the way he hit "she's" harder than the rest of the words, and judging by their guffaws, so did his friends.

Chris stared at his father, too pissed off to say anything in response, much less anything clever. At his dad, at himself for even entertaining the idea that anything would ever be different between them.

Dad looked away first, before Chris could read anything in his eyes—was he sorry, was he bored—so Chris did what he said he would.

He hefted Meg off the couch—she was a solid kid but nothing he couldn't handle—and she stirred a bit, snaking her arms around his neck and resting her head on his shoulder.

He trudged up the stairs and into Meg's room, laying her on the bed. He flipped on the little desk lamp and pulled off her shoes. She barely stirred. He debated whether to wake her up enough so she could put on her pajamas and brush her teeth but decided it wasn't worth it. He tucked her in, gave her a quick kiss on the forehead (she gave him a sleepy smile in return), switched off the light and closed the door.

He slumped against it, the dark broken only by the flickering night-light halfway down the hall, paralyzed by indecision. He didn't want to go back downstairs, he didn't want to hole up in his room with only his own thoughts for company. With a sigh he straightened up, went down the hall to his room, went to his desk and sat down, rummaging through the messy pile of research he dumped there until he found what he wanted. On the pretext of checking old stats for his piece on the upcoming school board elections—although he wondered later why he'd felt the need to lie to Ms. Price about it—she gave him the key to the morgue where old issues of both the *Dalesville High News* and *Ledgers* were kept. His gut had been correct, whomever had blacked out the name at the main and the school library hadn't thought about the journalism department. He'd scribbled down the blurb in his notebook, then spent the rest of the time going through old stories about local elections. He tore that page out of his notebook and stuffed it in his pocket, thinking maybe it might be a good time to share what he found with Veronica.

He grabbed his coat and slipped down the back stairs to the darkened kitchen. He had his hand on the doorknob when he heard, "No, no, I'll make some more. Hold that thought."

He froze as the kitchen flooded with light, his hand still on the doorknob. He turned to see his mom, empty pitcher in her hand, wry smile on her face. "Well, that's not remotely incriminating."

He dropped his hand from the doorknob and leaned against the door. "How do you know I wasn't going out for fresh air?"

She strode across the kitchen and set the pitcher on the counter, mixing up a new batch as she talked. "If you were, you wouldn't be sneaking out the back door."

Despite himself, he grinned. "Foxed by logic. Damn."

She uncorked a bottle of red wine and poured it into the pitcher. "Pick up some half 'n' half while you're out, *okay*? I think we'll all need coffee tomorrow."

He straightened up in shock. "Really?"

She put the wine bottle back down on the counter and turned, resting her left hip against the counter. "Look Chris, you've put in your time, got Meg safely into bed, you don't need to hang around anymore watching us make fools of ourselves."

Her tone was light, but her mouth was set in a straight line and no smile lurked in or around her eyes. He wondered if she'd overheard the remark Big Pat made and decided he didn't want to know. He crossed the kitchen and gave her a kiss on the forehead. "Happy Birthday, Mom."

She reached up and squeezed his shoulder, a little smile now playing on her lips that was remarkably similar to the one Meg gave him earlier. "Be back by midnight."

She turned back to the pitcher while he ghosted out the back door. Five minutes later he was driving down Sunset.

He tossed the half 'n' half on the passenger seat and slammed the door behind him, sat behind the wheel and lit a smoke. It was a risk, but he felt like taking it. He started the car again and kept going until he saw the City of Light Acres sign in the wash of his headlights, and smiled. He drove past the sign, feeling more energetic than he'd felt all day, despite the fact that he had no idea how to find her. He drove past endless rows of identical houses, wondered how anyone found their own. Worse, she'd never given him her address. Still, the almost manic energy he felt wouldn't diminish, even in the face of those realities. He was confident he could locate her. She'd dropped tidbits from time to time. He knew her room was on an alley and started looking for one.

Fourth time was the charm. He drove at parade float speed, alert for any clue. About three houses down he saw a light on and sure enough, there was Veronica's profile, sitting at her desk, head bent over a book with what looked like a slight frown on her face.

He continued down the alley, turned back on to the street, made a note of her address, then went in search of an unobtrusive place to park. Chris found what he needed in the form of a section of new construction about three blocks from Veronica's. He parked the wagon behind a half-constructed house and set off down the street.

He stiffened his spine, strode up to the window and tapped on the glass. Her reaction would have been hilarious under any other circumstances—she looked up, eyes wide, nostrils flaring, caught his eyes, said what looked like "holy shit!' and promptly fell off her desk chair—but he felt no urge to laugh.

She was laughing when she pulled open the window.

"I'm so sorry," was all he could manage. She, still laughing, stuck her head out the window, scanned the alley left and right and then helped boost him inside. She gestured him toward her recently vacated desk chair, and she flopped onto the bed, her laugh tapering off into snorts and gasps.

She finally met his eyes and sobered up. "I'm not laughing at you."

"Oh?"

"Actually, I was imagining how it must have looked from your perspective." She smiled again. "How did you find me?"

"I went door-to-door."

Her eyes went wide with fear in the instant before she realized he was kidding. "Bastard." She leaned over and smacked his arm.

"Is it...safe? Your Dad..."

"He was supposed to be back today, but he got delayed 'til tomorrow afternoon. We're safe. Enough." Now she grinned. "In fact, you couldn't have picked a better time, my nosy neighbor Mrs. Sneed is at her Saturday bingo game."

Then he could smile, it felt comfortable on his face. "Good, 'cause I can't imagine what reasonable excuse either of us could come up with to explain 'guy in your room,' even if your dad wasn't a religious n..." He stopped, felt the heat creep up his neck to his ears and stared down at the floor.

"Nut?" Her voice sounded amused, his embarrassment receded. She held out her hand and he twined his fingers with hers, finally looking up at her. Her smile was warm. "You're not saying anything I haven't thought before."

She tugged a little on his hand and he stood and joined her on the bed. "You've had a crappy day."

He straightened up, looked at her, struck again by her weirdness.

"It's written all over you. Slumped shoulders, this wrinkle between your eyes..." she reached her free hand and touch it lightly and he felt it ease, "hard lines here," the same gentle touch at the corner of his mouth.

Not quite sure what he was doing, he took her hand and kissed the tips of her fingers. Her eyes widened again, but she didn't pull away. Feeling bold, he leaned in and kissed her lips, barely touching them, then pulled away and looked at her. They stared at each other for what seemed like a long time. That think line Laine captured in his sketch looked chiseled between her eyes, but whether that was good or bad, Chris didn't know. Then she tilted her head and pulled him to her, kissing him back, clumsy but determined, lips parted, and her fingers tangled in his hair, pulling him closer, leaning into him so that her chest was pressed against his and he was sliding back, toward the jumble of pillows at the head of her bed and then, drowning...

He was alone on the bed, breathless and feeling drugged. He shook his head like he was clearing water from his ears. Veronica was leaning against the wall, touching her lips and looking as dazed as he felt. Her eyes seemed all blue, like there was no pupil at all.

He knew he should say something, but he didn't feel quite capable of speaking at that moment. His breath was ragged, his lips a little sore, the rest of him felt so relaxed he could slide down and fall into the deepest sleep on this bed. Instead, he splayed his hands on his knees and stared down at the bumps and whorls of his knuckles, listening to Veronica's own hitching breath nearby. He only looked up when she spoke, met eyes that looked dazed but normal.

"That was..." she started, her hands up and open, clutching at nothing, but then she stopped, her mouth shut and her hands dropped back to her side.

He felt his own lips widen into a grin and thought they might stay that way forever. "I know."

She touched her mouth again with her right index finger, straightened and started to walk back to him, then stopped so suddenly she lurched on the spot.

He held out his hand to her. "Want to do it again?"

A little smile. "Yes, but..."

He shrugged. "There's always one of those."

Her face flamed like a flash fire, and she sank onto the desk chair. "If I kissed you like that again, I wouldn't be able to stop."

Chris felt the same heat transfer from her face to his as they stared at each other. There were a thousand reasons why not, but there was this moment, this room. "That's kind of the point. What's wrong with that?" He heard his own voice, sharp with frustration, saw it reflected in the way her eyes flinched away from his, but went on anyway. "Sex isn't a bad thing. It's not evil."

Then she did look at him, her eyes narrowed, a spark of anger there. "I know that! It's...there are things you don't know about me. I..."

He rose up off the bed and strode across the room toward her and she scrambled off the chair and skittered toward the window. He stopped mid-stride. "I wasn't going to...hurt you."

She came toward him then, laced her hands with his. "I know, Chris. It's not in you. It's not me I'm worried about."

She pulled him down to her and kissed him again, aggressive and intense, like a closed circle where they held each other up and blocked out everything else. Finally, she broke the kiss, still holding his hands. "Can you meet me downtown tomorrow? Around noon, at the Blue Moon?"

He nodded, he would have promised to meet her on Pluto at that moment.

She let go then, went to the window, pulled back the curtain and stuck her head out the window. "It's safe."

He put the hood of his jacket up and slipped out the window. Only then did he remember why he'd risked this in the first place. He dug in his pocket, pulled out the paper, and reached up to hand it to her.

"Thought you might be interested in this." With that, he took off, only turning back when he reached the alley. She still stood framed in the buttery yellow light of her room, and he could make out the sad little smile on her face. He raised his hand in a wave and melted into the shadows to find his car.

He'd told her nothing, really, asked her nothing. That wasn't how he'd planned it to go.

It was better.

Chapter Twenty-Three

I don't know how long I stood there, staring out at the night Chris had disappeared into, the chill in the air cooling my face, still warm from his touch, his kiss, but the clock in the living room rang once when I finally rattled the curtains closed and turned back to a room that still vibrated with his presence. I sank down on my bed, exhausted, exhilarated.

I hadn't expected to see him, or anyone. I'd been using Dad's absence to write about Project M, Theo's warnings, full of bland words with no insight. Then Chris was at the window, the moon silvering his hair, his lips curled in a little crooked smile and what else mattered?

I stared at the ceiling, letting the moment play out in my mind, his face below mine, his hands...I stopped the fantasy by scrambling off my bed and taking a deep, shaky breath. Why did I stop him? Why did I stop myself?

You know why, a voice clambered deep in my head.

"I don't!" My own voice seemed impossibly loud in my little room. I closed my eyes, and my masochistic mind offered up a sensory replay of our kiss, his hand in my hair, the warmth of his breath on my lips in that moment before he kissed me, our skin transformed into warm wax ready for the other to leave their impressions everywhere. Oh, God, I wanted him.

I wanted to find Mom, that was the purpose of this.

Who was I kidding? I didn't know what I wanted anymore. I didn't know what was mine anymore. As I stared around my room—flower-stenciled vanity, the jumble of books in and around my bookshelf, worn-out stuffed animals littering the bed—it occurred to me that I was a child. Mentally sticking out my tongue at Dad and Faith Fellowship, drinking at *The* Club like that made me a grown-up. Playing with Chris, knowing too much about him and fobbing him off when he wanted to know anything about me. All under my control. Maybe I was more like Dad than I thought.

It was all mixed up—the feel of those soft lips, the taste of cigarettes and toothpaste, those eyes close enough to see the little flecks like panned gold mixed with the green—the taste of tin and coffee, leaves stained with blood, and the heave of a dying animal. The bile and burn of shame. Secrets I had no right to know.

I bounced up off the bed, out the door, and down the hall to the kitchen. I flipped on the light. The sterile white cleanliness of the floor, the counter, the appliances, was a reproach of the thoughts I'd left my room to avoid. How I felt about him, what we did, short-circuited everything, made me forget vital things, like the danger Faith Fellowship posed, or solving the mystery around Mom.

I'd worked so hard, I thought, as I gathered filter and coffee, not trusting sleep, pouring in water and scoops of coffee with little attention to what I was doing. Kept to the sidelines, avoided touch and talk so well that I knew people thought I was a snob and a bitch. I didn't want to know what I knew. I didn't want to be this way.

I watched the coffee stream into the pot like it was the most fascinating process in the world, thought about my wall. What had Chris said? "You're like a ghost." Neither here nor there. Mom would have said something about lights and bushel baskets, about wasting gifts.

Chris's note was still clutched in my hand.

The stream stopped. I grabbed a soup mug from the dish drainer, filled it, and took it with me into the living room. I had more immediate considerations. I deliberately burnt my mouth with the first swallow, trying to shock myself into thinking clearly, then set the mug on the table and flopped onto the couch and turned on the lamp. I unfolded the paper, *M (or Em?) Raynor picked up on Sunset, November 11, 1989; returned to Dalesville Hospital.*

The paper shook in my hand. This and the retracted police report, meant she'd been here. Had maybe even tried to see me. Proof I didn't need that she hadn't abandoned me, but how did she end up at Dalesville Community Hospital? And why?

And who owned the *Ledger* in 1989?

I picked up the mug and drained it. The James family, of course. You don't know what they're capable of. That's what Theo had said. You're putting him at risk. That picture, vision, whatever, surfaced again. Me leaving town, worn backpack riding heavy on my shoulders as I walked away, followed by Julian's expression at *The* Club, the one that said as loud as words, are you going to hurt him?

Cold crept up my spine as my own question, one I didn't want to acknowledge, rose from the depths, or put him in a position where others would? Robert James, staring at me with that smug little smile as he said, "No one will stand in our way."

I opened my eyes, reached for the coffee cup, took another burning drink. I knew what was next. I needed to try to show Chris—I didn't know what, but make him understand that there was something off—with me, with this place and then he could decide. To be honest, for once, about everything.

Mom had always said, when I complained about how people never seemed to get what they deserved, with a sad smile on her face, "Life isn't always fair, but we should always be. We can't know how things will end up, but we know how we behaved. If we're fair, if we're kind, that's what matters in the end."

"Mom," I said aloud, surprised at the shakiness in my voice. If that was true of dealing with people who wronged you, it was doubly so with someone like Chris. My mouth was numb with self-inflicted burning, the scratch of acid in my throat. Because it wasn't only about Mom, or Robert James, or Chris himself. It was Theo's warnings, vague and troubling, about me, about Chris, about his missing years. His reason he wouldn't talk about. It was Mom, pushed out so completely she couldn't make contact, reduced to a retracted police report and an item in the police blotter. I knew I needed to do the rest of this on my own.

I gulped the dregs of the coffee, not wanting to admit the last reason, the cut lines and flat brake petal speed of how things were between Chris and I. It was a distraction, an unnecessary risk. I stared at his scrawled words, burning them into my brain. If Dalesville taught me anything, it was that letting someone in—to your head, to your heart—made you that much easier to control.

Chapter Twenty-Four

S he was silent, sipping her coffee, as if she was trying to figure out what to say. Finally, she leaned in, her voice barely a whisper as she glanced around the Blue Moon. "Where did you find a clean copy?" He followed her glance, yet saw nothing but the usual crowd.

Being this close to her after the night before was making it hard to focus. He cleared his throat and tried to sound at least a little professional. He took a drink of coffee, unable to keep from grinning. "We've got copies in the journalism room, I figured whomever did this," he pointed at his scrawl, "wouldn't have thought or known about the ones there, they only hit the ones in the school library. Backer would be pissed if he noticed."

She folded up the paper, answered his grin with a wan smile. "Didn't get a chance to tell you last night, but this is great work, Christopher. I told you, you had skills."

He stared down at the table's warped wood, not sure how to respond. When he looked up, Veronica was staring out the large window, still streaked with water from the morning's brief squall. That vibe was coming off her again and he followed her gaze to the street. It was the same bench with its' "City of Light" slogan, empty except for an abandoned newspaper.

He was about to ask her what was up. Ask her all the questions he'd meant to last night. Before he could say a word, she turned, gave him a much brighter smile. "You wanna get out of here? We could get these," she pointed to their cups, "to go."

He shrugged. "Why not?"

Cups in hand, the two of them walked side by side through downtown, not speaking. It was, Chris thought, a comfortable silence.

"Hold on a sec." He stopped to dig into his jacket for a cigarette and his lighter. When he looked up, Veronica was still moving, nearly around the corner.

"Veronica!"

She jumped a little and he smiled as he watched her look to her left and realized he wasn't there, then finished her turn, facing him with a sheepish expression. She started back toward him.

So, not a companionable silence, he answered himself as he finished lighting up and slipped the lighter back into his jacket pocket, it was the silence of distraction. What the hell, they'd only known each other, been friends of unknown type, for what, a little over a month? Certainly not long enough to interpret the infinite variety of interpersonal non-verbalness. This one however, was getting more and more noticeable—she'd been in and out since they'd sat down at the Blue Moon. He'd ask her what she was thinking if he didn't hate the question on general principles.

Still, the little kernel that such a question sprang from wouldn't be denied. Add it to the list.

Maybe he was cynical, but he found little to surprise him in most people—they seemed absurdly easy to figure out within a few conversations. He supposed he wasn't that complex either, he knew what he wanted, to get out of this town and be Chris Mulligan—not Big Pat Mulligan's son or Megan's big brother, not a Catholic in Faith Fellowship's town, or a weirdo with a pierced eyebrow—just himself.

Veronica, however, remained an enigma. They seemed to talk about a lot of things, but he still couldn't quite figure her out. She was the personification of evasiveness as a perfected art form. Except the night before, in her room.

"Sorry," she said, when she was back in the circumference where shouting was no longer necessary. She pointed at her head. "Spacey."

He shrugged. "I'm getting used to it."

Her smile was sad, asked forgiveness. "Bad habit. You should see my childhood report cards—almost everyone has a comment like 'dreamy,' 'easily distracted,' 'needs to work on 'appropriate,'" she made air quotes with her fingers, "'interaction with peer group.'"

Chris rolled his eyes. "Be you, fuck them. You can be in my peer group."

The flash of a smile. "Best offer I've had yet."

He returned her smile. "Best offer I've had today, at least."

Chris took her arm, one part spontaneous and one part to keep her from drifting and they walked over to the middle of the square, sat under the tree where he'd seen her staring up at the sky, that night they'd met.

This, Chris decided, *was* a companionable silence. She leaned slightly into his side while they watched the various and sundry Sunday day crowd amble past. The sun had finally emerged, burning off the last of the rainfall, the air was almost warm and the people around them seemed less goal-oriented than usual.

He was so relaxed himself that the question he'd been chewing on slipped out before he could stop it. "So, are you finally going to answer the question I asked you at Sam's?"

"What?" A low murmur, as if she'd been half-asleep.

"You know. Why sometimes you get so," he paused, trying to find the right word, "jumpy?"

"You really want the answer?"

It wasn't even a question. "I do."

"Because it's dangerous. Because I'm dangerous." He tried to make his face a mask, like hers. Clearly, he didn't succeed, she looked almost angry. "I'm serious. You already known Raynor is my mom's maiden name, so it's likely the blotter was referring to her. That's enough to make anyone," she made quote marks with her fingers, "'jumpy'. And then there's Theo," she spat the name out like it tasted bad.

His head was spinning. "Theo?"

Her voice was ice. "He's the guy Faith Fellowship pays to follow me around. He was sitting outside the coffee shop half an hour ago."

"I thought it was only one time. Veronica, that's…" He didn't know how to finish that sentence. He thought getting these answers would bring some kind of clarity, instead, his brain was reeling. Too many layers bleeding into each other. He latched onto the most ridiculous. "Faith Fellowship is paying some guy to follow you? Why would they do that? It doesn't make sense."

Her face was motionless, like held breath. "I have my suspicions."

He wanted for her to continue, but instead, she drained her coffee cup and stood up, taking it to the trash can and dropping it in. She stayed there, her back to him, her hands gripping their sides like it was the only thing holding her up.

He hissed a sigh, trying to be patient. "Which are?"

"You don't want to know." She still hadn't turned around.

He stood up, took a step forward. "I do."

A new silence, one he couldn't name, stretched out between them. He took a gulp of coffee, and it burnt his mouth, he savored the dead feeling on his tongue as something real. Only gradually did he realize she'd turned and was staring at him like she'd done that first night at Sam's, her face still an impassive marble mask, a statue that breathed. That spoke. "Christopher."

He stared at her.

"I wasn't kidding about being dangerous. You really want to know why?" She came closer, her face pale except for two spots of color high on her cheeks. Chris nodded and she sat back down. "Will you take my hand?"

He did and closed his eyes in fear, in defiance. He felt her start to withdraw her hand and made his decision again by drawing her back in.

When he opened his eyes again and met hers, her expression was the twin of the one he'd seen the night before, pupils swallowed up by the dark blue of her eyes. The only difference was that cold marble look, the clipped tone of her voice, not blushed and breathless like she'd been the night before.

"You were eight," she said, looking at him without seeing him. "So small, but you felt big, that gun in your hand, your dad's grin, the crack of the leaves and crisp air. You were a man today, weren't you? And when that gun went off you liked the sound it made, even the bitter taste it left in the air."

He was fixed, that same crackle of energy coming off her he'd felt in the hallway, in the playground, but if that was the shock you got crossing the carpet and touching the doorknob, this was like being tazered. Frozen, and she was laying him bare.

"Until you saw what you did, the slow glaze in the eyes, the heave of the deer's breath bringing the blood slow and sluggish and the look in your dad's eyes when you puked."

"Stop it." That same sick shame feeling was rising in him again.

"Big Pat looked at you like he didn't want to know you, little boy, not man enough to kill."

"For Christ's sake, stop." It was nearly a shout and a woman ambling by pushing a stroller with one hand and holding the hand of the other child turned and gave him an angry look and sped up her walk. He pulled his hand away from hers and the world righted itself again. Now it was his turn to sit, head in hands, eyes shut tight.

"I'm sorry. I didn't think..." Chris lifted his head, and she was there, standing in front of him, eyes normal again, her own shame livid in her cheeks. "I should go. I should have never..."

She started to turn, to leave, and he grabbed her arm harder than he intended. She winced and he let his hand drop, ashamed.

"Don't." He wasn't sure what he meant by that, but she stayed, looking down at her feet.

He crushed his cigarette under his boot, heard the shake in his voice. "How could you do that?"

Her eyes were wide when they finally met his. "I don't know. I always could, but it's getting stronger."

"That not what I meant." His voice was steadier now, that was good. "How could you expose me like that?"

He watched her face grey, except for the dark smudges under her eyes. "I didn't..." She trailed off.

Not breaking the gaze, he said, "You're weird."

"I know. I needed you to know, too."

The admission seemed to take something out of her, and she flopped back down next to him. Out of the corner of his eye he watched her slump, saw her left hand twitch toward his, but instead, she wrapped her right hand around her left wrist as if to contain it. Chris was glad. In fact, if she never touched him again, that would be all right with him. There was some relief in acknowledging, at long last, that he was the coward Big Pat thought he was.

"You're not."

At that, Chris jumped, skittered sideways so fast he nearly fell on his ass off the bench. "Don't do that. Ever."

If she slumped any further into that bench, he thought, she would slide right out the back. "I'm sorry."

In the back of his throat, he could taste the sour bile of self-loathing. She couldn't help whatever the hell she was, but then again, he couldn't help his aversion, either. He felt...used.

"I gotta go." Yet he stood there, like he was waiting for permission. She didn't say a word, she stared ahead at the newspapered window of Happy Family Chinese across the street. He took a deep breath and thought he could still discern the faint tang of sweet and sour sauce in the air. She didn't say a word, didn't move at all, didn't even look his way. Chris supposed that was enough of a sign. She'd gotten what she wanted, right? He'd found some sign of her mom and was no longer needed. He adjusted his satchel on his shoulder and made his way down the street.

When he got to the corner by Lou's Used Records, he turned back. Even from that distance he could see she hadn't moved. He knew she'd gone away again, lost in whatever curse she lived with. It occurred to him, belatedly, that she'd let him in because she was lonely, that she was trying to be honest with him. And maybe he wasn't as smart as he thought, all those little things—the intense gaze, the emotional pre-guessing, even the there/not-there quality she had at school—they made sense. For a moment he knew he could take a step back, return to her side. The next moment brought a hot anger at her for exposing that memory so casually, for reaching in and pulling it out of him, without warning, without permission.

After a momentary paralysis where he wavered queasily between the two, he turned away from her again and made his way to anywhere else.

Chapter Twenty-Five

T he bench creaked. I opened my eyes, my heart beating a little out of rhythm, hoping it was Chris. It was Theo, looking every inch the Faith Fellowship insider. Hair slicked back, suit neatly pressed, pin shining on his lapel. I hated him. "You did the right thing, you know."

I shot up from the bench, wanting distance from the whole thing, but him in particular. "I don't know that." It was a lie, but I didn't care.

"Veronica, I told you. If you want to bring that place down, you can't take risks like him."

All the rage I felt—at myself, mostly—came out as I spun to face him "That's not what I want. That's what you want. I want out."

He took a step closer, I took a shaky step back. "You think they'll let you go? People who have files and keep tabs on you are gonna let you board a bus and hit the road?"

I shook my head. "I only have your word such a thing exists at all. Maybe you're a stalker and that's your cover story."

His face paled as he sat back down on the bench, rumpling his suit as he slumped. "It's all true, Veronica."

Without thinking, I stepped forward, looming over him. "Why should I take your word for it? You say they play these games, how do I know you're not a part of it?"

"You have to believe me." He reached up and took my hand before I could stop him.

The square disappeared. I was in a dim room, my (his) thoughts fuzzy, my (his) head aching. A man sat in front of me, his lips smiling, his eyes cold beneath the thin lenses of his glasses. "Help us understand, Theodore, why you'd want to act counter to the Lord's way."

"It's..." the words came slowly, both in mind and speech. "It's not. I am... how God made me."

I stumbled back, nearly falling onto the sidewalk, my head pounding, my stomach grinding as the connection broke. I bent over, fighting the nausea, gulping breath like it was water. I heard Theo stand up, come towards me, I shrunk away. "I'm *okay*. Just don't...don't touch me."

Finally, my stomach settled enough to risk standing up straight, but the headache and dizziness were still in play. Theo looked a little unsteady as well, his hands trembling at his sides, his face shiny. "What just happened?"

I knew. Not everything, but enough to understand. Some kind of bullshit counseling that seemed a lot like torture. That, on top of Chris, on top of what might have happened to Mom, was about a thousand times more than I could deal with.

A deep breath and I gave Theo a wide berth, retrieved my purse from the bench. "We all have secrets."

I left him standing there and stumbled out of the square.

By the time I reached Sunset I felt a little steadier, a little more myself, except for the ache in my head and heart. Every instinct said go home, lay down my aching head in a dark room, but I knew I couldn't rest until I had the last answer. The sign across Sunset said "Walk," but I ran, my head ringing with every footfall, not stopping until I stood in front of Dalesville Community Hospital.

I stopped at the door, catching my breath. My body refused to move. "You want answers or not?" I mumbled under my breath as two guys in scrubs came out the doors, laughing as they made their way over to one of the benches that lined the wide walkway. The sun was behind me, turning the doors into a mirror that reflected my sweaty, scowling face, my wind-tangled hair. I moved off to the side and took the bench opposite the guys on their break and ran my fingers through my hair to work out the tangles, armed the sweat off my forehead. I reached into my purse for a tie to pull my hair back, and ended up pulling out a cigarette instead.

As I sat there smoking, my mind kept up a steady stream of abuse. A coward, a bitch, a child. It wasn't wrong. What I had to know lay through those doors, I hoped, and I sat here smoking and staring at the scuffs on the toes of my sneakers like they were hieroglyphics to decipher, pretending my spine hadn't gone all iceberg at the literal point of entry.

"You know, sweetheart, the fear of the moment is always worse than the reality."

Mom's voice was so clear in my head I could be sitting next to her in our old white truck, with its sprung seats and tall stick shift one of us would always knock into getting in or out. We'd sat outside of school for what seemed like forever, the truck growling and rumbling as it idled. I hadn't wanted to go in, something bad happened—a fight with a classmate, maybe, or something embarrassing like my shorts falling off in gym class, too many humiliations to count—and I hadn't wanted to walk through those doors either. "Always?"

She leaned over, knocking her elbow on the stick shift, she ignored that and kissed me on the cheek. "I promise."

I took one last drag and stood up, dropping the butt in the ashtray by the door. I could disappoint Dad and drive off Chris, but I owed it to Mom to be strong.

The lobby was quiet enough to hear my own heart beating in my ears, the squeak of my sneakers as I crossed the lobby where an older woman sat, her hair pulled back in a no-nonsense bun. Her face, however, was lit by a warm smile as I approached. "How can I help you?"

"I," my lips formed the words, but no sound came out. I tried again. "I'm…I'm here about a patient. Marie Raynor? Is she here?"

"Let me have a look." The woman, Marjorie according to her name tag, typed rapidly on her keyboard. The idea that I might see her, whatever state she might be in, seemed to suck all the oxygen out of me. Marjorie shifted in her seat, giving me a fleeting glance as she typed, I knew I was staring at her, but I couldn't seem to look away. "Do you know when she was checked in?"

I drew a breath, shallow but enough to talk. "Not exactly. It would have been in 1989."

Marjorie's eyebrows shot up over her glasses for the space of a second before the calm, professional face she greeted me with reappeared. "Give me a minute."

She stood up and for a second, I was worried she was going to call someone. My body tensed, read to run. Instead, she went over to a filing cabinet, bent and opened the bottom drawer, flipping through the files until she pulled one and straightened up, holding it to her chest as she turned. "We're still transitioning older patient files to our computer system."

Her smile faded as she opened the file, she snapped it shut again. "May I ask why you're interested in this patient?"

My hands trembled on the counter. I shoved them in my pockets. She had been here. Was here. A lie would be the smart choice. Marjorie seemed nice, but my trust in my instincts was at an all-time low. I opened my mouth and the truth came out. "She's, my mother."

The words were a hoarse whisper directed at the counter and were greeted by silence. That made me look up. Marjorie stood perfectly still, the professional expression replaced with wide, sad eyes, and I knew—without touching her, without her saying a word—at least one thing the file said.

She came around the desk, placed it on the counter. "Are you Veronica?"

Whatever I thought she'd say, it wasn't that. My knees buckled and I grabbed the edge of the desk to steady myself. "I am." Silence. "I can prove it, I have my school ID."

She shook her head, her lips quirked in a small smile. "No need. I can see the resemblance. Marie was a long-term patient here. She...s he'd said your name more than once."

Every word hit me like a gut punch. The information came in a wave that felt like it would drown me. Long-term? She was here all this time?

That was the moment I was sure, when the most important word in that cascade finally crashed over me. Was.

I don't know how long I stood there, the hospital eerily quiet around us, my head pounding, an acid taste in my throat, on my tongue. Marjorie stood there, all sympathy and patience, until I finally came up with the only question that mattered. "When?"

Marjorie opened the file. "October 6, 1992."

I watched as her eyes narrowed, her jaw tightening under the softness. "Stay right here."

She bustled into the back and shut the door, leaving me clutching the desk as grief and adrenaline mixed a nauseating brew in my stomach. I was about to take off when Marjorie reappeared. She strode over to the desk, glanced down the hall before handing me a sheaf of papers. I stared at her instead of them.

She leaned forward, her voice low. "Something isn't right here, and you deserve to know." She straightened up, the professional demeanor back in place. "I'm sorry for your loss."

All I could do was nod before folding the papers and shoving them in my purse. I staggered out the doors and kept walking, the world a blur of noise and movement coming from all directions.

A car horn blatted, and I stopped, one foot on Sunset and the other on the curb. I scrambled backwards, my feet tangled under me as I fell, a hatchback blowing past where I'd been standing. The pole with its "walk, don't walk" buttons broke my fall, digging into the small of my back. The pain was enough to stop me, cleared my head enough to see where I was, the corner of Sunset and Florida. To the right, the cemetery I walked through on the way home from school, where I first told Chris about Mom.

And there it was, unable to be denied or ignored or run away from. She'd been here, calling out for me.

She was gone. I couldn't save her. And there was no one who could save me.

I stood up as the light changed and started walking again, with no real idea where I was going.

Erin Giannini has wanted to be a writer for longer than she cares to remember. She served as an editor and contributor at PopMatters, and currently writes both fiction and non-fiction, including books about TV shows like "Supernatural" and "The Good Place." She loves to read and hopes to eventually have room for all her books, read and yet-to-be read.

9 781961 967618